THE
MARRIAGE
ALLIANCE

THE
MARRIAGE
ALLIANCE

DEBRA CALHOUN

Cover design by Dar Albert
Wicked Smart Designs (www.wickedsmartdesigns.com)

Book design by Maureen Cutajar
www.gopublished.com

ISBN: 978-0-6482599-2-3

For my children,
Because you are my world, and I don't know what
my life would be like without you.

One

The first day of September dawns bright and clear. Fall is approaching, and it's the beginning of a new school year. Corrie tries not to think about what that means as she reluctantly throws off her quilt and pads barefoot into the next room. Her mother and little brother lie curled up in the large bed opposite the fireplace and Corrie steps silently out of their small two-room cottage into the cool morning air, hoping she hasn't disturbed them. She should have gathered wood for the fire last night but was too busy completing her last order for delivery today. The payment for that is all that stands between her family and destitution.

The woods are quiet this morning, unlike her thoughts, and Corrie lingers for a while to embrace the stillness.

Her family are outcasts of sorts, forced to live at the edge of the woods and away from the town, after her father joined a Rebellion designed to overthrow the Alliance. Left to scrounge for their survival, Corrie sews for the more privileged. During the summer many of the better off townsfolk travel, so there are fewer orders, which means less payment and less food. With the delivery of her order today Corrie hopes to be able to purchase much needed groceries for her family after school.

Education—or "re-education" as they like to call it—is the one thing the Alliance does provide. Its purpose is to ensure loyalty to the regime and prevent the possibility of future Rebellions. It is also used to further strengthen the Alliance by pre-determining the future of its citizens.

After the Rebellion a radical element in the Alliance had taken control, instituting a more oppressive regime. Under the new system the Alliance decide which children move on to higher education and which are forced to work in the fields or factories.

Corrie was chosen to move on. She is talented with language, and her lettering is exceptional; the Alliance might have a use for her.

Eventually, the remaining students will be chosen for another reason. They will be chosen for each other.

This is the Alliance method of orchestrating marriages to suit the purposes of the regime, ensuring the fittest thrive while they maintain control of the partnerships being established. It results in robust stock to build the future of their society, and propaganda to convince young people the Alliance is acting in their best interests. Indoctrination begins when the children start school and reaches its peak when the Marriage Selections take place in their final year.

This is Corrie's final year.

It doesn't take long to gather what she needs, and Corrie

returns to the cottage where she lights the fire and sets a pot of water over it to boil before moving across to the cupboard where their meager supplies are kept. She takes out the last of the grain to make weak gruel with warm water. It isn't much, but it will have to do.

When it is ready, Corrie places the softened gruel into three bowls and helps her brother to sit up so her mother can begin feeding him.

Her brother, Joseph, suffered from a lack of air when he was born. By the time the Midwife forced the first cry from his lungs the damage was already done. Joseph is slow, and his movements uncoordinated. Speech is difficult for him, and Alliance schools don't entertain such children. They are left for their families to rear in ignorance, but Corrie's father was determined, and Corrie is even more so.

Her mother never fully recovered from the difficult birth and four years later, when Corrie's father was lost in the attempt to overthrow the Alliance, Corrie became the family's sole provider. That was six years ago, when Corrie was ten, and she continues to do what her family, and the Alliance, expect of her.

After eating breakfast, and stoking the fire again, Corrie returns to her room to get dressed. Her worn cotton dress lies on the chair beside the bed with her grandmother's shawl draped alongside it, and her one pair of sturdy scuffed leather shoes lie underneath.

Slipping the light summer dress over her underclothes, Corrie realizes she hasn't grown much over the summer. The dress is the same length, and the shoes will probably still fit her, too. At least she won't look like she's wearing clothes she has outgrown. At sixteen, going on seventeen, Corrie is maturing more slowly than other girls, standing just over five feet tall with a boyish figure only now giving way to nature's intentions.

Pulling her thick dark hair into a ponytail Corrie ties it with a green ribbon, the one exception to her timeworn outfit. It was the only luxury she could afford after working all summer, and she chose it to match the color of her eyes. Unable to afford new clothes or shoes, Corrie could afford a small length of ribbon which now adds that something extra she needs to lift her spirits.

Gathering her bag and books Corrie returns to the main room where her mother's sympathetic gaze communicates what neither is able, or willing, to say. She knows what this final year will mean. They both know it isn't what her father would have wanted. Corrie hastily kisses her mother and brother goodbye, telling them she will be home with a nice treat later, and warns Joseph not to stray too close to the fire. She tells him this every day, and every day she is grateful when she comes home to find him unharmed, sitting beside her mother in the bed or on the armchair by the fire.

The walk to school is normally invigorating at this time of year with fall leaves blazing a colorful trail through the trees, but Corrie doesn't feel very invigorated today. She is weighed down with thoughts of what this new school year will bring, wondering how she can possibly avoid what the Alliance is planning for her.

In the Selection Process designed by the Alliance, those found to be unsuitable for marriage are assigned to other

4

roles, the girls destined to become Housekeepers helping to run other people's households, the boys enlisted into the Army. Both appointments lay somewhere between the status of being assigned to an Alliance-sponsored marriage and working in the fields. The Alliance make the final decision on each student's status, and it won't be long before they will be deciding for Corrie.

Approaching the school, Corrie observes the four roads radiating from the center of Brookstown. One runs in a straight line ahead of her, turning right in the direction of the Mill. Another runs horizontally through the town where, to the left, it travels to the capital city of Louisville and, to the right, it leads to the next County. The road behind her leads toward a fork in the river and the woods. It leads to Corrie's home.

Agricultural land surrounds the Mill, while in and around the town center, apart from the shops and official Alliance buildings, there are two- and three-story townhouses where the more privileged townsfolk live. In the early morning light, the townhouses glow with muted colors of cream, brown and mustard as the town begins to come to life. Shopkeepers are putting out their signs, office workers are heading purposefully toward the official Alliance buildings, and young people are making their way to school. Corrie doesn't join anyone on her walk to school. She doesn't have a lot of time for friends.

When she reaches the gate to the low wooden building that accommodates about one hundred students and enters the yard where groups of students are already gathered, the bell rings to indicate the start of the day. Corrie allows the other students to rush past her before taking a deep breath and making her way to class.

Entering the classroom, her eyes go immediately to Nate who is looking fresh after the break, tanned and much stronger. He must have grown another foot over the summer because he is now towering over her. His father is the town Blacksmith and Nate helps him in the family business. The Alliance chose him because he is strong and athletic. He is also naturally handsome, with blond hair and blue eyes, and Corrie is attracted to him. Nate's eyes meet hers and she quickly looks away, not wanting him to think she has any interest in him. It won't be up to her in the long run who the Alliance chooses as her Marriage Partner, and she doesn't want to become too closely attached to anyone. The fact that Nate is friendly with everyone doesn't help. He flirts with all the girls, so no one knows who he might be interested in anyway. Nate would be quite a catch, but Corrie doesn't know if he will be her catch, and she doesn't want to get her hopes up.

Sitting at the back of the class is Samuel, chosen by the Alliance because he is good with figures and mathematics. Samuel is slightly taller than her, not well built, with a soft complexion, dark hair, and deep brown eyes. He has a long fringe that hangs over one eye, making him seem somehow mysterious. Corrie knows he uses it to help cover the marks from his father's drunken beatings. Samuel's head is down, and he is already studying the books they have been given for the new school year. He is the least sociable of her classmates and rarely attempts to engage Corrie in conversation. Instead, he just peeks up at her occasionally from under his long fringe and searches her eyes as though asking a question that will never be answered. Corrie can't answer him because he doesn't speak to her at school, and only in a perfunctory manner when she goes to buy grain at the Mill.

Corrie takes the seat next to Nate to show she isn't afraid to sit next to the most handsome boy in class, regardless of whether she will be married off to him or not. And for another reason that she can't quite put her finger on. It just seems like the right thing to do. Classes begin, and Corrie keeps to herself as the first day goes by quickly with the usual input about the Alliance's goodness and the need for people to understand their place in society.

She is startled during the final lesson when the teacher announces the date of the Alliance Winter Ball for the Marriage Selection Procedure to begin. Corrie isn't expecting to be confronted with this news on her first day back at school. It brings her future into sharp focus. The Alliance's "drip, drip, drip" of indoctrination, filling up the dam of her education and school life, is coming to a head. With the dam is about to break, Corrie realizes she can't hold back the waters threatening to course over her life. The Alliance is going to marry her off to someone of their choosing.

It's not that she doesn't want to get married one day or have a family. It's that she won't have a choice in who she marries. That thought really frightens Corrie. There are attractive, outgoing boys, like Nate, and quiet, shy boys, like Samuel. There are boys who boast about what they will do to their wives once they are married, and she finds them the most disturbing of all. She doesn't want anyone to "do" anything to her. She wants someone who will be there for her, as she will be there for them, someone who will watch over her, and her family, in the days ahead. Most of all, Corrie wants to marry someone she loves. A person chosen by her, not the Alliance.

There's a lot of murmuring among her classmates, and Corrie sees other students beginning to size each other up as they wonder about their prospective partners. She notices some of the boys looking in her direction and can't wait to get out of the classroom. It's too soon to be talking about the future. Corrie wants, needs, only to live for today, and getting her order to the buyer will be her priority after school ends for the day.

When the bell rings, she doesn't stop to talk to her classmates but rushes out the doors in her haste to escape the drowning waters of Alliance edicts, blindly making her way to the client's townhouse. The lady is expecting her, and invites Corrie in as she tries on the dresses. They spend some time together deciding if the clothes need any last-minute adjustments before Corrie finally takes her payment and heads back into the town center to buy what she needs for her family.

The luxury of the town homes always leaves her feeling smaller, lesser, somehow. In many ways she is lesser because the Alliance has decided she is, and because her father was a soldier in a war that was fought against them. She is lesser because her mother is unwell, and her brother is "simple". Corrie is lesser because she is Corrie and she has no one else in the world to look out for her, her mother, or her brother.

Deep in thought, Corrie purchases her supplies at the main store and puts everything into her bag, except the eggs.

She carries these in her hands as they are precious, and she doesn't want them to get broken. Her last stop will be at the Mill for the grain they need to make gruel and cookies. She crosses the main street, taking the side road out of the town to get there.

The walk is calming, and Corrie tries to enjoy the final scents of summer, breathing in the aroma of lavender bushes scattered along the side of the road and occasionally leaning down to pick a daisy or two to bring home to her mother.

Her mother loves daisies, and her father never failed to bring some home to her whenever they were in bloom. The flowers would sit proudly in a miniature vase on the small table beside the bed, adding a real brightness to their home, and her mother would give them fresh water every day until even fresh water wasn't enough to keep them alive.

When Corrie gets to the Mill Store, Samuel is behind the counter serving customers. She always feels awkward around him but, as they are both in the same predicament when it comes to the year ahead, Corrie decides to make an effort.

"Hey, Samuel," she says cheerily as she puts her eggs on the counter and her bag on the floor. "We need some grain, but I can only carry about a pound today as my bag is already getting heavy."

Corrie isn't going to tell Samuel that she can only afford one pound of grain, and he doesn't ask any questions. Maybe he already knows since she only comes into the Store every couple of weeks. For some reason, this makes Corrie feels annoyed. This boy she is asking for grain, this boy she might be forced to marry, accepts that to feed a family of three for two weeks only requires one pound of grain.

"Will that be all?" Samuel asks her politely.

"For today." Corrie answers him curtly. For today. For the next two weeks. Why would Samuel care? It's not his problem. Corrie knows Samuel has problems of his own.

"OK. That will be two shillings," he says.

Corrie knows a pound of grain is worth four shillings and looks at Samuel in surprise. He shakes his head slightly to indicate she shouldn't argue with him in the Store. Flustered, she hastily tries to get the money from her purse, in the process accidentally knocking the eggs from the counter and onto the floor.

"Oh, no!" she cries. How could she be so clumsy? They are the only eggs they might have until she gets her next payment, and now they are broken, splashed across the floor and over the top of her shoes. Corrie is angry with herself, and then she is angry with Samuel. If he hadn't offered her the grain for less, she wouldn't have rushed to get the money from her purse. He moves to the other side of the counter to see if he can help.

"I'm sorry," he says.

Corrie knows he has nothing to be sorry for but before she can tell him it's not his fault, and she is the one who is sorry for being so clumsy and making a mess on the shop floor, her eyes begin to fill with tears. She has worked so hard for so little, and now even that is gone. Corrie doesn't want Samuel to peek up from under his long fringe and see her tears, but he does anyway. Without hesitation, he tells her he will clean up the mess and she should come back tomorrow. He will have the bag of grain ready for her then. That way he hopes she has enough money to replace the eggs that are now broken.

Joseph has been looking forward to his treat, and Corrie doesn't want to disappoint him. He would find it hard to understand. She manages a quick and choked "thank you" before rushing out of the store and running as quickly as she can back to town for the eggs. Corrie doesn't know how she will come back tomorrow, but she must. And she will also have to face Samuel in school tomorrow knowing that he has done her a favor and she has hardly acknowledged him, ever.

Two

The following day Corrie enters the classroom with some trepidation. She isn't sure how she will react when she sees Samuel, but as she scours the room there is no sign of him and she takes her seat again next to Nate. This seems to be her place now. She claimed it on the first day back to school. It looks like the others have taken her claim seriously with no protests from her fellow classmates. Nate gives her a grin as she sits down and Corrie smiles back, not sure if the grin means he is happy to see her or if it means he is happy to contemplate another conquest in what she is sure is the long line of conquests Nate has enjoyed. Corrie looks to the back of the class again in case she has missed seeing Samuel, with his head down hiding under his fringe. After confirming he is nowhere in sight, she gets on with the day.

There is much chatter about the upcoming Ball and Corrie can't stand to listen to it. Most of the girls are excited to think about the possibility of their upcoming weddings, even though they don't know who the Alliance will choose for them. Corrie thinks they are naive. Why are they in such a hurry? What if they get someone they don't like, or who treats them badly? They don't seem to be thinking that far ahead and lack the sense of oppression that plagues Corrie. Is she the only one who wants to have a choice in life and not have someone else decide who she will marry or what her future will hold?

Corrie spends the time between classes on her own, away from the hushed conversations of the other girls and their furtive glances directed at Nate and other boys. She sits behind the school building and looks down the road that takes townsfolk to the city of Louisville, wondering if children there are forced to comply with Alliance edicts, too.

A presence suddenly appears beside her and Nate blocks the sun with his large frame.

"Not in the mood for company?" he asks.

"Not really," Corrie replies. She looks down at the ground and waits for Nate to speak again.

"Me either," he says.

The two of them sit there for a while, side by side, silent and comfortable in their agreement not to speak. Suddenly, the bell rings and it's time to go back. Nate gets up first and offers Corrie a hand, a hand she doesn't want to take in case Nate gets the wrong idea. He tries to coax her.

"C'mon. I won't bite. I promise." His words bring a smile to Corrie's lips as she finally accepts his offer and puts her hand in his.

Nate seems friendly enough, but Corrie has other things on her mind. She needs to go back to the Mill after school and isn't looking forward to seeing Samuel again. She's sure he saw the tears in her eyes yesterday and is embarrassed to have been so vulnerable in front of him. No one had ever seen her cry before, at least not the other children at school, and Corrie feels uneasy about exposing her vulnerability. There's always a chance it could be turned against her.

The town is rife with people hoping to garner favor with the Alliance, desperate enough to share information to gain a reprieve from their own suffering—whether it be a deliberate oversight on a payment, or extra goods for their family. In fact, isn't that what Samuel had been offering her? He could be an agent of the Alliance. Corrie will have to be careful.

As she walks into the Mill Store after school, Corrie sees Samuel standing behind the counter. His head is down, and he doesn't look up as she comes in. Corrie clears her throat to get his attention.

"Hmmhmm."

Samuel lifts his head slightly and Corrie can see the bruising and swelling around his eye.

"Oh, Samuel! What happened?" Corrie asks before she can stop herself. She knows what happened.

"Just a little accident, last night. It's nothing. I'll be back at school tomorrow."

"I'm sorry," she murmurs, truly regretful of bringing attention to Samuel's circumstances, and maybe embarrassing him.

"Are you here for your grain?"

"Yes. But I'll only take it if you let me have a look at that eye."

Corrie feels that would be a fair exchange and coaxes Samuel from behind the counter into a back room where there is a basin. She pours cold water into it and finds a rag to soak as Samuel watches her, before putting it against his badly bruised eye. He flinches at first, then lets her tend to him as best she can.

"Did your father do that?" she whispers quietly under her breath.

"Yes," he mumbles.

"You won't get into trouble for giving me the grain, will you?" she asks, concerned that Samuel's father could beat him again if he found out. She doesn't want to be the cause of Samuel's suffering. He is already suffering enough

"No. He doesn't work here, so it's got nothing to do with you."

Corrie is taken aback. It sounds like an insult, or as if there's more than a bag of grain between them. She quickly takes the cloth from Samuel's eye and tells him he should keep applying something cold to it to help bring down the swelling. They move back to the counter, and Samuel hands her the bag of grain. Corrie gives him two shillings from a deposit she has received for her next order and tells him she will give him the rest when she is paid. Just in case Samuel is working for the Alliance she'd rather not take any favors.

Three

After her initial unexpected encounters with Samuel in the lead up to the Winter Ball, Corrie continues to see him every couple of weeks outside of school when she goes to buy grain, but she always has the correct money, putting it on the counter before Samuel can offer to sell her the grain for less. It's a matter of pride and integrity. She won't take any favors from the Alliance, or anyone else she suspects might be working for them. For all she knows the Alliance will give him her hand in marriage. Then what? It doesn't bear thinking about, the Winter Ball and all it might mean for her future.

Nate, on the other hand, is a different story. They have become friendly, both in class and outside, and Corrie continues to sit next to him in school where he provides a welcome distraction from the humdrum of the Alliance's indoctrination. He sometimes slips her little notes under the desk and waits for her reply or pulls faces when the teacher's back is turned. He draws Corrie out of herself, and makes her laugh at the most inappropriate times, which just makes her laugh even more. They spend their break times together, and often go behind the school building as they did on that first day where they look down the road in the direction of Louisville contemplating how people there live.

Corrie continues to wonder if children there are being married off during their final year at school or being forced into different sectors of work for the Alliance. She feels sure that is the case as under the Alliance everyone has, and knows, their place. It makes life simple. It also makes it maddeningly endless. Those who "have not" generally will never "have", unless they have a special gift or talent. The Alliance is always scouting for such people, as they had scouted for her, Nate, and Samuel, and the divisions between these various groups mean they can be ruled effectively. The last time the rule of the Alliance was challenged Corrie lost her father.

The chill in the air increases as the time for the Winter Ball approaches and Corrie must soon focus on preparing a dress for the occasion. This means buying material, an expense her family can hardly afford, so she has taken on more work to pay for what she needs, often having only three or four hours sleep as she tries to complete her orders sooner.

A month before the Ball, Corrie visits the fabric store in the town to check on materials and prices. The selection is overwhelming. There are multiple fabrics in colors ranging from glistening gold and shimmering silver to varying hues of blue, green and burgundy. She touches them, feeling the soft velvet and smooth silk, rough cotton and rich taffeta. It's a dressmaker's dream, but Corrie can only afford the most basic material.

Choosing a green silk, which will match her eyes, she asks the shopkeeper what it will cost to get several lengths to make a gown. The shopkeeper quickly tells her that it would cost three pounds and ten shillings for the material. Corrie's heart sinks. Twenty shillings buys their meager fortnightly supplies, and the material is more than three times that amount. She can't afford the asking price and, as there is no suitable fabric which she can buy for less, Corrie thanks the woman and walks out of the store feeling dejected.

Her spirits haven't lifted much when she enters the Mill Store where Samuel is again serving behind the counter. Corrie waits in line for her turn and when it comes Samuel tells her he has something he wants to give her. He says it in a hushed tone, like the two of them are conspirators and Corrie begins to feel uncomfortable. She has no idea what Samuel is talking about as he beckons her across to the back room.

Once inside, he closes the door and picks up a carefully packaged item from the floor, handing it to her. It's light, lighter than grain anyway, so Corrie knows it's not food Samuel is offering her. Good. She has made it clear she wants to pay in full for whatever she orders from him. She looks up at Samuel again, and sees he is watching her expectantly, waiting for her to see what's inside.

"Open it!" he says.

"OK . . . ," says Corrie, feeling a little reluctant to step into the unknown with Samuel. What is in the bag, and why is he giving it to her?

Corrie carefully unwraps the outer layer and can feel that whatever is inside is soft and full. As she slowly opens the inner layer, gossamer and tulle, silk and pearl adornments burst out to reveal a dress, the like of which Corrie has never seen before.

"Where did you get this?" she asks, breathless in her surprise.

"It was my mother's," he tells her, as a little sadness creeps into his voice.

"Oh, Samuel, it's beautiful," she says as she lifts it out of the bag and holds it up to look at it more closely. A delicate perfume emanates from the dress and Corrie places it against her cheek, feeling the soft material while breathing in its heavenly scent. It's the scent of another world and, for a moment, Corrie is transported out of her suffocating, Alliance-controlled existence into the ballrooms of a past era where people danced because they wanted to, not because they were forced to as part of a Marriage Selection Process ordered by the Alliance.

"I want you to have it," Samuel says matter-of-factly.

"Oh, I can't!" Corrie says. "It was your mother's. Your father would never part with it, I'm sure, and you shouldn't part with it either."

"My father is a drunkard who probably doesn't even know this dress has been lying in a trunk in the attic for years. It's yours now, Corrie. I want you to have it."

Was this Samuel's way of enticing her to consider him

when it came to the Selection Process? None of them had any control over the outcome. Maybe Samuel was hopeful, but Corrie didn't want him to get his hopes up. She wouldn't choose until she could truly choose, and her choosing wasn't part of the Selection Process.

Samuel senses her reluctance and makes her an offer that Corrie finds hard to refuse.

"What if I lend it to you for the Selection? Would you consider borrowing the dress, just for one night? My father will never know it's gone. He doesn't even know it's still there . . . ," Samuel reminds her sadly.

"If I can borrow it for that one night and return it to you the next day, I will be happy to wear your mother's dress to the Ball, Samuel," Corrie tells him. Samuel can't possibly know her desperation at this moment and how much this gift means to her. Corrie can't tell him either.

His face lights up and he flashes her a brilliant smile, one that sends butterflies fluttering in Corrie's stomach. She realizes she needs to leave as soon as possible. She quickly repacks the dress and goes back to the counter where she places her four shillings for a pound of grain. Samuel doesn't try to argue with her but offers to help her carry the load home. Corrie refuses. She feels confused and elated at the same time. No one had ever given her anything as substantial as this, and the dress is beautiful. More substantial in Corrie's mind is the smile she has just received when accepting Samuel's offer. It was a gift in itself, and has created an excitement in her she can't understand. For some reason, it also spells danger. Corrie decides she needs to distance herself a little from Samuel, even though he has given her a dress for the Ball. She doesn't like the way he is making her feel, confused and uncertain of herself. His actions also have the potential to unravel the plans the Alliance is making for both their lives, and Corrie knows she is the only one who can keep her family safe.

Four

Over the next couple of weeks, Corrie doesn't exactly avoid Samuel, she just keeps him at a distance by spending every spare moment with Nate while they are at school, laughing loudly with him whenever the opportunity presents itself. She knows why she is doing it, but at the same time it doesn't help dissipate the confusion she is feeling. It just makes it worse. Corrie knows she is hurting someone who has tried to help her. She just wants the Ball to be over, so she can give the dress back to Samuel and be done with the whole ridiculous mess.

Samuel keeps his distance, as Corrie had planned, and Nate pays more attention to her than ever—which isn't part of her plan at all.

When the night of the Ball finally arrives, the girls are each to be collected by one of the local soldiers who will escort them to the local Town Hall. Corrie has made a few simple adjustments to the dress Samuel gave her which is a full-length gown in stunning emerald green. Its plunging neckline is studded with pearls, and puffed sleeves taper at the elbow where the material narrows in a tight-fitting fashion to her wrists. A hooped underskirt makes the dress expand out from Corrie's waist, and she shows her mother and brother what the dress can do with a special twirl. Suddenly there is a knock at the door, and Corrie's mother opens it to welcome the Escort before handing her the gossamer shawl to place around her shoulders.

Corrie hugs her mother, who has tears in her eyes, and kisses Joseph on the forehead leaving a lipstick mark, before she goes. It's the first time she has worn lipstick and it feels better now that some of it has rubbed off onto Joseph's forehead. Perhaps she will get a few more kisses tonight which will remove it altogether. Corrie knows a lot of the boys and girls find secret places to indulge their passions on the night of the Ball before it's too late and they are betrothed to another, but she doesn't think she will be one of them. She doesn't even want to be part of this Selection Process. Yet, as she steps outside to see snow lying softly all around and stars glittering in the sky, Corrie wonders if this night might just be magical after all.

When they arrive at the Town Hall, brightly lit lanterns hang suspended above a walkway of deep blue carpet guiding them to the entrance. The sound of an orchestra carries on the brisk night air inviting them into the Ball.

In the lead up to the Winter Ball the students were given dance lessons, and an opportunity to dance with each of their classmates. This is because at some point during the night the Selectors will be pairing the students with one another to help determine their suitability. Dancing isn't one of Corrie's strong suits, but she's discovered that if she has the right partner it can be so much easier and more enjoyable.

When Nate had the opportunity to dance with her at school, he led her around the gymnasium in a whirl of missteps and laughter. He obviously wasn't much of a dancer either. When Samuel took her in his arms, he was serious and focused. Holding her lightly, with an arm placed behind her back as she rested one on his shoulder, he took her right hand in his and drew her into an otherworldly place. Gently guiding her in time to the music, Corrie's found her focus was soon on his face, not on her feet, and then Samuel had smiled at her again.

Broken out of her reverie by the Escort as he introduces her to several Town Officials, Corrie is polite, but in a hurry to find a familiar face. After being offered a glass of punch by her Escort, she's able to enter the hall to meet her classmates. As she moves toward them, Corrie catches sight of herself in one of the long mirrors placed strategically along the wall. She sees a vision of a girl who looks much older than her seventeen years, a woman in fact, and a beauty that even Corrie finds it hard to recognize. She has swept her thick dark hair up into a generous bun leaving strands, twisted into curls, to fall on either side of her face. The faux pearl earrings she bought with her meager savings drip from her ears. Corrie looks like a princess and she scans the room looking for her prince.

She spots Nate by a table laden with a selection of bite-size snacks, and he is hungrily helping himself to the

Alliance's offerings. Corrie heads across the floor and, as Nate sees her approaching, he stops mid-bite to slowly lower his food back to the table.

The Selectors are sitting at a long table which is on a raised dais at the top end of the hall, and Corrie can feel their eyes on her as she walks toward Nate to greet him. When she does, Nate takes her by the hands and holds her arms out from her sides taking in the full vision of her beauty.

"Corrie, you look beautiful."

"Thank you."

"Your dress is stunning."

"I know," Corrie says without thinking. It's stunning because it isn't hers. It's stunning because Samuel had given it to her, and she suddenly wonders where he is. She's been too busy looking at herself in the mirror and being self-conscious about the Selectors, too busy searching for her prince, to look around for Samuel. Nate takes her hand and leads her along the table, showing her the array of goodies laid out for their special night. The aromas are delicious, and Corrie chooses a pastry with a creamy filling to settle her rumbling stomach. She was too nervous to eat during the day and suddenly she is starving.

Biting into the snack, Corrie sees Samuel in the mirror as he enters the hall behind her. He is wearing tailored black trousers with a low-cut black vest under a long frock coat. His shirt is white with a high collar, and the green cravat he has chosen matches the color of Corrie's dress. Samuel's trademark fringe is brushed back from his face and, as Corrie takes in his appearance, he catches her eye in the mirror and smiles.

Caught off guard, Corrie looks down just as a shy smile crosses her lips. She can feel her cheeks flush and places her hand on one of them as the music strikes up again. Not knowing where to look or what to do, Corrie takes Nate by the hand to lead him to the dance floor. At the same time, she sees one of the other girls cross over to Samuel to speak to him. He looks so different, so much more mature and open now that he has pushed his fringe back from his forehead. Samuel looks more approachable than he has ever been, and the sharks are beginning to circle. Corrie wonders if she is a shark as well, holding onto Nate's hand as she pulls him toward the dance floor. Other couples are already dancing with no restrictions for now on their choice of dance partner.

After a few minutes, Corrie feels dizzy and asks Nate if he could get her another drink. It's probably because she hasn't eaten much today, so she snacks at the table again while she waits for him. Corrie notices Samuel on the dance floor with the girl who spoke to him earlier, and she watches them glide around, seeming to enjoy each other's company. Nate comes back with Corrie's drink and comments on Samuel.

"Samuel seems to be enjoying himself. He's quite a talented dancer by the looks of things, too."

Corrie wonders if Nate has noticed her watching Samuel, but decides he's just making a general remark as normally Samuel is the least likely of their classmates to make an impression.

"Yes. I wonder where he learned to dance?"

"I think his mother came from quite a well-to-do family in the city, so I'm guessing he might have learned from her," Nate replies.

She hadn't thought much about the woman whose dress she was wearing. It was beautiful, and Corrie looks beautiful in it. Maybe Samuel's mother had floated across the dance floor with his father before he became the drunkard that he was today. Perhaps losing her is what pushed Samuel's father over the edge and into alcoholism, but he is a mean drunk and Corrie thinks that mean streak must have always been in him. There is no sign of that in Samuel, and she decides Samuel must be a lot more like his mother.

Corrie feels better after enjoying more snacks but wonders if there isn't just a little bit of alcohol in the punch they have been drinking. Maybe the Selectors want the young people to relax so they can get a better idea of who they really are, and who they might be best suited to. Corrie decides to stay off the punch after this glass, just as Samuel walks over and asks her for a dance. Nate has turned away to talk to one of the other boys, so Corrie doesn't see the harm. She is wearing his mother's dress after all.

Samuel clasps her cool hand in his warm one and draws her out onto the dance floor. Positioning them both in time to the music, he gently leads her around the dance floor as Corrie stares into his deep brown eyes. What she sees in them is appreciation, and maybe something more. Corrie needs to make sure she doesn't read too much into it, as the reminder of his mother could be making Samuel look at her this way tonight. She stays in step, enjoying the music, and waits for Samuel to speak first.

"Corrie, you look beautiful," he says.

If it wasn't for the dress he had given her, she wouldn't look nearly as beautiful.

"It's your mother's dress that's making me look beautiful. Thank you so much for giving it to me to wear."

"She would have wanted you to have it. She loved to dance, and when we danced at school together you reminded me of her. You dance so well."

Corrie hadn't even noticed. They'd been dancing for a while now, and she'd only looked at her feet once.

"I think it's you that makes me dance well," she says, giving Samuel a smile. It is a genuine smile and he returns it with one of his own, making her heart flutter again.

"Who do you think they will choose to marry you off to after tonight?" Samuel asks her candidly. It must be on his mind, too.

"I don't know. In some ways, I don't want to know. It's out of our hands, so we just have to deal with the decision as best we can," says Corrie.

"That's very prudent of you" says Samuel. "I guess some people fall in love after they get married".

"I don't think the Alliance is concerned with feelings. Certainly not love. Who knows, at our age, what love is anyway?"

Corrie isn't expecting Samuel to share his thoughts on love with her, but he does anyway.

"I think love is when you feel drawn to someone and want to spend as much time with them as possible. When you're with them, you feel like you can't breathe, and when you're apart, all you want is to be with them again. Somehow, their happiness becomes even more important than your own . . ."

As Samuel tapers off, his words breathe life into something that has only been an abstract concept to Corrie until now . . . love. She wonders how he is able to stir things in her that no one else can and is relieved when a tapping on glasses indicates it's time to take their seats for the meal.

The girls sit on one side of the hall, the boys on the other. They are given a rich soup entrée with small parcels of bread. Corrie doesn't particularly like the fishy soup but feels she must eat it so as not to appear impolite or ungrateful. After forcing the last of it down she looks across at Nate who pulls a face to make her laugh. For mains, there is roast beef. Corrie loves beef. It's a rare occasion when they get to eat it, and now she feels guilty for enjoying all this good food while her family survives mainly on grain and its various offerings.

When it's time for dessert, Corrie thinks she can't fit in another bite and might even burst the seams on Samuel's mother's dress, but it looks so incredible she just has to try some. Chocolate is the rarest treat of all and, after sampling her desert, she slips what she can into a handkerchief to take home to her mother and brother. That makes her feel better. Just then the Head Selector comes to the podium.

"Girls and boys, or should I say, young men and women . . . " Some of the other Selectors snicker at his attempt at humor. "You all know why you are here. In a few weeks, the Alliance intends to place you into couples, and this time next year you will be given to each other in marriage. Tonight, we want to determine which of you are most suited to each other, so we will call you out to dance together. We have arranged six suitable couplings for each of you, so there will be six dances now as we watch you together and discuss the merits of your partnerships. For the first dance . . . " the

Selector goes on, and suddenly Corrie's name is coupled with Nate's and they are required to meet in the middle of the dance floor.

Nate looks happy, and Corrie feels comfortable with him, so she walks confidently to the middle of the dance floor and waits with him as the other couples take their places. The music begins again, and Corrie looks up at Nate who swirls her around energetically, occasionally sweeping her off her feet to entertain the crowds. Corrie is forced to stifle a giggle as Nate works to impress the Selectors.

Soon, their dance is over, and Corrie is called to dance with her next partner, Jeremy. Before long she has danced with Nate, Jeremy, Bartholomew, Anthony and James. She felt most comfortable with Nate and is undecided on the Selectors other choices who are all just classmates to her and nothing more. None of them are terrible to look at, but some of them can be immature, and Corrie isn't a big fan of those boys.

The last call takes Corrie by surprise. Samuel. She wonders why the Selectors have chosen to put the two of them together, and Samuel must notice the look on her face because he walks toward her slowly, with his head down, to meet her in the middle of the floor. He takes her in his arms and, while the music plays, doesn't look at her, but instead surveys all the other couples as he safely guides her across the floor until their dance is over. She can't look at Samuel now either and mumbles her thanks as she walks back to the table.

Something inside her makes Corrie want to cry. For Samuel, for herself, for all the people in the world who may never get the chance to experience true love, thanks to the Alliance and its edicts.

More casual dancing is allowed after the Selection Process is completed, and small groups gather to dance jigs in the middle of the dance floor. It is the merriest part of the evening, when partners can choose each other again, and they forget the Selectors are still watching them as they dance, deciding on their futures. Nate draws Corrie onto the dance floor again, not noticing how pensive she has become. Corrie notices Samuel is nowhere in sight.

At the end of the night, as they gather at the doors for their homeward journeys, Corrie finally spies Samuel. He has let his fringe fall over his eyes again, and they are both downcast as he makes his way toward the door. It hurts Corrie to see him this way after he had looked so proud when he first walked into the hall. She can't let him leave like this, and moves across to where he is standing, preparing to leave.

"Samuel" she says.

"Yes?" he answers her quietly.

"I really enjoyed dancing with you tonight."

If that was true, she would have danced with him more. Corrie knows it and Samuel knows it, too.

"I think I enjoyed dancing with you more," he says.

"I'm not a very good dancer, and I was afraid I would make you look bad."

"I think you are an excellent dancer, with the right partner. I hope the Selectors pick the right partner for you after tonight."

You could be my partner, Corrie thinks. They could pick you. But she doesn't say it out loud. They won't pick Samuel because he didn't look at her and she didn't look at him. They would be the two most incompatible people in the world, and they showed the Selectors that tonight.

"I hope the same for you, Samuel," Corrie blurts out just before she makes a run for the door, wanting to put distance between them. At the same time, she longs to put her arms around Samuel, to comfort and reassure him, to tell him everything will be alright. She can't. She and Samuel are not compatible. And the closest Corrie came to being compatible with anyone tonight, was with Nate. They had developed a comfortable friendship over the last few months and she trusts him. Corrie still doesn't know if she can fully trust Samuel. The less they see of each other, the better. No point in getting Samuel's hopes up after all his talk about love tonight.

Then, just as she takes the Escort's arm, Corrie remembers. She has to return the dress to Samuel tomorrow.

Five

In the early hours of Sunday morning Corrie is woken by the sound of alarm bells ringing everywhere. She jumps out of bed to check on her mother and brother. They've been woken, too, and she tells them not to worry as she grabs a coat and runs outside to see what is going on. Full of trepidation, Corrie runs up the dirt road toward the town, forced off it as several horsemen gallop by. They are going at speed, heading deeper into the woods, and Corrie's heart is racing as she continues toward the town center, taking cover closer to the trees.

Rifles crack in the distance as the smell of gunpowder begins to penetrate the woods. Reaching the outskirts of the town, Corrie sees soldiers running in all directions. There are bodies lying in the street, and soldiers shouting at people to return to their homes. It's a chaotic scene. Suddenly, Corrie sees a man run from behind a building to take aim at a soldier. He fires, and the soldier crumples, falling from his horse. More soldiers materialize, and one puts a gun to the shooter's head. Corrie has already turned around and is running back to the cottage when she hears the fatal shot.

As soon as she enters, she bolts the door from the inside and climbs onto her mother's bed, gathering Joseph in her arms. Trembling, and in shock, Corrie "shh's" Joseph and tells him everything will be alright. She isn't sure what's happening, but knows it isn't good. She also knows it's not the first time people have reacted violently to the oppressive measures of the Alliance.

The shouting, gunfire, and sound of hooves along the track continue through the night until eventually Corrie's eyes become heavy again, and she nestles further into the covers before falling asleep.

A sudden loud rapping on the door wakens her, and Corrie stiffens in fear. Could this be soldiers at their door? Rebels?

"Open up!" a voice shouts from the other side.

"Who is it?" Corrie shouts back.

"The Alliance!"

"I'm coming" she says as she wriggles her way out of the bed and unbolts the door as quickly as she can. Her hands are shaking.

"Who lives here?" the soldier asks.

"Just me, my mother and my brother" Corrie answers.

"Where is your brother?"

"Over there" she says pointing.

"How old is he?" asks the soldier.

"He is ten," she tells him.

"Where were you last night?" the soldier wants to know.

"We were here. There was a terrible commotion during the night, but we were too afraid to go out. What's happening?" Corrie asks.

"You don't need to worry your pretty little head about that," says the soldier. "You're ordered to stay indoors for now and not to open the door to anyone," he instructs her, "unless it's the Alliance." As the soldier rides away, Corrie bolts the door behind him.

She lights the fire and gets breakfast ready, telling her mother and Joseph not to worry; they are safe for now. She mixes an egg with a little milk and cooks it over the fire in a pot. It comes out nice and fluffy and Corrie spoons it over some gruel cookies to give to them. She pours a little milk into a cup for her brother, then puts a cup of water beside her mother before preparing to go out again, in defiance of the soldier's orders. As much as she doesn't want to leave her family, Corrie needs to find out what is happening.

"I'll be back as soon as I can," Corrie says as she runs out the door. Just as she turns the corner to head up the path she runs into Nate.

"What's going on?" Corrie asks with urgency.

"There's been a Rebel attack on the town. A lot of the Rebels were killed, but some escaped into the woods. Soldiers are looking for them now. Where are you going?" Nate asks curiously.

"I just wanted to find out what was happening."

"The Alliance has closed everything down. They are probably going to call a meeting, but I don't know when. Everyone has been ordered to stay indoors until then."

Corrie suddenly thinks of Samuel. She doesn't know why. Perhaps it's because she's supposed to return the dress to him today. Nate tells her he will come back if he can with any news but says that she should stay in the cottage for now, especially with Rebels taking refuge in the woods.

Six

orrie spends the day indoors with her mother and Joseph, anxiously waiting for news, and tries to take her mind off what is happening by sewing. The days are short now that the winter has set in, and it isn't long before darkness descends. She lights a lamp, stokes the fire again and sets a pot of water with gruel over it, adding two small potatoes to make it more filling. She has managed to find some spinach growing at the side of the path which she tosses in as well. It adds a touch of color and flavor to the meal, and she thinks anything green must be good for them. Her father had told her that.

Since the Rebellion, people had been unable to grow their own food, as the Alliance forced an increased dependency on the populace. The privilege of farming went to loyal supporters and the produce could only be sold to the Government who determined its price. This caused the prices for basic items to soar and Corrie tries to supplement their diets with occasional foraging expeditions in the woods. It's the best she can do, and she sometimes wonders if it might not have been better if she'd been sent into the fields or factories to work. At least that way a meager income could be relied upon, rather than having to rely on the whim of privileged people seeking her out to create the latest fashion at the lowest price.

She sits by the fire in the big armchair while she waits for the stew to warm as Joseph sits beside her. He leans against her, and Corrie tells him a story—one of the stories her father told her long ago. It helps to pass the time and keep their fears at bay.

Her father had told her when he was a boy there was a day during the summer when everyone would participate in competitions, down by the river. There were competitions for swimming, fishing, skipping stones on the water, and for finding hidden treasure. All the families from the town would come together and enjoy a picnic on the banks. It was a colorful event and people usually wore their best clothes. They even had competitions for that: Best Dressed Lady, Best Dressed Man and Best Dressed Child. Of course, the well-to-do people usually won those competitions, as they spared no expense in having outfits made which they hoped would outdo all the others. It was the busiest time of the year for his mother, a seamstress, when the Summer Social came around.

She often had offcuts from various dress materials and normally used these to make rag dolls for children in the orphanage. He said she never wasted a scrap. One year, his mother decided to enter him in the children's section of the

Best Dressed competition at the Social and used the offcuts to create a garment with mythical overtones. It was based on story of a cloak, an amazing cloak of many different colors, which attracted the attention of Kings. The cloak was said to have magical powers which would cause a King to bow before whoever wore it, thus making the wearer of the cloak all-powerful. Of course, the King had to be tricked into inviting the wearer of the cloak to his castle, otherwise he would never do so.

His mother was not the only one who knew the story, so when her father appeared wearing what looked like the magical cloak from the story, the crowd immediately bowed to his superior presence, and to his mother's superior skills. He won the competition, and his prize was a children's storybook and a bag of sweets of his choice. Corrie always loved hearing that story and imagining the world before the Alliance came to power.

As the stew begins to boil, Corrie ends her story and helps Joseph up onto the chair, so she can feed him his dinner. She hands a bowl to her mother, whose eyes have lit up at the memory of her father and the stories he told. Corrie likes to see her mother happy. It is a rare occurrence these days.

After dinner, Corrie realizes that she hasn't returned Samuel's mother's dress. She wonders if Samuel has forgotten about it because of everything else that has happened. She can't go out, leaving her mother and brother alone. It would be too risky. What if any of the Rebels showed up at the door while she wasn't here? No, Corrie must stay put for now, and wait for someone to bring her news of any developments.

As the evening wears on, it's soon time to make sure Joseph is in bed and her mother is comfortable. When they are settled, Corrie goes back to the sewing machine and begins her nightly work. The sound of the machine never seems to disturb her mother or brother and, as the fire burns down in the hearth, they are both soon fast asleep.

Close to midnight, Corrie hears a light knocking at the door. It's so light, she wonders if she's heard anything at all, but stops the machine to listen again. There it is. A light tapping sound. Not the type of banging that soldiers at the door would normally produce, but a clandestine tap-tap-tap and the sound of her name being whispered through the door with a kind of urgency.

"Corrie!"

Corrie doesn't answer.

"Corrie!" a little more loudly.

Who could it be? If they know her name, it must be someone she knows, so she goes to the door and asks quietly from the inside:

"Who is it?"

"Samuel."

Corrie is startled. Why would Samuel be at her door at this time of night? He lives closer to the Mill, on the other side of town, and he has no reason to come knocking . . . unless it is to pick up his mother's dress.

"Hold on," she tells him as she unbolts the door and lets him inside. His trademark fringe is covering his eye, but she can see a red mark on the side of his face.

"What happened?" Corrie asks with concern.

"Oh nothing. My father wanted some liquor, and when I

told him all the stores were closed, he hit me and told me to go out and find some."

"We don't have any liquor here," Corrie tells him.

"That's not why I'm here. I walked into the town anyway, just to see what was happening, and the only place that was open was the Blacksmith's. Nate and his father are tending to the soldiers' horses after the search for the Rebels."

"Oh," says Corrie.

"I came because Nate asked if I could get a message to you."

"Oh," Corrie says again.

"He wanted to come himself, but he can't leave, so I told him I would bring you the message."

Corrie waits expectantly for what Samuel is about to tell her.

"He overheard the soldiers say that the Rebels are more numerous than they thought, and the Alliance is going to hunt down anyone who may be connected to them. He wants you to be careful, especially with the search still going on for Rebels in the woods. He said it wouldn't be good if the soldiers find any Rebels in the vicinity of your home."

What did he mean? Rebels in the vicinity of their home? Does Nate think there are Rebels hiding in their home? Her father had been a Rebel, but they'd had no further contact with the people who had garnered her father's support and wouldn't help them now.

"He thinks Rebels might be hiding in our cottage?!" Corrie says in both amazement and anger.

"I don't think that's what he meant . . . "

"Well, there are no Rebels here. You can see there's only my family—my mother and my brother—and no one else has been near the place all day!"

"Corrie, he didn't mean . . . " She doesn't let Samuel finish.

"It doesn't matter what he meant. There is no one here, and I wouldn't even have let you in, except you called me by name. I wouldn't even think of opening the door to anybody else."

"I believe you," Samuel says matter-of-factly.

Corrie can see Samuel's cheek beginning to swell and, as she has had enough of the conversation about Rebels, she offers to tend to it for him.

"Let me get something for that cheek," she offers.

"No, that's OK."

"Samuel, you've come all this way on a freezing night to bring me a message. You didn't have to do that. Now, let me look at your cheek."

"OK," Samuel says reluctantly, and Corrie can see he feels foolish for running what turns out to be a fool's errand. What was Nate thinking?

Corrie takes a cloth and tells Samuel to wait while she unbolts the door and collects some snow in the cloth for him to hold to his cheek. When she comes back in, she holds the ice pack to Samuel's face before taking one of his hands telling him to hold it there for a while to help stop the swelling. The first thing she notices is how firm and strong his hand is, while at the same time being soft and gentle. It is a man's hand, the hand of a gentle man, a man who will carry a message in the middle of the night without fear or favor. Samuel wasn't afraid to bring her the message, even with Rebels hiding out in the woods, and he has nothing to gain from his visit to their home tonight.

Then, Corrie begins to wonder . . . has Nate really sent him? Has Samuel come of his own volition to make sure she is OK? Has he come because he is an Alliance agent, and his real job is to spy on her?

As the thoughts swirl around in Corrie's head, she begins to look at Samuel with suspicion. Are his motives as altruistic as they seem? She can't be sure and, as the thoughts continue to crowd her mind, she notices Samuel beginning to sense her discomfort.

"I think I should go now." He stands and prepares to leave.

Corrie feels bad that Samuel has to go home to an angry father who will have no alcohol now to soothe the raging beast inside. She wants to tell Samuel to stay. What if Rebels are close by? What if soldiers suspect him as he comes out of the woods?

"Samuel . . . " Corrie begins hesitantly.

"It's OK. My father will probably have fallen asleep by now, so he should be harmless by the time I get back. He won't hit me again tonight."

"It's not just your father that worries me," says Corrie. "What about the Rebels, or the soldiers? They might think you're a Rebel when they see you coming out of the woods."

"It's alright, Corrie. The Captain on duty knows me. He knows my father and that he keeps books for the Alliance," Samuel says.

They know him, Corrie thinks. How well do they know him? Well, if he is a spy he can go and tell them now that there is no one hiding out in the cottage and there never will be. They have suffered enough already not to invite more suffering on themselves. Then she remembers.

"Oh, I nearly forgot!" says Corrie. "Your mother's dress . . . "

"You keep it," says Samuel. "You looked so beautiful last night. It should belong to somebody who appreciates it, and it looked like it was made for you."

Corrie tries hard not to blush. Thinking of the first thing that comes into her head, she says:

"I had to make some alterations, but they were only small ones."

Samuel replies without hesitation.

"As long as you never alter yourself."

Alter herself? How could she alter herself? Corrie never thought about being anyone except Corrie. What was there to alter?

"I won't," she tells him, not really knowing what he means.

"Good," Samuel says as he heads out the door.

After bolting the door, Corrie goes to her bed with Samuel's cryptic words still hanging in the air. "As long as you never alter yourself."

It could only mean one thing. Samuel likes her just the way she is.

Seven

Early next morning, a soldier comes to their door to call them to a meeting in the town. Corrie tells her mother to stay in their cottage and look after Joseph while she goes to the meeting. There is no need for them all to go. She can tell them what they need to know when she gets back. As she leaves, her mother warns her to be careful.

It's usually a thirty-minute leisurely walk, but today Corrie is in a hurry, and reaches the town center in half that time. She arrives panting and pushes her way through the crowd to get a better view of the gathered Officials. She sees some of her classmates in the mass of bodies, as well as familiar faces from the stores where she normally shops, but there is no sign of Nate, or Samuel. A tall, well-dressed man stands atop a podium that has been erected hastily in the middle of the Town Square.

As she waits for the meeting to begin, Corrie takes in the townspeople and the Officials. Their town is normally a simple place, inoffensive, trouble-free. But she knows life is not so simple, and such an appraisal of her town is not true now and would be less true after today. The tall silver-haired Official takes his place at the microphone and clears his throat. On his left is the Town Mayor, wearing his full regalia, and on his right the Head of the Military Garrison in full uniform. Corrie begins to feel nervous but knows she must stand her ground to hear what they are about to say.

"The Alliance has issued a decree in relation to the Insurrection which occurred in your town, and several other towns, overnight. The actions by local Rebels, and those who entered the towns from outlying areas, was an affront to our well-ordered society and the Alliance's response has been swift and sure. Several Rebels are dead, and we have captured many others. There is now a curfew in place which will be explained to you by Colonel Thomas. From today, all businesses will be overseen by the Military. This is to ensure there is no disruption to vital services. For this purpose, we are bringing in extra troops, and we will also be organizing a system of rationing. People considered loyal to the Alliance will receive a Ration Card entitling them to a generous portion of goods and services. Those whose loyalty is in question will have to prove their loyalty before receiving a Ration Card. The Mayor will instruct you in terms of how that will be done."

Corrie looks around at the people now cowed into silence by the suggestion that, without proof of their loyalty, they might just starve. As the Mayor makes his way to the microphone to spell out the terms of this decree, the crowd waits expectantly and Corrie spies Nate to her left and closer to the back of the podium. He is almost a head taller than the rest of the people standing in front of him, and Corrie wonders how she missed seeing him earlier. His gaze is fixed intently on the Mayor, and she decides she will try to speak to him after the meeting is over. There will be a lot to talk about.

"I know most of the people standing here today are loyal to the Alliance," begins the Mayor. "Unfortunately, those who are not have created problems for our town, and now we must all pay the price. The price will be highest for those who are unable to prove their loyalty to the Alliance, so I urge you all to show your support and engage with the Officials who will be coming to your homes to question you. You have nothing to fear and should cooperate as a way of ensuring your own safety and that of your family. After these visits, within a short period of time, you will be issued with your Ration Cards which will be an indication of your current level of loyalty. This, of course, can always be improved, so I urge you once again to be cooperative with Officials. Thank you."

Corrie senses that the Mayor is under duress, unhappy about the outcome of the Insurrection, which has put the whole town under the microscope. It isn't enough to put the Rebels down. Now, everyone will pay the price for the Rebel's rash deeds. People are beginning to mumble to one another about what it could all mean when Colonel Thomas finally takes the microphone.

"As you have already been informed, the Army will be taking over the running of this town and imposing a curfew. No one will be allowed out after dark and, if you are discovered breaking the curfew, prepare to pay with your life." Thomas pauses for effect before he goes on. "We will be organizing the rations and greatly appreciate the Mayor's assistance in providing us with the information we will need to do so. There is nothing to fear if you have done nothing wrong, but those who wish to test the patience of the Alliance will be punished severely. We desire your cooperation and will work toward securing your town and your homes from the Rebels." He gives a slight cough as he walks back to his seat. The Alliance Official returns to the microphone to tell people to return to their homes and to wait for Town Officials to visit them.

Corrie is dumbstruck. She runs a business of sorts, unofficially of course, and it has been the mainstay of their survival. How will they manage if the Alliance shuts it down? How will she prove her loyalty and gain the rations her family needs? It's all too much to take in and Corrie tries to find Nate in the crowd again. People are beginning to move off, going back to their homes and their families.

"Corrie!" She hears a harsh whisper beside her. Corrie turns to see who it is.

"Samuel!" Relief floods over her at the sight of him.

"I saw you from the other side of the podium. We can't talk for long or these people will get suspicious."

Suspicious of what? Corrie wonders. She guesses they are suspicious of everyone and everything after what had taken place last night. There is bruising on Samuel's cheek now, which is less swollen than it would have been if she hadn't put the snowpack on it when he came to see her.

"Is your cheek sore?" she asks him, not wanting to focus on the dread now tying knots in the pit of her stomach.

"A little, but it's not me I'm worried about," Samuel says.

"What do you mean?" Corrie asks innocently.

"I overheard my father talking this morning with an Alliance Official who came to the door. The Official said the Alliance is going to be looking closely at people who have Rebel connections in their past, as well as people they currently suspect of being involved with the Rebels. I just wanted to warn you."

Her father. Her father had fought clandestinely to topple the Alliance, which means she and her family will now be in their sights. They'd had nothing to do with the Rebels since her father's death, but maybe that wouldn't matter now. She looks at Samuel and sees the concern in his eyes. Why is he telling her this? Can she really trust him?

"Samuel, it's best if you aren't seen with me then," she says. "Please, I don't want you to get into trouble."

"I'm going to see what else I can find out," Samuel replies. "If there's anything I can do to help you, I'll do it," he says with a great deal of sincerity.

Corrie still doesn't understand why Samuel would want to help her, why he is always trying to help her. She has done her best to discourage him, trying to ensure her family's safety, but Samuel is insistent in his efforts and Corrie must make sure her resistance doesn't wane. Especially now, when the Alliance has her family in its sights. She needs to go home and explain to them what is happening. She doesn't know what she is going to tell them, but she isn't going to involve Samuel in her family's problems.

Corrie tells him she is grateful for his concern and hopes his family will be OK, too. She also hopes Nate is OK and wonders how his father will react to the news of the Army taking over his business. None of them has much choice, but she hopes there won't be any more trouble, and that this blanket edict won't last very long. It has the potential to cause an enormous amount of suffering.

Eight

C orrie takes her time going home, trying to work out how she will tell her mother and brother the news. The curfew will have little effect on them because they rarely go out after dark, and Corrie is normally too busy working on her sewing projects at night. The curfew won't be a problem.

What is a problem is that Corrie doesn't know what questions the Officials will ask, or how her answers will affect the family's entitlement to rations. She also has no idea what will happen to her sewing endeavors. Corrie likes to sew and wants to keep her independence. There are just too many unknowns, and she doesn't want to cause her family any concern right now until they know more. Corrie decides to tell her mother only about the curfew. It seems like standard procedure after the events of the previous night and is easy to understand. For now, she can protect her mother from the knowledge that there might be worse to come.

As she takes a bend in the path leading back to the cottage, Nate suddenly appears before her.

"Nate! You scared me!" Corrie cries as she steps back and takes in his tall, muscular figure. He looks at her with an uncharacteristic seriousness. Taking her hand, he leads her off the path and into the trees.

"Corrie, I'm not supposed to be here, and I can't stay long, but I just want you to know that I will do my best to help you and your family with anything you need."

It was slightly different to what Samuel had said, but it carried the same sentiment. Corrie had two people who cared enough about her and her family to take risks to ensure they would be OK.

"Thank you, Nate. I don't know what's going to happen yet, I just know we're going to get a visit from Alliance officials, and we'll have to answer their questions. I don't know what the questions will be about, but if they ask about my father . . . ," Corrie trails off. Samuel had already warned her that might happen.

"Corrie, your father has been gone a long time now, and your family hasn't caused any problems for the Alliance since then. They have no reason to suspect you of disloyalty," Nate reminds her.

Corrie isn't sure if that's how she wants to be thought of . . . someone who doesn't cause problems for the Alliance. Her father had aligned himself with the Rebels previously for a reason. Corrie isn't going to insult his memory by accepting that she is not a troublemaker like him.

"I'm not sure I like what you're implying," Corrie snaps back.

"I'm not implying anything. I'm just saying that the Alliance has no reason to think you're connected to the Rebels, so hopefully they'll treat you fairly."

Corrie hopes so, too, and knows she must be careful, for her family's sake. She tells Nate she will find out soon enough.

"Are they going to take over your father's business?" Corrie asks.

"Yes. My father and I will still have work, but the soldiers from the Garrison will be overseeing the work we do and making sure it isn't connected to the Rebels in any way. My father isn't happy about it, of course, but he'll accept the directive for now until we see what that might mean. He hopes things will settle down soon, and we can go back to doing what we normally do."

Nate doesn't seem to be too bothered by what they "normally" do. Corrie hasn't been either, up until now. But things are changing. She is beginning to think for herself, and with the prospect of an Alliance orchestrated marriage hanging over her head isn't sure she wants to play along with the Alliance's plans. Maybe she is more like her father than she previously thought.

"You'd better go, Nate, and thank you. I'm sure they'll have to open the school again soon, to make things seem as normal as possible, so I will see you then if I don't see you before."

Nate heads back up the path as Corrie continues on her way home, distracted. She has a lot on her mind.

Nine

The Alliance Officials come to Corrie's home two days later. Even though she is expecting them, she's only partially prepared when they arrive. Her next delivery of clothes is hidden under her bed. How much do they know? She doesn't want to take any chances, and wonders if there is a way of keeping her business going in a clandestine fashion. The most important thing is to play it safe for Joseph's and her mother's sake. Unfortunately, she hasn't been able to hide her sewing machine and will have to explain that to the Officials if they ask. She reminds herself to wait for them to ask, rather than offer them information.

She lets the two officials into the cottage and explains to her mother that they just want to ask a few questions about the family, so they can arrange the provision of rations while the town is under military supervision. The explanation seems to satisfy her mother who, nevertheless, watches suspiciously from her bed with Joseph by her side.

"Please give us your names," says one Official.

"My name is Corrie Tennant. This is my mother, Alice, and my brother, Joseph."

"We believe you still attend school, Corrie. Is that correct?"

"Yes. I am in my final year."

"So, you attended the recent Winter Ball in the town?" the other Official asks.

"Yes."

"We are calling people up to work for the Alliance. It won't affect the Marriage Selection Process, but as a student in your final year you are qualified for call up. We are here to request your presence for testing tomorrow."

Their request is totally unexpected.

"I'm not sure what you mean," answers Corrie.

"We need people who can attend to documentation and provide support with communication. The work of the Communication Office has tripled since the Insurrection. We've been led to believe you are very good with language, and that your writing is exceptional."

That's true. It's the reason she had been able to continue with her education, and why she is soon to be married off to a "suitable" partner.

"I have been told that," says Corrie.

"We would like you to come to the Town Hall tomorrow and sit a test. The test will indicate if what we have heard about you is true. If it is, we can promise you a generous supply of rations for your family."

It wasn't really a choice, just like everything else the Alliance engineered. It was blackmail. At the same time, it was like music to Corrie's ears. She would still be able to support her family, and it also meant the Alliance didn't seem to be seeking further retribution for her father's "crimes".

"We need your response before we leave today," the first Official says. It's a take it or leave it offer, and Corrie decides to take it.

"I will come to the Town Hall tomorrow," is all she says.

She wonders if anyone else has been invited to go to the Town Hall. Nate already has his work decided for him, helping his father at the Blacksmith's. They will need his skills to tend to the soldiers' horses. Samuel's father helps the Alliance keep their books. Maybe he will be apprenticed to his father in the same fashion as Nate. He is good with numbers and it seems only natural.

The Officials leave the cottage without further comment, and her mother looks at her with concern after Corrie closes the door.

"Corrie, I'm not sure that's a good idea," she says.

"What? Working for the Alliance?"

"Yes. Your father fought these people because he was against everything they stood for. He knew one day it would come to this, and the Alliance would engineer a way to gain more control."

"But, it's only because of the Insurrection. It might not even last that long. Just until things settle down again, and then . . . " Corrie doesn't know what then. Back to struggling to survive, married off to a chosen suitor, maintaining a status engineered by the Alliance? Corrie's "and then . . . " is left to hang in the air as she ponders her mother's words. It seems like the Alliance can never have enough control and that she, herself, can't have any. Well, she did have some control over the outcome of her visit to the Town Hall tomorrow. Corrie knows she has a choice to make, she just hopes she makes the right one. If she doesn't get this job, she might not be able to sew either and then they would most certainly starve.

Ten

The next day Corrie arrives at the Town Hall, which no longer glitters after the Winter Ball. The main hall is divided into four sections. Signs indicate the different sections: Language, Mathematics, Science and Geography. These are the immutables. With them, there is no room for free thought which could challenge or incite. These studies are to be used precisely, and for the Alliance's purposes. History and Politics are only for the elite who are destined to become the future leaders, and obviously it's the Alliance's own version of both which is served up to them in abundance. Philosophy is out of the question. It's by far the most threatening of all topics, capable of challenging the Alliance's agenda, and the status quo. Philosophy is for free thinkers and radicals, and the Alliance want none of those.

Corrie sees tables and chairs arranged around the room, with an Official sitting at the head of each section attending to paperwork for the candidates. So far, not many candidates have gathered, but Corrie knows where she needs to go and heads to the section for Languages.

"What is your name?"

"Corrie Tennant."

The woman marks her name off a list, gives her the necessary paperwork, and directs her to a seat at one of the tables. The paperwork is in a sealed envelope, and she is told not to open it until the test begins. Corrie waits nervously as other people, including students from her class, enter the hall, gathering their paperwork and taking their seats. She suddenly remembers that Samuel might be coming, too. Inexplicably, this makes her feel better. She has a co-conspirator with whom she can compare notes, but not until the test is over. They are not allowed to talk until then.

Samuel walks in oblivious to Corrie's presence. The Mathematics section is in front of hers. As he turns around after being given his papers, he catches her eye and looks surprised. So, Samuel isn't expecting to see her here. Corrie wonders if that's because of the warning he had given her about her family, or if he didn't think she was a suitable candidate. He nods his head slightly in her direction, his trademark fringe falling further over his eyes, before he takes his seat. The chair makes a loud scraping noise as he pulls it back, attracting everyone's attention. Samuel coughs slightly in embarrassment before he sits down, preparing for the test that will help determine their futures.

A bell rings, signaling that they are to open their envelopes. The candidates have five minutes to read the papers before two more rings will indicate it is time to start the test. Corrie looks at her papers. There are questions relating to

Grammar and Comprehension, a section presenting an opinion piece to which the candidates must provide arguments for and against, and finally an essay to be written on the 'goodness' of the Alliance. For this she must choose one example of how the Alliance has benefited the people. This will come straight out of the propaganda lessons at school, to be presented "parrot-like" and without critical thinking.

Corrie knows she will have no problem with this part of the test, but the opinion piece tempts her to share her true feelings about the Alliance. A thousand alarm bells begin ringing in her head, telling her to answer the way the Alliance would expect, while she hears the concerned voice of her mother asking her again if she should even be here. Well, it's too late now, Corrie decides, and the only thing left to do is what is required of her. She feels torn between protecting her family and telling the Alliance what she really thinks. She wishes she was Samuel who just had to calculate a few numbers and wasn't required to expose his thinking to these oppressive Alliance officials. Maybe that's why they have chosen her.

They have three hours to complete the test, and Corrie moves through the first section on Grammar and Comprehension in an hour. She leaves the opinion piece and moves straight to writing the necessary praises of the Alliance, which takes her another hour. Throughout the test she occasionally looks up at Samuel's back to see him diligently working through his answers, every now and again putting the pen to his mouth as he thinks about his calculations. She can almost see his mind ticking over and wishes that she could rely on tried and trusted formulae, rather than her own impulsive thinking.

The opinion piece, to be written in this final hour, now looms in front of her. Corrie, at last, decides to dive in. They are asking her to discuss the merits of an article, giving her leeway to share her opinion, but she knows it needs to be in a muted fashion, so that she doesn't hurt her family. The question rests on the issue of marriage, and the piece they have been given to read extols the virtues of Alliance imposed marriages—the type of marriage in which Corrie will soon be enjoined. She has been indoctrinated enough to know how to present the argument in favor, but it's not long before Corrie must consider the arguments against. Of course, they are many and varied, but Corrie decides to focus on the reality of love.

Samuel had gotten her thinking about it when he shared his thoughts with her at the Winter Ball. He was a type of philosopher in his own right. Not many seventeen-year-old boys would be thinking about the meaning of love . . . what it was, how it made you feel, what it could mean for the people concerned. Corrie looks up at Samuel's back again, and decides to borrow his words in expressing what she thinks is probably the human heart's deepest desire . . . the desire to love and be loved.

She writes, extoling the virtues of love, not removing them from marriage, but insisting that they should be the reason for marriage. It is only a deep love between two people and a yearning for the other that will enable a marriage to last, to be successful, to produce the intended consequence of faithfulness, and the fruits of coming together.

As she writes, tears begin to swim in Corrie's eyes. She thinks about all these things, of how her own parents had managed to find love, only to have it ripped away from them again. Maybe love is more tenuous than she imagines, and maybe it's too painful because the consequence of losing it can break your heart. Corrie doesn't want to think any more about love.

The bell rings twice to indicate there are five minutes to go before the candidates must put their pens down.

At the final bell, Corrie gets up from her seat and hands her paper to the official at the head of her section. Samuel has also gotten up to hand his paper in, and Corrie decides it's better to wait for him outside where the Officials won't be watching them. She stands to the side of the building and this time it is her turn to whisper loudly to him.

"Samuel!"

He turns immediately and walks across to where Corrie is standing.

"Corrie. I didn't expect to see you here," he says.

"And why would that be?" Corrie asks, annoyed at the inference for a second time that Samuel is surprised to see her.

"Well, I wasn't sure what happened after I talked to you the other day. I didn't know what the Officials might have . . . " Corrie stops him.

"Said? Done? Samuel, you warned me about the Alliance investigating people who had Rebel connections in their past, and I hadn't even thought about that. I got all worried about what that might mean, and what they would ask me . . . I even hid my sewing under the bed. And do you know what? The only thing they said was that they were calling people up to work for the Alliance and requested I come here for testing today! You didn't need to warn me at all."

Corrie's hands have balled up into fists by her side and she is not only upset, she is angry. Why had Samuel warned her when the Officials had not even asked her about her father? She didn't understand.

"Corrie. I told you what I heard when they were talking to my father. I thought it was only fair to warn you. Just in case . . . "

"Well, I didn't need your warning. I'm a candidate for an Alliance position, just like you, and if they select me then I won't have to worry anymore about feeding my family, or how we are going to survive every day!"

Corrie knows she isn't being fair to Samuel, but she doesn't know how else to react. It's all right for Samuel. His father already works for the Alliance. They are never going to go hungry.

"I'm sorry if I worried you. I was just trying to help, and I wanted you to know what to expect if they did start asking questions about your father," Samuel tells her.

Corrie tries to see it from Samuel's point of view. She knows, if he had been right, the situation could have been a lot more precarious for her and her family. He wasn't trying to hurt her.

"You're right. It could have been worse. Now we will both have to wait and see what the results of the tests will be," Corrie tells him, relenting. "How do you think you went?" she asks Samuel.

"Fine. For some reason figures just come easily to me, and I finished before the time was up, but wanted to wait until you had finished, too. I was hoping we might be able to talk after it was over."

There it was again. Samuel's ability to catch her unawares. He had waited for her to finish, but would she have waited for him if she had finished sooner? Corrie would have been glad to leave before the others if she'd had the chance. She hated being watched over by officials, especially officials who were testing her. Maybe Samuel hated it, too, but he waited for her anyway. The truth is, Corrie is glad he had waited. She didn't want to admit it to Samuel. She didn't even want to admit it to herself. But that was the truth, and it confounded her.

Corrie decides it's time to go home before she says something that she will regret . . . like she was glad Samuel waited.

"Samuel, I have to get back home. My family will be wondering where I am."

"I know. I have to go to the Mill and help out now that they have begun the rationing program. I think school is back next Monday, so I guess I will see you then."

The thought of going back to school cheers her up immensely for some reason, and Corrie gives Samuel a smile before taking her leave. He smiles at her in return and, feeling as if the sun has just shone on her, Corrie heads back to the cottage to tell her mother about the test. She hopes she will hear something before school begins again next week. All the waiting and anticipating is starting to fray her nerves.

Eleven

When school begins again the following week, there is still no word about the test results. Corrie wants to see Samuel to ask him if he has heard anything. In the meantime, she has delivered the last of her current orders, packaging them tightly and carrying them in her shopping bag, spreading out her deliveries in case the soldiers became suspicious. She also carried loose change in her purse in case they asked her why she was going into the town. Until the Ration Cards were given out, people could still use their own money to shop, but soon the only type of collateral would be Ration Cards, and that was what the shops must accept.

Corrie walks into the classroom and sees Nate sitting in his usual place. She is hesitant about taking her seat beside him but doesn't know why. Maybe it's because she's only seen him once since the Insurrection, and she wonders if he's made any attempt to come to the cottage in the meantime. She hasn't made any attempt to see him, so Corrie assumes they have both been unsure about the right thing to do. She takes her seat, and Nate gives her a grin. He doesn't seem too upset that she hasn't tried to call on him either. Just as the class is about to commence, Samuel walks in and mumbles his apologies. He takes his usual seat at the back and the day begins.

When the lunch bell rings, the students have a chance to go outside and get some fresh air. In winter, they take their morning and afternoon breaks in the classroom because it is so cold outside, but at lunchtime they go out to stretch their legs. The snow on the ground crunches underfoot as Corrie makes a beeline for Samuel, who is walking over to the far side of the yard to eat his lunch. Nate has hung back to talk to other boys and is soon kicking a ball around the yard with them. Corrie will walk with him after school and talk to him then.

"Hey, Samuel," Corrie says.

Samuel looks up and gives her a smile. Everything else around them is caught in the frozen chill of winter, but not Samuel's smile.

"Hey, Corrie."

"I was wondering if you had heard anything about the test yet?" she asks.

"No. Not so far. I asked my father when he thought they might be giving us the results and he said it should be sometime this week. I hope so. People will be relying on those results for their rations," he says.

Corrie will be relying on those results for her rations. She hasn't taken any more orders, for fear of repercussions, and is hoping a positive test result will mean she doesn't need to either.

"Yes," she says without giving her thoughts away.

"Do you want to sit down?" Samuel asks her.

Corrie sees Nate is still busy with his friends, so she takes a seat beside Samuel who offers her some of his lunch. He has cheese sandwiches with a kind of pickle on them, and there's an apple too. Corrie is hesitant, but the cold is making her hungry and the food looks delicious.

"Are you sure?" she asks him, not wanting to take food out of Samuel's mouth. He is a little on the lean side, and she wonders if it's because he doesn't eat enough, or if it's just his natural physique.

"Yeah. Go ahead. My father has his Ration Card already and the best part about that is they will be rationing his alcohol, too!" he says without hesitation. "That means we will have more food and ... " Samuel trails off. His father not being able to buy as much alcohol might give Samuel a reprieve from his beatings and Corrie feels happy for him.

"I'm glad. How many brothers and sisters do you have?" she asks.

"A younger brother and sister. They are both in Junior school," he tells her. "I saw your brother when I called around the other day. What's his name?"

"Joseph. He's ten. He has a condition that was caused by a lack of air getting to his lungs when he was born. His speech and co-ordination are affected, but he is bright, though he has never been allowed to go to school," Corrie answers wistfully.

"I'm sorry. That must be hard for you all."

"It is, but we manage. He's a contented child and makes very few demands. I just wish my father was still here to take him out sometimes. He used to take Joseph everywhere, but now he's gone, and Joseph is getting too big for me or my mother to be able to do that. Nate comes over sometimes and takes him out into the woods, so he can get fresh air and sunshine. My mother really appreciates that." Corrie realizes she is revealing too much to Samuel who probably doesn't want to hear about her family anyway. He has his own family to worry about.

"Nate's very good with people, isn't he? says Samuel.

Corrie isn't sure if that's a general comment or an insult toward Nate. Nate had never said anything bad about Samuel.

"Well, we should all make the most of our gifts and talents. Nate has plenty, and isn't shy about using them," says Corrie making a point of the fact that Samuel seems too shy to do the same.

Her point hits its mark as Samuel looks down again at his lunch and doesn't reply. Corrie realizes her words are hurtful but can't bring herself to apologize. She has a point, and Samuel can't go around implying things about Nate just because he doesn't have the same confidence. She gets up.

"Good luck with the results," says Corrie, indicating that she won't have much to say to Samuel in the meantime. She can't. Every time they get into a conversation, it ends in a misunderstanding, and Corrie feels like she needs to keep apologizing to Samuel. In fact, she's never felt she had to apologize to someone so much in her life. Nate doesn't make her feel like she needs to apologize when they talk.

What is it about Samuel that seems to bring out the worst in her? Heaven forbid that the Marriage Selectors choose Samuel to be her husband. Corrie doesn't want to spend the rest of her life apologizing!

Twelve

Corrie spends the rest of the week in Nate's company . . . in class, during the breaks, and on walks with him after school as far as the Blacksmith's. She has told Nate about the Alliance's offer of work for rations, and Nate seems happy that at least Corrie and her family won't have to go hungry for now. It's the best any of them can hope for as the Alliance tightens its grip on their small town.

At the end of the week, Corrie decides she needs to spend the last of her money getting supplies, while at the same time hoping that their Ration Card comes soon. Getting supplies means going to the Mill where she will probably see Samuel. She can't avoid him forever, so after getting what she needs in the town, she heads out along the Mill Road. On the way, a group of soldiers passes and stops just ahead of her. Corrie isn't concerned. She isn't doing anything wrong. One of the soldiers gets off his horse and blocks her path.

"What's your name?" he asks her gruffly.

"Corrie."

"Corrie who?" he asks.

"Corrie Tennant," she tells him.

"Well, Corrie Tennant, I don't think I've seen you around the town. Where do you live?"

"Down by the woods," Corrie answers. Why is he asking her all these questions? What did it have to do with him?

"People who live by the woods normally live there because they don't belong in the town," he says arrogantly.

What is he getting at? Corrie isn't sure.

"What is your point?" Corrie replies disrespectfully.

The soldier moves in more closely, his manner menacing.

"My point is, it means you come from Rebel stock, and from now on we will be watching you." He calls out to his men. "This is Corrie Tennant who comes from Rebel stock. She's not to be trusted, and I want you to keep an eye on her. You have my permission to question her whenever you see her . . . and you can do whatever else you like with her as well" he says threateningly.

Corrie is afraid, and the men are laughing. Some of them are not much older than her, and they snicker to impress their Sargent. Rather than hang her head, Corrie holds it high, as if daring them to follow their Sargent's orders. The Sargent, seeing this, grabs her arm and whips her around to face his men. Grabbing the top of her dress from behind, he rips it downward, exposing the top of her breasts. Some of the soldiers look shocked, and Corrie feels hot, wet tears begin to spill down her cheeks. No one has ever treated her this way before. The Sargent wraps an arm across her chest from behind, resting it on her bare skin, and holding her close as he breathes down her neck.

"We will be watching you, Corrie Tennant. I will be watching you," he says, finally releasing her.

Corrie clutches the top of her dress and holds it together as she watches the Sargent mount his horse. He throws her a look of contempt before leading the other soldiers away. Shaking and dazed, Corrie gathers her bag up from the ground with what is left of her dignity, hoping the soldiers don't turn back. Not wanting to walk back through the town looking disheveled, she decides to walk the short distance to the Mill wondering if Samuel will let her use the back room to tidy herself up a bit.

He is behind the counter when she walks in and has no other customers right now. As Corrie gets closer, he looks at her with concern before coming toward her.

"Corrie, what happened?!"

"Soldiers stopped me on the road," she says breathlessly. "A Sargent asked me questions, before telling his men to watch me. Then he ripped my dress ... " Tears spill down Corrie's cheeks as she stands there shaking, holding her dress in place. Without hesitating, Samuel puts his arms around her, telling her she is safe now. It's the first time a man has put his arms around her since her father died. Rather than recoiling from Samuel's touch, she clings to him as though clinging to life itself. Corrie allows her tears to flow freely as Samuel holds her. When her sobs finally subside, she slowly releases him to wipe the tears from her face. Samuel takes her by the hand and leads her into the back room, telling her to take as long as she needs to tidy herself up. Corrie uses the basin to wash her face but feels dirty all over. The best she can do is pull her dress together and try to pin it somehow. She peeks out from behind the door.

"Samuel," she whispers quietly. He comes across and she asks him if he has anything that can be used to pin her dress. As she does, Corrie notices something new in Samuel's eyes. Something she has never seen there before. Anger.

"We have clips we use to hold the paperwork together. I'll get you some of those," he tells her.

He comes back quickly and hands the clips to Corrie. When she is ready, Corrie comes out of the back room and crosses to the counter where Samuel is now staring angrily at a page in the ledger.

"Corrie, you need to report that Sargent for what he did to you!" he says fiercely.

"No, Samuel . . . I can't. It will only cause more problems for my family. They know my father was a Rebel . . . that's what he told me . . . because we live down by the woods."

"He shouldn't be allowed to get away with that, Corrie. It's not right. If he did that to you, he will do it to other girls, too. I know how men like that think."

"Maybe it won't happen again," Corrie says as she remembers why she is here. "I was coming to get my grain."

"I'll get your grain, Corrie, but I'm not letting you walk home alone. It's starting to get dark, and it's dangerous," Samuel finishes.

Corrie doesn't argue with him. She doesn't want to walk home alone and accepts yet another generous offer from Samuel as he closes the Store and prepares to walk her back through the town.

The night is bitter, causing Corrie to wrap her coat more tightly around her. As they walk toward the gas lit town, Samuel tries to take their minds off what has just happened by saying that any day now they should be hearing about the results. Corrie isn't sure which results he is talking about, so she asks him.

"You mean the ones for the Alliance positions?"

"Yes," he says.

"I hope so. I've spent the last of our money today to buy what we needed."

"When do you think we will hear about the Marriage Selections?" Samuel wonders next.

Corrie knows they can't avoid the topic forever.

"Soon. They're obviously going ahead, and it's usually within a month after the Ball."

"Hmm," is all Samuel says as they continue to walk, lost in thought.

They avoid the areas where they see soldiers gathered in the town, and Corrie tells Samuel he can leave her when they reach the woods.

"No. I'm not leaving you. Not until we get to your front door."

"OK," says Corrie meekly. She's glad Samuel is going to bring her all the way home.

As they get closer to her home, Corrie stumbles and Samuel grabs her hand to keep her from falling. For some reason, she doesn't try to take her hand away. Samuel's hand is warm and comforting, just like his embrace in the Mill Store.

When they reach Corrie's front door, Samuel slowly releases her hand.

"Well, here you are."

"Thank you, Samuel. I don't know what I would have done if you hadn't been at the Mill," Corrie says appreciatively.

"I'm glad I was there," he says. He means it. Corrie can tell. Nothing is too much trouble for Samuel.

"See you at school next week," she says.

"OK," Samuel says, flashing her one of his winning smiles.

"Oh, and Samuel?"

"Yes?"

"Be careful." Corrie means it. She wants Samuel to be safe.

Thirteen

On Monday Corrie heads to school as usual. The Garrison is on the outskirts of the town, so Corrie feels she can safely walk through the center of town to get to school. Her heart pounds when she sees several soldiers gathered by the entrance to the Town Hall. She keeps her head down and hurries by. Thankfully, they are deep in conversation, and don't notice her. She was never nervous around the soldiers, but now things have changed. She thinks about asking Nate if he can walk her home after school, if his father doesn't need him at the forge right away. Samuel did her a favor last night, but walking her home would take him too far out of his way if he needs to be at the Mill after school to serve customers.

Corrie enters the classroom and notices Nate is absent. She wonders where he could be. It wasn't like him to miss school, but she imagines he must have a good reason. Samuel is sitting in his usual place at the back of the class and she smiles at him as he looks up. Samuel smiles back. As the morning wears on, Corrie finds she can't keep her mind on the work, wondering when the officials will let her know about the Alliance position. It's also the week they will probably hear about the Marriage Selections. She doesn't know which one she is more nervous about right now. One means survival, the other entrapment, and both will have an enormous impact on her future.

Just before the lunch bell is due to ring, the Principal comes into the classroom and whispers something to the teacher. Corrie overhears her name and sees the teacher look up at her. She calls Corrie forward and asks her to go with the School Principal. Corrie does as she is asked, turning to look at Samuel as she leaves the room. The Principal's office is at the end of a long corridor, the door is open, and an Alliance Official is standing there waiting for her. He's dressed in the gray uniform that all Alliance Officials wear and is a man of about fifty with a slight paunch and balding head. He studies Corrie as she comes into the office. The Principal asks Corrie to take a seat.

"Miss Tennant," the Official begins, "I have called you here to inform you about the results of your test."

Corrie's heart skips a beat. This is the moment she has been waiting for. She tries not to look nervous.

"We were very impressed with your results, and the school has obviously done an excellent job in educating you." He pauses to allow the Principal to take in the Alliance's praises. "We've come to a decision about the role you might play in assisting the Alliance during these troubled times."

Corrie is holding her breath now.

"I would like to welcome you to the ranks of the Alliance, Miss Tennant."

As Corrie releases her breath, the Official has one more thing to say.

"We hope you will be a more loyal citizen than your father."

The initial smile of success dies slowly on Corrie's lips. It was a mistake to think the Alliance would allow her to put the past completely behind her. Corrie feels a sudden flush of anger but, unable to show her reaction, forces herself to smile again and thank the Official. It's the reprieve she's been hoping for. Her family won't starve, but she knows the offer is in no way an act of forgiveness for her father's crimes. If it wasn't for her talent with language and writing, Corrie knows it would be a very different story. She is forced to shake the hand of the Official as he offers it at the end of the meeting. It is cold and unyielding, just like the Alliance. She walks away as quickly as she can.

The bell has rung for lunch, and Corrie goes to find Samuel. She sees him sitting in his usual spot on the other side of the yard and, without hesitating, Corrie walks across and sits down beside him.

"Hey," Samuel says.

"I've been offered a position."

"Really?" Samuel responds. "That's great, Corrie. Congratulations!" he says giving her a smile. "That means you'll get your Ration Card and you won't have to worry about how you are going to feed your family."

"I know," she says quietly. She feels compromised and wonders if Samuel would understand.

"Is something the matter?" he asks her.

"It's just. . . the Official mentioned my father, and how he hoped I would be a more loyal citizen than he was." Corrie's bottom lip trembles. She doesn't want to cry, and if Samuel says anything understanding to her, she probably will.

Instead of saying anything, Samuel just takes her hand and holds it tightly. His gesture is more powerful than words, and Corrie's eyes fill with tears. She feels so alone in all this, but Samuel's gesture reassures her. She wonders whether he will also get a job with the Alliance. Brushing a tear away from her eye, she asks him.

"Have you heard anything yet?"

"No, not yet. I'm guessing they will call us out one at a time to give us the news."

That's probably true, and Corrie hopes that Samuel will be chosen, too. They stand up as the bell rings again, releasing each other's hands, and walk back to their class-room.

During the afternoon, several more pupils are called out of class, not in any particular order, and Corrie grows more anxious as the school day nears an end. She doesn't know why. Samuel already has part-time work at the Mill, and his father works as an Accountant for the Alliance. He won't be relying on his entitlement to a Ration Card like she will. It must be because she wants to share this journey with someone. Finally, at the end of the day, Samuel's name is called.

Corrie decides to wait for him outside the building after school. She wants to know. She needs to know the outcome. When Samuel steps out, she can see from the smile on his face that he has been selected, too. Corrie wants to throw her arms around him, but can't, so she just returns his smile. They chat as they walk together and as they turn the corner, Corrie and Samuel come face to face with the Sargent who had accosted her on the road.

"Well, Corrie Tennant. Fancy seeing you here . . . in the town. I thought you might be hiding out with Rebels in the woods," he says with a smirk.

Corrie's cheeks flush red and Samuel steps in front of her.

"What's your name?" the Sargent asks Samuel.

"I'm not giving you my name, until you tell me yours" Samuel retorts.

"I don't have to give you my name, but you do have to give me yours," says the Sargent threateningly, putting his hand on the pistol at his waist.

Corrie takes Samuel's arm and whispers "Tell him". She doesn't want Samuel to get into trouble because of her.

"My name is Samuel Jacobs."

"That's better" says the Sargent, smirking again. "I'm Sargent Jonathon Seymour, and I have the power to arrest you if I think you are a threat to the peace."

"He's no threat." says Corrie.

"We'll see. If he's a friend of yours, he may well be. I will keep that in mind, Mr. Jacobs, and I'm sure I'll see you again soon."

Corrie tugs on Samuel's arm. She wants to hurry him away from there, from any trouble that might be brewing because of her. She doesn't talk as they make their way to the edge of the town, and when they get there, she releases Samuel's arm.

"Samuel, I don't want you to get into trouble because of me," she tells him angrily.

Samuel is angry, too.

"It's not OK what that Sargent did to you the other day, Corrie, and I'm going to make sure it doesn't happen again. My father knows people and, if I give him a name, there's a good chance that Sargent will be dealt with properly. An Army is supposed to be disciplined and trusted by the people. There's no excuse for his behavior," Samuel retorts.

"I know that," says Corrie. "But now that I am going to be working for the Alliance, it shouldn't be a problem. We'll both have a new status, and Seymour won't be able to touch us. Please be careful, Samuel. He's not worth it."

Samuel turns the thought over in his mind before telling Corrie what he's thinking.

"But you are . . . " he says, tilting her chin up and looking into her eyes. Corrie thinks he might kiss her. She has never been kissed before and something deep inside makes her want Samuel's kiss. But Samuel just takes her hand and walks her the rest of the way home.

Fourteen

Next morning, before Corrie leaves for school, the family's Ration Card arrives. It entitles them to shop for necessities to the value of one pound and five shillings per week. An accompanying letter states that Corrie is to continue attending school and is to report to the Alliance Offices every day after school to perform her duties. Excitedly, Corrie shows the letter to her mother who hugs her, and thanks Corrie for everything she is doing to help their family. There are tears in her mother's eyes, and Corrie hopes they are grateful tears, not tears of regret— regret that Corrie must to do this and is now going against everything her father had stood for.

Nate is in class when she arrives, and Corrie tells him the good news. He gives her a hug and congratulates her on her success. She goes on to tell him about Samuel. He doesn't seem as enthusiastic about the fact that Samuel has been able to get work with the Alliance. Corrie wonders why.

"Aren't you happy for Samuel, too?" Corrie asks.

"Sure. It's just . . . ," Nate hesitates to finish.

"What?" Corrie asks impatiently.

"Well, it's just that it means you might be spending more time with him," Nate says.

"And?" Corrie responds.

"And I'm not sure if I want you spending any more time with Samuel," Nate finally gets out.

"Why not?" she asks, unable to comprehend what Nate's problem with that would be.

"No reason," Nate finishes, not willing to say any more.

Corrie is confused. What is Nate's problem with Samuel? He's never expressed any concern about Samuel before. Was there something he knew that he wasn't telling her? Corrie makes up her mind to coax it out of Nate when she gets a chance. Surely, he isn't jealous of Samuel? And why would he be? Unless . . . Corrie puts the thoughts out of her head. There is no reason for Nate to be jealous of Samuel, and she has enough to concern herself with right now, including her upcoming job with the Alliance and the looming Marriage Selection. It will be happening any day now.

Corrie prepares to attend her first evening of work at the end of the school day. The office is only a couple of doors down, so she is there before she needs to be, and is seated outside a door with a sign that says Communications. She tries not to fidget while she waits nervously as other workers and officials pass her by in the corridor looking at her with both curiosity and contempt. New workers are bound to be looked upon with suspicion, especially now.

Suddenly, the door beside her opens and Corrie is invited into a medium-sized office with several desks. They are piled high with stacks of paper alongside quills and ink wells. Cabinets line the walls to the left and, just beyond these, Corrie sees a large desk with a rather large man sitting behind it. It's not the official who came to the school, but a more robust man with an eyeglass and mustache. He's holding a fat cigar in his hand and leans back in his chair, eyeing Corrie with a look of amusement. She isn't sure what to make of him but feels drawn to him as he smiles at her and offers her the seat opposite.

Paper shuffles in the background as he takes a puff of the cigar and coughs slightly before introducing himself.

"I'm Silas Caine, Miss Tennant, and you will be working for me" he says, looking at her more seriously now. "I don't want you to be nervous, we are all nervous when we start in a new position, but let me assure you we will take good care of you . . . even better care if you do your job well. I'm going to let Maisie show you what we need you to do for now. Don't worry, it won't be anything too daunting. We just want you to get used to how the Communications Office runs, and we'll start you off with minor tasks. Feel free to ask any questions, either of myself or the other staff. There are three of us, including myself, and you will be taking the table in the corner beside my desk."

Corrie looks to her right and sees the small table in the corner, grateful there's another cabinet between it and Silas Caine's desk. She would feel very exposed if she had to sit

84

under his watchful eye the whole time. The idea of sitting in the corner doing minor tasks gives Corrie some comfort, as does the smell of Silas Caine's cigar. Corrie remembers that smell. When she was a child, her father would occasionally bring home one or two cigars if he had a good week at work. He managed the supplies coming into the town for the shops, offices, factories and the Army Garrison. All the supplies went into one large storage facility, and it was his job to ensure they all went to the correct buyers. It was also his job to make sure there was no illegal trading ... or worse, illegal shipments of arms. When he joined the fight against the Alliance, the latter had been his undoing, and he had paid for it with his life.

Corrie is drawn out of her reverie as Silas Caine calls Maisie over to introduce her and indicates the other staff member, Tilly. Corrie realizes that all their names all end with an "e" sound, including her own, then wonders what else they have in common. Maisie and Tilly both look young, probably in their early twenties, and Tilly continues writing as Maisie shows Corrie around. She has a high-pitched voice with a drawl that makes Corrie think she doesn't come from their town, but it doesn't matter. She seems friendly and Corrie is grateful. Her first evening at the Alliance Offices isn't what she'd expected, and Silas Caine isn't as she'd expected him to be either.

Corrie knows the Alliance has a way of lulling its citizens into a false sense of security, acting like a benevolent parent until you had either the foolishness or audacity to cross them. She also knows she can't afford to cross the Alliance. With Seymour watching her, and her family dependent on the Ration Card now provided by the Alliance, she is more trapped than ever. The Marriage Selections will be the final nail in the coffin of her autonomy, and Corrie will never be able to make the choices she wants to make for her own life.

Two hours at the Office pass quickly, and staff finish at 5.30pm on the dot. Silas Caine doesn't like to be late for his dinner and dismisses them before he closes the Office for the day. The girls all head in different directions, and Corrie is the only one going in the direction of the woods. She hopes no one notices.

It's a bitterly cold evening, and the wind is fierce, so Corrie hurries toward the edge of the woods. Suddenly, as she turns the corner that will set her on the path to home, somebody grabs her from behind. She gasps and pushes at the hands holding her around the waist. When the assailant finally releases her, Corrie whips around to see Nate standing in front of her.

"Nate! You scared me!" Corrie says angrily.

"Sorry, Corrie. I just wanted to see how your first day at work went," he tells her, looking at her in an injured fashion, as though she was the one who had frightened him.

"It was fine," she says, still feeling injured herself.

"Well, what did you do?"

"Lots of things. Whatever they asked me to do. Filing, mostly, and putting items into envelopes. It was easy."

"Well, that's good. What are the other people like who work there?"

"Their names all end in an "e" sound. Tilly and Maisie! If you add me to the mix what you've got is a bunch of "e"ducated women "e"nsuring the "e"xistence of the current regime," Corrie finishes and puts her tongue out at Nate who laughs out loud. They can always make each other laugh, and have such "e"asy conversations, Corrie thinks. Whereas with Samuel, things just seem so much more serious with Corrie always feeling the need to apologize to him.

Nate offers to walk Corrie the rest of the way home and she accepts. Darkness has set in and only a pale moon is shining in the sky tonight. Corrie reminds Nate to be careful on his way back, as she remembers the soldiers have been given permission to shoot on sight anyone they suspect of being involved with the Rebels. She is always worrying about the people who are worrying about her. Maybe that's what friendship is, and maybe that's what she has with both Samuel and Nate. Corrie isn't sure which of those friendships will last, but she cares about them both, and wonders how Samuel's first day at his new job has been.

Fifteen

Corrie is able to ask Samuel the following day. He tells her he is working with special machines that are used to do calculations and create codes. There is a lot to learn, but Samuel says he is enjoying the challenge. He also tells Corrie that he will continue his work in the Mill on three days during the week—Monday, Wednesday and Friday—because he's only required to work in his new role for the Alliance on Tuesday and Thursday, but could be called on at short notice any time of the day or night. Samuel's work sounds secretive, and it's kept away from the other offices where Corrie works. It seems they won't be spending as much time together as Nate had predicted.

Time passes quickly, and finally the day arrives for the announcement of the Marriage Selections. Her new job has taken her mind off the concerns around marriage, but now Corrie is forced once again to confront the reality of her future under the oppressive Alliance — the Alliance for which she is now working.

Students must attend the Town Hall where Alliance officials are waiting to announce the names of the students to be betrothed. The officials are in their usual spot on a podium at the front of the hall, and the students are asked to line up—girls on one side and boys on the other. There is some nervous chatter and coughing before silence quickly falls over the gathering.

After giving an initial welcome, and acknowledging their reason for being in attendance, a female official begins to read out the names. First, they read the names of any young people found to be unsuitable for marriage. There are three boys assigned to the Army—Jeremy, Dan and Freddie. Corrie can see Freddie's bottom lip begin to tremble, but he manages to remain stoic along with the other boys, and they are told to wait at the right side of the podium. Next, three girls are assigned to the position of Housekeeper—Jane, Agnes and Helen. Stoicism isn't a feature of the girl's reactions as two of them begin to cry, and one collapses to the floor. An Official chosen for the task moves swiftly to wave smelling salts under that girl's nose before removing all three girls from the hall so the proceedings can continue uninterrupted.

Corrie feels every muscle in her body tense up and holds her breath, as she waits for the official to begin reading out the names of those about to be betrothed. The girl's names are called first, and Corrie watches the reactions of other students whose names are called before hers. Their responses range from delight to dismay and, in what seems like no time at all, the Official calls Corrie's name. She must walk to the center of the hall, adding to the line of couples which have already been created, and there are six couples in the center now. Neither Nate's nor Samuel's name has been called yet.

Corrie keeps her eyes downcast. She doesn't want to look at either Nate or Samuel right now. Maybe they wouldn't partner her with either of them.

"Nate Daniels," comes the Official's voice from the podium.

Corrie looks up to see Nate coming toward her with a huge grin on his face. He is pleased with the Committee's Selection and it shows. Nate is her friend, Corrie thinks. He is handsome and charming, and he has been good to her family. But she feels her heart sink and struggles to bring a smile to her lips. She tries, wondering if her attempt is successful, as Nate comes to stand by her side and takes her hand. His grip is firm and sure. Corrie's is tentative, and less convincing. Nate won't notice, though, Corrie thinks. He is too caught up in the moment.

Two more couples join them and then, with four people left to choose and only two couples left to be created, Corrie sees that Samuel has the prospect of Selena Prescott or Molly Jones. Selena Prescott is the girl that Corrie had seen approach Samuel when he first made his appearance at the Winter Ball, the one who had gone gliding around the dance floor with him, unafraid to enjoy his company.

"Selena Prescott." Selena walks to the middle of the floor to join the others.

"Samuel Jacobs."

It was decided then. Selena will marry Samuel, and Corrie will marry Nate. It doesn't matter how any of them feel, it isn't about feelings. It's about a calculated decision based on . . . what? Corrie doesn't know. She didn't look at Samuel that night when they danced, and he didn't look at her. She didn't think they were compatible then, and now the Alliance doesn't think so either. If Corrie and the Alliance agreed, what was niggling at the back of her mind, making her feel restless and confounded?

Corrie looks across at Samuel. He lifts his head at the same time to look at her. Neither of them are smiling. It's too hard to read what is in Samuel's eyes at this moment . . . it could be sadness, it could be pain . . . and Corrie wonders if he sees the same thing in her eyes. It doesn't matter. The Alliance has decided. Corrie now has to focus on Nate, and the Official gives them the details of what will happen next.

"Your marriages will take place in exactly eleven months in this hall. That will give you time to prepare, and you will be allowed supervised visits once a week with a Chaperone. These visits can occur on a Saturday or Sunday only, and an evening visit will require a special request. We will do our best to accommodate you. You are to honor the decision the Alliance has made on your behalf, and you are not to be seen spending time with any of the other boys or girls in your class unless it is for business purposes only. Students, you are now betrothed, and we congratulate you. We also offer our full support in relation to your future marriage."

This is the indication that it is now time to leave the Ceremony and go back to the classroom. Nate keeps hold of Corrie's hand possessively, but she notices that Samuel is not holding Selena's hand. He was always so shy. She hopes he will be happy. In class, she takes her seat again beside Nate, who can't take the foolish grin off his face. Corrie tries to respond to the pleasure he seems to have derived from the announcement by smiling back at him. Inside she just feels like crying. What is wrong with her?

After school, Nate tells her he will see her on Sunday, because he has to work with his father all day on Saturday. Corrie just says "OK" and goes to the Alliance Offices to finish her week at work. She needs to shop for supplies, and fortunately they finish at the office at 4.30pm on Fridays.

Her workmates know the Selection has taken place and surround her to congratulate her when she returns to the office at 3.30pm. It's an hour of babbling on about weddings and dresses, relationships and children. Oh, my! Children! Corrie hasn't thought that far ahead and doesn't want to think about it now. She tries to appear excited about the prospect of her future marriage and, at one point, notices Silas Caine looking at her with a kind of fatherly concern. Maybe he can sense her lack of enthusiasm, so Corrie tries harder to join in the celebratory air surrounding her.

At 4.30pm, Corrie exits the building breathing a sigh of relief. How will she survive the onslaught of advice and merriment that always seems to accompany talk of marriage? It's going to be a long eleven months. Corrie takes her Ration Card from her bag as she enters the main store and purchases her usual supplies with a few extra treats for the family. She gets soft sweets for Joseph and special blend of tea for her mother. It cheers her up to be able to buy these things, and then she heads for the Mill.

It's Friday, so Samuel will probably be working, and Corrie

doesn't know what she will say to him when she sees him. She can only see him for business purposes now, or in class, and once upon a time that wouldn't have bothered her. But now, for some reason, it does. Corrie despises the Alliance for the control they apply to people's lives, control that doesn't allow for the freedom to choose, especially who you will spend the rest of your life with.

When Corrie enters the Mill Store, she joins the queue. It's long, and the more she waits, the more anxious she becomes. What is she going to say?

Eventually, it's Corrie's turn to be served and thankfully there are no more people waiting in line, no more people to interrupt this moment Corrie feels she needs to have with Samuel, this moment when she needs to say goodbye.

"Hey, Samuel." Corrie tries to sound cheerful.

"Hey," Samuel says, not elaborating in any way.

"Congratulations on your Marriage Selection today," she says hoping that she sounds sincere.

"Congratulations to you, too," Samuel says in a perfunctory manner.

Corrie doesn't know what else to say right now so she orders her grain. As Samuel brings the bag to the counter, Corrie feels the need to say something more.

"I'm sorry," she says. She is sorry for all the times she has ignored Samuel, neglected him somehow, refused his friendship and turned him away. Corrie is starting to feel it may be her biggest regret, but Samuel doesn't hold it against her.

"It's OK, Corrie. You and Nate are meant to be together. I know you feel comfortable with him, and that's how married couples should be. Comfortable."

Corrie isn't sure if that is the ultimate ideal for a marriage, but she has nothing to counter it right now. She asks Samuel if he can help her with her bags, which are more than she normally has, and he comes around the counter to see what he can do. As he moves to her side, Corrie turns to face him. He has grown taller over the last few months and she lifts her head to look at him. Corrie doesn't know what words are resting on her lips, waiting to be shared, probably for the last time, but as Samuel looks into her eyes and tilts her chin, she doesn't get a chance to say them. His lips are on hers, and Corrie feels herself falling . . . falling into a chasm that is frightening in its depth and exhilarating in its majesty. She doesn't want to draw herself out of it. She wants Samuel to catch her at the end.

As he gently breaks their kiss, Corrie can see the desire in his eyes, and the pain. It will be their first kiss, and their last, and Corrie has to let him go. She doesn't say goodbye, she can't. She just brushes her hand over his and thinks the three words she hasn't been able to say.

"I love you."

Sixteen

Corrie is glad of the privacy of her small room in the family cottage that night. There, she sheds the tears she has been holding back since seeing Samuel at the Mill. Tears of sorrow and frustration, tears for lost opportunities, and lost dreams. Where are the tears of happiness she is supposed to be shedding on this night?

When she is all cried out, Corrie finally goes to sleep. It is a deep sleep, releasing her from some of her despair, and in the morning, Corrie tries to put the meeting with Samuel out of her mind. She spends the rest of the time, until she sees Nate the next day, telling her mother about her new job and avoiding the topic of marriage. She knows her mother is happy about her Marriage Selection, and Corrie doesn't want to give her any cause for concern, but they both avoid the topic, understanding that neither of them have a choice about the situation and must make the best of it.

Nate comes around on the Sunday evening with the

Chaperone and asks Corrie if she would like to go out for a walk. The Chaperone walks a few steps behind to allow them some privacy, but Corrie is glad to have the Chaperone with them. She will ensure that the couple don't become too close before their marriage takes place and this is a relief for Corrie. She doesn't want anyone else to kiss her right now.

"How are you feeling, Corrie?" asks Nate.

Corrie hesitates for a moment before she gives the expected answer.

"Good. Everyone at work wants to talk about the wedding and I don't even know where to start. I will be able to make my own dress, so I should probably start looking at patterns soon. I might even go to the city to look for materials if I can," she says, as she imagines seeing the world beyond their small country town.

"I wish we could go together," says Nate.

"I think my mother might like to come with me if she's well enough. Now that we're eating better, she seems to be getting stronger, and maybe we can see a doctor while we're there who can help her."

"That sounds like a good idea, Corrie."

Nate is being understanding, and she feels like she is betraying him by feeling the way she does. He isn't a bad person and he's her friend. Corrie feels like she needs to try harder. It's not his fault they are now betrothed, and he seems genuinely pleased. She should be happy that he is happy with the Alliance's choice, which is her.

They are allowed an hour together and then it is time for Nate to go, but not before he entertains Joseph with a story, and gives her mother some flowers they picked while they walked in the woods.

The next day at school Corrie takes her usual seat and tries not to look at Samuel as he takes his seat at the back of the class. There's no point in engaging with Samuel now, except for business purposes, and the less contact they have, the better. Otherwise, it will only hurt them both.

Corrie tries to remain stoic as the weeks pass, and winter finally turns into spring, bringing with it the usual wonders as new life bursts from the once frozen landscape. Before long, a heady mix of aromas fill the air outside Corrie's home as flowers begin to bloom. Daffodils are Corrie's favorite. Their smell is so audacious, filling the places where they grow, and Corrie often wants to sit and stay a while wherever she finds them. The change of seasons makes Corrie realize how precious life is, reminding her that she shouldn't take anything for granted, and that she should enjoy every moment, in case there isn't another. And that makes her think of Samuel.

She has fallen into a routine with her work and school, adjusting to all the talk around her upcoming marriage and makes an effort to engage with Nate when they have their weekly "dates". He is good company, and her mother and brother adore him. Corrie has decided to stop going to the Mill when she knows Samuel will be there and goes on Thursdays instead. She has to rush there after work before the Store closes at 6.00pm, but she has no other choice.

Seeing Samuel at school every day is hard, but he must also come to terms with the choice the Alliance has made for him.

Corrie wonders how that is going. Almost every time she is out with Nate, she thinks of Samuel and Selena. It creates a strange sensation in her stomach, like a tightening that travels all the way to her chest. Then, in her chest, she feels a crushing sensation, as though an invisible creature has her heart in its grip and is squeezing it tight. So tight, sometimes she thinks she could scream. She wonders if Samuel feels like screaming sometimes, too.

Toward the end of spring, Corrie decides she has saved up enough money to travel to the city and arranges for Joseph to spend the day with Nate, while she and her mother go to Louisville to shop. They will also visit a Specialist Corrie has been able to contact. The girls in the office have given her the names of doctors who understand "women's problems" and Corrie's mother has agreed to go. Corrie is spending less time at home, due to her new job, and her mother is going to need to assume greater responsibility for Joseph. Maybe they could get advice on how to help him, too, although Corrie isn't sure there is much doctors can do. There is no cure for Joseph's problem, but maybe there are ways to help him to become more independent and strong.

The Saturday of their journey finally arrives, and Nate comes to collect Joseph and take him to the forge early in the morning. He is still small and Nate lifts Joseph easily to carry him up to the town. They have a place prepared for him with a comfortable seat in the corner of the shed where he can watch Nate and his father work. Joseph loves animals, so it's an extra treat when Nate allows him to pat the horses and offer them hay. The horses seem to like Joseph, too, and they nuzzle up to him, tickling his skin and making him laugh. This makes Corrie smile, and she thanks Nate as she and her mother leave for the station.

The train arrives at the station at 8.30am. It will take them to Louisville—about a two-hour journey. They will have plenty of time to do what they need to do and be back in time for dinner. Corrie and her mother are waiting to board the train when, out of the corner of her eye, she sees Sargent Seymour making his way onto the platform. Corrie doesn't know if he is getting onto the train but pulls her mother further along the platform to avoid him. They climb into the front carriage and settle into their seats. The windows of the train are grimy, but that doesn't lessen Corrie's excitement at the prospect of seeing the world open up before her.

As the train lurches forward, Corrie hears the door between the carriages open behind her. She turns to see Sargent Seymour step in and quickly looks away, hoping he hasn't seen her, but sensing he already has and is making his way towards them.

"Well, Miss Tennant, we meet again," he says as he takes the seat beside her.

Corrie doesn't say anything but continues to look out the window at the scenery now passing by.

"Is that any way to greet an old friend?" he asks.

"You are not my friend, and I have no reason to greet you," says Corrie.

Out of the corner of her eye, she sees the shocked expression on her mother's face. Corrie hasn't told her what happened with the Sargent. Samuel is the only one who knows about her encounter with Seymour, and that's the way Corrie wants to keep it.

"I hardly think that's any way to speak to a soldier of the Alliance, a Sargent no less," Seymour says.

"I am also an employee of the Alliance now. I work for Silas Caine in Communications and he is the person I answer to, not you," Corrie tells him.

"You will answer to me because I am the Law and we oversee your town now. I can make problems for you if I want to, Miss Tennant."

Corrie knows this is a threat and decides not to respond.

Seymour speaks to her mother instead.

"I assume you're Corrie's mother?"

Her mother nods mutely.

"I suggest you bring your daughter into line as far as the hierarchy of the Alliance is concerned. She doesn't seem to realize who's in charge around here," Seymour finishes, before getting up to exit the carriage. Corrie is shaking and, once Seymour departs, her mother turns to ask her what is going on.

Corrie tells her about the confrontation with the Sargent on the Mill Road, explaining that it was an unpleasant experience, and that she had been very afraid at the time. Her mother asks why she didn't tell her. Corrie says she didn't want to worry her, but they are both worried now. She doesn't want any trouble, but her dislike of Seymour is strong. She remembers how Samuel confronted him, and she wonders if Samuel has come across Seymour again. She hopes she hasn't caused more trouble for herself, or for Samuel.

Corrie doesn't take in the scenery on the journey. She's too distracted after another encounter with Seymour. There is no further sign of him as they alight the train at Louisville, and Corrie hopes they can enjoy the city now that he is gone.

As they exit the station, the first thing that Corrie notices is the grandeur of the buildings. They are made of stone, and have huge pillars, making them look imposing and authoritative. It forces Corrie to realize again the power of the Alliance. Here in Louisville there are rich people, educated people, who embrace what the Alliance stands for. She imagines them to be something like the buildings—imposing and impenetrable.

Louisville is divided into four sectors. The train has delivered them to the business sector, which is also the seat of Alliance power in their County. The Alliance rerouted the train line to this sector so that anyone arriving in the capital would be aware of their immense power. It is all around them, and Corrie feels its suffocating effect as she moves her mother quickly through the main streets toward the shopping sector. Before long, the oppressive shadow of Alliance buildings gives way to brightly lit stores and shops selling goods of all kinds. Generous displays in the windows draw eager shoppers in from the streets, offering whatever money can buy.

Corrie has exchanged the weekly value of her Ration Card for real money at a special stand as they exited the station. In Louisville, there is no need for Ration Cards, and real money continues to change hands.

They won't have time to visit the other two sectors today which are the market sector, for fresh food where both businesses and families could buy what they need, and the entertainment sector, where people can enjoy food already prepared, along with music, dancing and even shows. Corrie assumes this last sector is the one least concerned with Alliance business . . . a place where the Alliance takes a back seat to citizen's dreams and laughter, maybe even love.

In the shopping sector, Corrie revels in the selection of beautiful materials on offer, admiring the myriad of colors, and enjoying the sensation of the fabrics as she runs her hands through them, often touching them to her cheek to fully appreciate their softness. Her dress will be white, of course, so it's just the type of material she needs to select. After visiting several stores, Corrie eventually finds one with prices she thinks they can afford and chooses a white silk material that she knows will provide a beautiful sheen as it catches the winter sunlight on her wedding day. She can only put a deposit on it today. Several trips to the city will be required to make payments before she can take the material home.

After stopping in a small café for cake and tea, they visit the Specialist. His office is on the way back to the station, among the official Alliance buildings. The Ration Card allows up to four doctors visits in a year, but a visit to see a Specialist was the equivalent of two. It is important for her mother to get well right now; there is little they can do to improve Joseph's condition, and her mother's health must improve if she is going be spending more time looking after him. She hopes they won't have to use up the remaining doctor's visits too soon.

On arrival, they are seated in a comfortable waiting room with old brown leather chairs, from which the nurse ushers them in to see the doctor when he is ready. Corrie explains to him the difficulties her mother has been having. He sends Corrie out, and summons the nurse. A short time later, the nurse returns to her desk, and tells Corrie to go back in. The doctor explains that her mother needs to increase her iron intake which will, in turn, increase her energy. He says she can do this by eating certain foods more regularly, foods which Corrie knows they might be able to afford now. He gives her mother a bottle of medicine, and prescribes another tonic for her mother's mood, saying that it is common for a person to become despondent after a difficult experience. Corrie knows that her mother has been needing this kind of tonic for a while and feels reassured, knowing that her mother may yet be able to care for Joseph.

There is a sense of hopefulness in their mood as they walk back to the station, but as they board the train for Brookstown Corrie grows more pensive. She realizes that by putting a deposit on the material for her wedding dress, she has taken the first steps toward fulfilling the future the Alliance has planned for her.

Seventeen

Corrie sees Nate the next day with the Chaperone. He seems happy things are moving along as they are, and Corrie continues to try to reconcile herself with the inevitable. And it is inevitable. As inevitable as the sun rising. Corrie is going to be married to Nate . . . she might as well get used to it. Soon, the long summer holidays will begin and then she won't see Samuel at all unless it's a chance encounter. Corrie wonders if Samuel ever thinks about her. But, that's not fair to Selena who is due to marry Samuel soon. She wonders if Selena has chosen her gown for her wedding, if she is telling Samuel excitedly about what she is planning. The thought creates a tightening in Corrie's chest. She has to stop thinking about Samuel.

Maybe she needs to talk to somebody about it. But who? She can't confide in her mother. That would only upset her. She doesn't have a sister or an aunt, a grandmother or even a friend that she can discuss Samuel with. Maybe she can ask the girls at work about their husbands, and what it was like for them when they were betrothed. Corrie is sure it would be informative, and that way she doesn't even have to say anything about Samuel. She makes her mind up to talk to one of her colleagues at work tomorrow. Which one should she choose? Maisie and Tilly are both young, so they have probably been through the Selection Process recently. Neither has children yet, and Corrie wonders about that, too. If they were married at seventeen and are now in their twenties, wouldn't they have children by now? Corrie decides to ask Maisie, who has taken Corrie under her wing and who is always happy to talk. Maybe her colleagues have already talked about their husbands, but Corrie must have blocked those conversations out in her desperation not to have to think about marriage.

An opportunity arises the following evening at work when Corrie and Maisie go to the storeroom to gather more supplies. Corrie isn't sure how to broach the subject, so she just dives straight in.

"How long ago did you get married, Maisie?"

"Four years ago, when I was seventeen," Maisie tells her.

That means Maisie is about twenty-one, and her marriage took place about two years after the Alliance implemented their new edicts.

"So, your marriage was compulsory then?" Corrie asks.

"Oh, yes. Just like yours. It was such an exciting time and I can't thank the Alliance enough for choosing such a suitable partner for me. He is wonderful," says Maisie.

"I'm so glad," says Corrie. "Do you love him?" she asks innocently.

"Love? Oh, well, of course I love him . . . " Maisie seems a bit uncertain now that she has been asked.

"I'm just not sure how I am supposed to feel about the boy I am going to marry. He is my friend and we get along just fine, but is that enough when you're actually going to be spending the rest of your life together?" Corrie asks her.

"Well, of course it is. I hardly knew my husband, but we got to know each other gradually as we were being chaperoned and he seemed like a decent young man. I don't really think 'love' has anything to do with a suitable marriage."

Corrie doesn't know if that is Alliance propaganda talking, the sort Maisie had been brainwashed into believing, or if Maisie is just playing it safe, telling Corrie what is expected. Either way, it's time to go back to the office with the supplies. Corrie had hoped to get a better insight into her situation, but the talk with Maisie hasn't really helped. She will have to try somebody else.

The week is busy at work, and Corrie is asked to stay back on Thursday to finish the filing. Maisie stays, too, and they are able to leave by 6.00 pm, but Corrie won't be able to go to the Mill to get her grain on the day that Samuel isn't working there. This creates a dilemma for her. She doesn't want to see Samuel, but she needs to get grain. In the end, Corrie has no choice. She will have to go tomorrow.

The next day, Samuel isn't at school. She thinks he might not be at the Mill tonight either and breathes a sigh of relief. The day goes by quickly, as she attends work after school, then goes into the town to buy supplies.

The walk to the Mill is pleasant and peaceful, so Corrie tries to relax a little, hoping she doesn't have to encounter Samuel on his own again. It's a moment she's been avoiding, for his sake as much as hers.

When Corrie arrives, she sees Samuel is in his usual place behind the counter. His trademark fringe still falls over his eyes and he doesn't see her immediately as she walks in. He is focused on his calculations and Corrie just watches him for a few moments. She doesn't want to disturb his thoughts. She doesn't really want to disturb him at all. She has no right being here, without Nate, without a Chaperone, without a hardened heart. When Samuel looks up, Corrie sees the bruise on his cheek. It's one his fringe can't hide. She rushes over to the counter.

"Samuel! What happened?! Did you father do that to you again?" she asks him with alarm in her voice. She hadn't seen a mark on Samuel since his father had received his Ration Card and been unable to buy his usual supply of alcohol.

"Don't worry about it, Corrie. It's not your problem," he says.

But Corrie is stubborn.

"Samuel, I want you to tell me. Who did that to you?"

"Seymour."

"The Sargent?"

"Yes. He came across me on the way home last night and I confronted him about what he had done to you. He didn't like it, so he hit me."

"Oh, Samuel. You didn't need to do that. He knows I am working for the Alliance now, so I don't think he will bother me again."

"I heard he was bothering you on the train."

How did Samuel know that? She hadn't told anybody about it.

"Samuel, I told you. I don't want you to get into trouble because of me. Besides, you have Selena to think about now. Does she know what happened?"

"No, it only happened last night, and I haven't seen her today. I'm seeing her on Sunday, so maybe it will be better by then."

"Let me look at it for you, please. I bought some ointment in the town today for Joseph. He gets a few bruises because he can't walk properly, and he fell again last night. It's a new remedy to help with bruises and swelling . . . takes the pain away, too." Corrie tells him.

"Don't waste your ointment on me, Corrie. Joseph needs it more"

"Please, Samuel. Let me help you. I'm the reason Seymour hit you after all."

Corrie finally gets Samuel to agree. She takes him to the back room and inspects the mark in the light. It is quite raised and Corrie wonders what Seymour used in the assault.

"What did he hit you with, Samuel?"

"The back of his hand. It could have been worse. He always carries a pistol as well."

Corrie knows. She saw the weapon again when he was traveling on the train. Taking out her pot of ointment, she dips two fingers into it, pulling out a generous amount. She slowly smooths it across the bruise and Samuel flinches, but only slightly. When she finishes, Corrie holds her hand to his cheek and looks into Samuel's eyes. Samuel gently places his hand over hers. They hold each other's gaze for a moment before Samuel leans down, and the sudden sensation of his lips on hers is tantalizing. It transports Corrie to that place again, that mysterious, dangerous and exhilarating place, where it feels as if the breath is being drawn from her lungs, and her heart is about to explode. As their kisses become deeper, Corrie feels tears begin to slide down her cheeks. Samuel can feel them, too. He stops to wipe away the tears, and finally tells Corrie what she has been longing to hear. What she wants to tell him, too. Samuel tells Corrie that he loves her.

Before she can respond, the Store bell rings. Another customer has just entered, and Samuel puts a finger to his lips motioning Corrie to wait there. The customer notices Corrie's bags on the floor and Samuel says they must have been left behind by accident. He puts them behind the counter, out of sight. When the customer leaves, Samuel appears in the doorway of the back room again.

"I have to go," says Corrie.

"I know."

Corrie throws her arms around his neck and Samuel buries his face in her soft, dark hair. They embrace for a long time. What are they going to do? They are betrothed to other people, and the Alliance won't tolerate dissent. Corrie reluctantly breaks their embrace smoothing her hand over Samuel's cheek one more time before telling him:

"Be careful."

There is a pained expression in his eyes as he promises her that he will. They will both need to be careful from now on. Corrie's life has turned a corner, with her job and her betrothal. Nate will be a good husband . . . and father. The way he looked after Joseph was proof of that. Corrie knows she isn't being fair to Nate, and Samuel isn't being fair to Selena. She picks up her bags and the load she carries home feels ten times heavier than it actually is. Just like her heart.

Eighteen

The last week of school before the summer break finally arrives. Every time Corrie sees Samuel now, she feels a stabbing pain in her heart, coupled with a longing that literally takes her breath away. She can't look at him, and yet the vision of his face, his eyes, his smile, appear before her uninvited. Corrie can still sense the touch of his hand, feel the softness of his lips and the comfort of his arms as he held her in their final embrace. Samuel's words . . . "I love you, Corrie," . . . still ring in her ears. She hadn't told him that she loved him, but he knew. Because she let her lips meet his, savoring the sensation of his kisses, and let her tears of sorrow fall, for Samuel to see. Finally, she had warned him to be careful. They both needed to be careful now.

The rest of the week goes by in a blur as schoolwork is completed, and classrooms are packed up for the holidays. Everyone is looking forward to the break and continuing with their plans for their weddings. They're also looking forward to the long, hot summer. Corrie must work at the Alliance Offices for the duration of the summer except for a two-week break, one at the start of the holidays and one at the end. She's glad she will be busy because it will help take her mind off everything else. Including her wedding. Fortunately, Samuel works in a different building. The work he does is far more secretive, so it is kept away from prying eyes. Corrie wonders if he'll still be working at the Mill during the summer, and if his hours will change. She doesn't want to arrive there while Samuel is working. It would be too much for both of them.

On the last day of school, classmates offer their goodbyes until school returns at the end of the summer. They will return for one term after that until the weddings take place, to ensure their indoctrination continues to the end. Corrie avoids Samuel and walks out with Nate at the end of the day. She has to go to work but tells Nate she will see him on Sunday as usual. He's happy with that and doesn't seem to have noticed that she's become quieter, more pensive, over the last few weeks. Normally, they laugh together over silly things, but not anymore. Maybe he doesn't miss those moments, the moments of connection, that they used to share. When they did connect, it didn't engender anything more than a sense of friendship in Corrie. She realizes she is going to be marrying a friend. She's not sure if Nate is.

It's a short hour of work before her week-long holiday, and Silas Caine calls Corrie over to his desk for a meeting. She likes Silas Caine and doesn't hesitate to sit opposite him while he puffs on one of his favorite cigars that remind

Corrie of her father. He looks at her across the desk with curiosity and doesn't begin speaking immediately. Corrie shifts a little uncomfortably in her chair wondering if she has done something wrong. She hopes not, because she likes her job, and her family is still desperately in need of their Ration Card.

"Corrie, I want to talk about your work but, first of all, I want you to tell me how you like working with us."

Corrie doesn't hesitate.

"I enjoy working here, with you," she tells him. "It's interesting, and the other girls have been very helpful in showing me what I need to do."

"That's good. You have excelled in the short time you have been with us and I want to put you on higher duties during the summer while Tilly is on holidays, see how you go. Would you like that?"

"Yes, Sir. I'm willing to learn whatever you would like to teach me," says Corrie.

"That's good. I'll have Tilly begin your training next week."

"Excuse me, Sir, but I am on holidays next week. I'm going into the city to pay for the material for my wedding dress," she tells him.

"Ahh . . . the wedding. Of course. Tell me Corrie, how do you feel about your upcoming marriage?"

His question takes Corrie by surprise. Why would he be interested in her marriage, the one the Alliance has orchestrated, and which Corrie is now beginning to dread? She realizes she must tread very carefully and takes her time before she answers.

"Ah . . . fine, I guess. I mean Nate is a fine young man and we are friends. He is very good with my brother, too, and my mother loves him." Corrie flushes, wondering why she is telling Silas Caine so much about Nate and her family.

"Do you love him?" he asks.

Taken by surprise again, Corrie tries to read the expression in Silas Caine's eyes. Is he fishing for something, trying to catch her out? Searching for something that will give him an indication that she really isn't a suitable candidate for the job he is about to give her? Is he privy to her exam entry, and her eloquent exposé on love in marriage? Corrie doesn't know, but quickly counters Silas's question with the propaganda she has learned so well to repeat.

"He's my friend. Friends can love each other, like family. I know he will support me, and my family. So, I'm not really sure what other kind of love matters. And, of course, the Alliance has its own criteria for determining the Selections which are far superior to any knowledge I might have about such things." Corrie has given it all she's got. She hopes Silas Caine won't ask her any more questions.

"Love comes in all different forms, Miss Tennant. Most of them good. But the best kind is the kind you choose yourself, or rather that chooses you. It sneaks up on you when you least expect it and grabs you . . . ," Silas Caine gestures in a grabbing motion " . . . in a way that makes you feel you have no choice, but at the same time you realize it's what you want." Corrie wonders how he knows so much about love, and why the pain in her heart is threatening to overwhelm her as she thinks again about Samuel. She doesn't want to cry in front of Silas Caine or give away her

114

deepest secrets away to a man she hardly knows, even though she feels she can trust him.

"It's a wonderful notion, but not very practical for the world we live in today," says Corrie.

"That may be so," he replies, "but the beauty of the notion can't be done away with, in spite of what the Alliance says."

This sounds like dissent to Corrie. She sees the flare of passion in Silas Caine's eyes, but dare not encourage it. There is too much at stake, and Corrie knows her place.

"Well, I suppose I will never know," says Corrie meekly, trying to defuse the usually affable Silas Caine. And she will never know because she needs to protect her family, and Samuel, too.

"Hmmm." He gives a gruff snort and then dismisses her to finish her work for the day. Corrie is relieved. She doesn't want anyone encouraging her thoughts about love, not now, when it is the furthest thing from her reach.

Nineteen

The following week, Corrie plans her next trip to the city. Since their last visit, her mother has gained quite a bit of strength with the tonics she's been given and is now helping around their home as well as with Joseph's care. Corrie tells her mother she will collect another dose of the tonic while she's in the city and reassures her that she will be fine traveling into the city on her own. Corrie is seventeen now. She turned seventeen a month before the Winter Ball, on the day Samuel had given her his mother's dress. It was like a birthday gift, but Samuel hadn't known it was her birthday. The Universe had known, and it had also known exactly what she needed on that day. The Universe must have spoken to Samuel, too, Corrie thinks.

She and Nate spend their scheduled hour together on Sunday, and she tells him she is being given higher duties at work over the summer. She doesn't tell him about the rest of her conversation with Silas Caine. That's between her and Silas

Caine. Nate tells Corrie that the work in the Blacksmith's has increased tenfold with the extra soldiers now stationed at the Garrison, and there's only himself and his father to do the work. She can tell he has been working hard. Strong muscles ripple beneath his shirt, and he is maturing much faster than Samuel. Right now, Nate is clean shaven, but he could grow a beard easily and sometimes Corrie feels the roughness of his cheek when he picks her up in a friendly gesture to hug her. She doesn't mind his hugs, but they aren't the kind of embraces that she and Samuel shared in the Mill. Corrie can't explain the difference, any more than she can explain love itself. It just is. And it's for her and Samuel.

When Corrie gets to the train station, she hopes not to see Sargent Seymour again, and wonders if he followed her the last time, waiting and watching to see where she might be going. He said that's what he would do, but she hadn't taken him seriously at the time. She thought it was just a display of bravado in front of his men. Only weak men have to display that kind of bravado, Corrie thinks.

There is no sign of Seymour as the train pulls into the station at Brookstown, and Corrie is grateful. She is also grateful to see Tilly at the station. She must be catching the same train. Corrie walks across to her as she steps onto the train and says hello.

"Oh, hello Corrie. What are you doing here?"

"I'm just going into the city to put some money on the material I'm buying for my wedding dress."

"Oh. That should be exciting. So, you've chosen the material. Do you have a pattern yet?" Tilly asks.

"Yes. I have a pattern and I'm going to sew the dress myself.

I'm hoping to pick the material up before the end of the summer and get started on it then."

"You must be very talented if you're able to sew your own wedding dress. Mine cost a fortune. My parents paid to have it made, so I only had to worry about the fittings."

"Did you go into the city to have your dress made?" Corrie asks her.

"Yes, of course. In the city, there's a huge choice of designs and fabrics. It was actually hard to decide in the end with all there was to choose from," Tilly says.

"I can imagine," says Corrie. She'd had the same problem, but expense had to be spared which made her choice a lot easier.

"When did you get married?" Corrie asks.

"Three years ago," Tilly replies.

Corrie wants to ask her about the Selection Process.

"Maisie told me she hardly knew her husband before the Selection Process took place. Did you know your husband?" Corrie asks.

"Oh, yes. I was lucky that way. Johnny and I had been friends growing up and he seemed to be the perfect choice . . . at the time."

Corrie notices how Tilly says, "at the time", and wonders if things have changed. She decides to probe gently and see if she can find out more.

"And was he perfect?" Corrie asks. "I mean, as perfect as you hoped he would be?"

Tilly looks at her in way that makes Corrie think Tilly wants to confide in her but isn't sure if she should. In the end, she obviously decides she can trust Corrie.

"For a while. He treated me like a real princess and would always be home straight after work, picking me up as he came in the door and hugging me. I would have a dinner ready for him, and then we would sit and maybe play a game of cards or chat. After about a year, he started coming home later. Sometimes he doesn't come home at all now. I don't know what happened, but I think it might have something to do with the fact there is no sign of us having children together. That's why I'm going into the city today, to see a Specialist about the difficulties we've been having. Johnny and I both want a baby, but so far there's no sign, and we spend less and less time together . . . " Tilly tapers off.

Corrie realizes that Tilly has been very generous in sharing this with her and promises, in her own mind, that she won't share it with anyone else. She can tell that Tilly is devastated at the way her marriage is working out right now, but then Corrie is sure sometimes people who love each have these kinds of difficulties, too. Maybe if they did love each other they would be able to overcome their sadness more readily. People who didn't love each other also had children together, so Corrie knew having children wasn't always about love. The ideal, in Corrie's mind was two people who loved each other having a baby together. She could imagine how that baby would be loved. Otherwise, a child would just be another task to complete, like the marriage itself. Having a child within an Alliance-sponsored marriage gave you more status, and it didn't matter whether people were in love or not. Children provided status just like marriage.

What would have happened to Joseph if their parents hadn't loved each other? Would he have known such fierce protection? And how would their mother have gained her father's understanding after Joseph's difficult birth? People who didn't love each other would become distant in the circumstances Corrie is sure. Love gave people strength to overcome the difficulties, and tragedies, in life. She had seen it herself. Was the love of two friends enough? Maybe in Tilly's case it won't be, and maybe in her and Nate's case it won't be either.

The colleagues fall silent until the train brings them into the city, where they go their separate ways. Corrie doesn't want to wander the streets of Louisville alone and once she has made her payment, and collected her mother's tonic, she is soon on her way back home. Tilly isn't at the station for the return trip and, after two hours, the train pulls slowly back into Brookstown. It's quiet, but still bright, and a little breezy. Corrie decides to walk down to see Nate, but she needs an excuse to be there. If anyone asks her, she will pretend the tonic she has is for him, and say that she is just delivering it but, hopefully, no one will ask. As Corrie walks toward the forge she sees Nate's father talking to a soldier.

"We need your son to help us fight the Rebels," the soldier is saying.

"My son is needed here," Nate's father replies with vigor.

"The Alliance requires all able-bodied young men to be called up to help us fight these people."

"My son is certainly able-bodied, but he is needed here. Who else do you think is going to shoe your horses?! Nate is apprenticed to me, and when he finishes school, he will be working here full-time."

"Is he your only son?" asks the soldier.

"Yes!" replies Nate's father. "There's no one else to carry on the work, and as far as I know people in business are able to nominate one child to help maintain their business or trade."

"That's true. I'll need to report back to the Officer-in-Command and tell him that is your answer," the soldier replies.

Nate's father turns his back on the soldier who hasn't seen Corrie standing there watching them. So, the Army needs new recruits and they are trying to get Nate to join up. It doesn't sound like his father is going to accept their offer, even if it comes with a generous remuneration, and Corrie doesn't want Nate to join the Army either. Working for the Alliance for the sake of a Ration Card is one thing. Joining the Army to do the Alliance's bidding is something else entirely. Corrie doesn't want that for Nate and, obviously, neither does his father. She wonders what Nate thinks, but he isn't there, so she turns around silently and makes her way home.

Twenty

Corrie must wait until Sunday to see Nate again, so she fills the rest of her week with walks in the woods, sometimes stepping down to the river to cool her feet in the slow-moving water. She remembers her father bringing her here with his fishing rod, and she would sit just like this while he cast the reel out to catch fish. The fish weren't normally very big, but if he caught a couple, it was usually enough for a family meal. Her father would prepare the fish for her mother to cook over the hearth and they would eat it with a dob of butter. Corrie's mouth is watering just thinking about it. The woods also offer her some respite from her concerns as she allows nature to minister to her. The world would keep turning, no matter what, and she must let things take their course, just like nature did. Nature is a great teacher, and a great healer, she thinks.

On Sunday, promptly at 3.30pm, Nate comes with the Chaperone. After overhearing the conversation the soldier was having with his father, Corrie is anxious to know what Nate thinks and what he plans to do. She doesn't think he will go against his father, and she doesn't think Nate wants to be a soldier fighting in the Alliance's Army. She will have to be careful that the Chaperone doesn't overhear their conversation, though.

Corrie says she'd like to go for a walk in the woods. After that, maybe they can bring Joseph down to the river and let him enjoy the fresh air and sunshine. They head off, with the Chaperone trailing behind, and Corrie asks Nate about the soldier.

"I went into the city during the week to put another payment on my material, and on my way home I stopped by the forge," she tells him.

"I hope you had a good excuse," Nate says.

"I did. I had my mother's tonic and was going to pretend it was for you," Corrie says cheekily.

"I see," says Nate. "So now I am an underfed forty-year-old woman in need of a dose of iron!" The two of them laugh together, and Corrie takes Nate's arm.

"I wanted to see you. There is so much to tell you about the city, and I traveled with one of my work colleagues on the train as well. We had a good chat which helped to pass the time."

"What did you talk about?" asks Nate. "Wedding dresses?"

"Yes." Corrie isn't going to tell him that they talked about a lot more than that.

"And I saw a soldier at the forge when I stopped there on the way home," says Corrie.

Nate frowns. Corrie can see that he is not happy about the soldier being there, or that Corrie saw him either.

"They want to draft me into the Army, but my father told them they can't. He needs me to work with him," Nate says.

"Would you want to join the Army?" Corrie asks out of curiosity.

"Not this Army," Nate mutters under his breath.

Does that mean he would want to join another army? Corrie wonders. The thought troubles her and she is reminded again of her father.

"I'm glad your father stood his ground. What would happen to me if you joined the Army?" Corrie says.

"I'd take you with me," Nate teases her, lifting her up and twirling her round, much to the Chaperone's consternation.

Corrie laughs, then leads him back to the cottage so they can bring Joseph out to enjoy the sunshine on the banks of the river.

When they get to the river, Nate finds stones for Joseph to throw and they hear them "plop" into the water while they watch the ripples move out from the center. There are ripples in people's lives, too, Corrie thinks. Ripples that are caused by the choices people make, and the consequences of those choices. Whatever you decide to do, it's going to impact on other people, especially the people you love. That's why you need to do your best to make the right choices, if you have a choice in life. Corrie hopes she will be able to do that. Nate skips stones across the water. He is very good at it and encourages Corrie to try. She does and fails miserably. Corrie wonders if there is a way to skip to the other side of life without making any ripples. Maybe if you move quickly enough, you can.

Corrie returns to work that week and prepares to take on new tasks while Tilly takes her holidays. Corrie will take her desk, and there she will help oversee correspondence relating to the requests that come in from Officials arranging the necessary duties under their care, including less sensitive paperwork from the Coding Office. Samuel is never the one to deliver the requests and Corrie is glad. Things are complicated enough already.

Twenty-One

The summer progresses quickly and Corrie spends as much time with her family as she can. Once she is a married woman, she will have to move into a new home with Nate, a home the Alliance will provide, and she just hopes it is nearby.

One Sunday, when Corrie and Nate meet, they decide to walk into the town with their Chaperone to enjoy some refreshments at a local café. It's a lovely, balmy evening and they want to do something different, something more grown up, like they see other couples do. As they walk into the café, Corrie sees Samuel standing at the counter. He is using his Ration Card to pay for a pot of tea and plate of delicate pastries. Then, she notices Selena sitting at a table in the corner. Nate waves at Selena, and Corrie looks away. She doesn't know how to react and wants to pull Nate out of the café so that they can go somewhere else, but it's too late as Samuel turns and sees Corrie and Nate standing in the doorway.

Samuel looks at Corrie first, and she feels a sudden rush of excitement and happiness to see him again. He smiles at her, and Corrie's heart soars. She can't help but smile back at him. Then Nate goes over and slaps him on the back.

"How are things going, Samuel?" Nate asks him.

"Fine," Samuel tells him, not elaborating.

"I see you and your lovely lady are out for an afternoon tea. Corrie and I had the same idea, didn't we, Corrie?" Nate says to her.

"Yes," answers Corrie, not knowing where to look now, and still not willing to acknowledge Selena.

"How would you like to join us?" asks Nate. "Maybe we can spend the hour catching up about what we've been doing on the holidays?"

Samuel looks across at Selena who is eyeing Corrie suspiciously. Corrie and Selena had not been friends in school, and Corrie is certain they will never be friends now.

"That's OK," says Samuel. "I think Selena likes to spend the time that we have alone. We don't get much of it when they only allow us an hour a week."

Corrie notices the Chaperone sitting at another table and she is glad the Chaperone is there. She doesn't want to imagine Samuel alone with another girl, and Corrie knows the Chaperones won't allow any "hanky panky" as they call it. For now, Corrie hopes she is the only girl Samuel has kissed. She can't imagine him kissing anyone else the way he kissed her, or her kissing Nate the way she kissed Samuel.

"That's true," Nate agrees. "Well, maybe another time then."

"Right," says Samuel as he carries the tea back to his table.

Corrie takes a seat at the table closest to the door and as far away from Selena and Samuel as possible. She doesn't want to know what they talk about, the things she and Samuel could be talking about if the Selectors had chosen Samuel as her Marriage Partner. She feels that creature stir again, the one that lives in her chest and puts a stranglehold on her heart, digging in its claws and making her heart bleed.

Nate brings the tea across, and Corrie can see Selena talking animatedly to Samuel. She is showing him something. It looks like it could be drawings of wedding dresses, and Samuel is just nodding and agreeing with her. She can't tell if he's really interested because Samuel has his back to her. Corrie wishes she had her back to him, so she didn't have to watch the two of them together.

Nate disturbs her thoughts by asking her if she wants one lump of sugar, or two, in her tea. Corrie answers him curtly, telling him she wants one, and then remembers that it's not Nate's fault she's in this predicament. She reaches across to him and tells him she is sorry, then takes the teaspoon to stir her tea. She stirs it over, and over, and over, lost in her thoughts, and not in the mood to talk. Nate hungrily eats up one pastry, then two, of the plate he had bought, while Corrie just sips at her tea. He finally asks Corrie if she wants the last pastry and she tells him that he should have it. She doesn't feel like eating right now. The two Chaperones have joined each other for tea and seem to have become distracted. In the end, it seems like well over the hour that they are sitting there, and Corrie can only watch Samuel's back while he listens to Selena talk.

The Chaperones eventually look at their watches and begin to get up, indicating it is time to leave. Corrie can't wait to get out of there and exits the shop ahead of the Chaperone. Nate follows her, and Corrie is halfway down the street before he can catch up.

"Corrie! Wait up" Nate says.

She stops to let him join her, and sees the Chaperone rushing behind. She also sees Samuel and Selena exit the café, with Selena linking Samuel's arm as they walk out. Samuel looks up at Corrie and she turns away quickly, not wanting to encourage another smile which will only rip a bigger hole in her heart.

"What's wrong?" Nate asks her. "You hardly ate anything and now you're rushing to get home."

"I don't know. I just get a bit overwhelmed sometimes with this whole marriage thing, I guess."

"What do you mean?" asks Nate.

"Well, it's just seeing Samuel and Selena together makes it all seem more real, that we've been made into couples, betrothed to one another, and there is no room for friendship anymore. Everyone belongs to somebody else, and they have to stay in those pairings whether they like it or not," says Corrie.

"Are you saying you're not happy with the Selection, Corrie?" asks Nate.

Corrie wishes she could be honest with Nate, but years of indoctrination, and fears for her family, prevent her from telling him how she really feels.

"No, I'm just not happy with the process. The way it divides people, so that they can no longer be themselves, but must in some ways pretend to be people that they're not, just because the Alliance says so."

Corrie is beginning to understand that people are not just divided from each other but are also divided within themselves as they try to live up to Alliance expectations. It's an internal division between who you are and what you want, and who the Alliance decides you are and where you fit into their agenda. The Alliance don't take into account the inner workings of people's minds and hearts and, while the outer trappings might indicate one thing, the soul and spirit of a person could never be captured and held by them ... well, only if you let them. She doesn't want the Alliance to manipulate her to the point that she doesn't know who she is anymore, and right now she's feeling confused.

Nate is shaking his head, not really understanding what Corrie is trying to say. She knows Nate isn't much of a thinker and maybe that's why she can enjoy the lighter side of life with him. If you didn't dig too deep you could be happy and satisfied with what you had. Maybe she should just stop digging and lay her love for Samuel to rest. Bury it and leave it where it belongs, in the past. And then she thinks about putting flowers on the grave of her and Samuel's love. Daffodils, Corrie decides. They are her favorite.

Twenty-Two

Corrie has her second week off work at the end of the summer. She is going into the city to make the final payment on her material and, once she brings it home, she will start working on the dress for her wedding. She hasn't told Nate much about it, and he hasn't asked. Corrie wonders if Samuel asked Selena about her dress that day in the café, or if Selena was just so excited she wanted to tell Samuel all about it. What Corrie knew was that Samuel listened. Was he really interested, or was that just Samuel's nature, to be kind hearted, whether he felt like listening or not? Corrie doesn't know and needs to stop brooding about Samuel and Selena. She needs to focus on Nate and their plans. It's the only way to move forward.

Corrie arrives at the station, not knowing how long it will be before she has a reason to go to the city again. There are parts of it that she enjoys, but in truth Corrie prefers her small, sleepy town without the imposing buildings and the sense of threat that seems to accompany them. She likes things to be simple and uncomplicated. Then Corrie wonders why things don't seem as simple as they should be . . . as uncomplicated they had always been. When did everything change?

As she stands there, mulling everything over, the train pulls into the station. There are quite a few people waiting, making the most of the opportunity to travel during the summer holiday period, and the train is crowded. Corrie manages to find a seat eventually and, after the train departs, she enjoys watching the countryside go by in a vision of greenery, broken occasionally by golden fields or the colorful hues of summer flowers. As the train passes towns closer to Louisville, she begins to take in less pleasant sights. There are buildings burned to the ground with only a few blackened stumps remaining as testament to their existence. Further along, broken wagons are scattered, some with the bloated bodies of dead horses still attached to them. The train rushes past these scenes of devastation before a final horrific vision sears itself into Corrie's memory. Two men hanging from a makeshift scaffold.

Something is wrong. Something is happening that reminds Corrie of what happened in their small town just a few months ago, but this is on a much bigger scale. No buildings were destroyed in her town, and the wreckage left after the Rebels were scattered was cleared away in a couple of days. Some of the Rebels escaped into the woods, and those who didn't were dead. Since then the town had accepted the imposition of Ration Cards and the Rule of Martial Law. Corrie's hope that it was just temporary, that the Rebels would disappear, and they could go on living their quiet lives of desperation, was not being played out in the scenes appearing before her. Corrie recognizes now what she had known intuitively when she'd investigated the ringing of alarm bells in her town. There were those, like her father, who saw rebellion as a necessary response to oppression.

As she steps off the train and moves to exit the platform, someone gently takes her arm from behind. Corrie turns in a swift movement, fearing Seymour has followed her and is going to accost her again. She didn't expect Samuel to be here. She didn't see him get on the train.

"Samuel!" Corrie breathes, after realizing she has been holding her breath, thinking Samuel could be somebody else.

"Corrie," he says, holding her eyes for just a moment, before turning her around and whispering in her ear: "follow me."

He releases her arm and walks briskly ahead of her. Of course, the two of them are not meant to be seen together, but Samuel is leading her somewhere and she feels she must follow. After what she has just seen on the way into the city, Corrie is worried. Maybe Samuel knows something important, something she needs to know for the sake of her family.

Samuel moves through a number of busy city streets, and Corrie tries not to lose him in the crowd. She sees him moving away from the official Alliance buildings and into the market area, finally entering a narrow alleyway at the back of some stalls. She hopes he isn't going to take her too far out of her way, worried she might not find her way back, and knowing she still needs to pick up the material for her dress. As Corrie enters the alleyway, she sees Samuel standing by a doorway that leads into some kind of storage area. As she catches up with him, Samuel takes Corrie by the hand and hides them both in the recess.

"Corrie," he murmurs, gazing into her eyes. Corrie needs him to keep talking, or she is going to want him to kiss her again, and the pain in her heart is already excruciating. "We need to talk. Did you see what's happening outside our town on the way here today?"

Corrie just nods her head. She's not sure what Samuel wants to tell her, or if she really wants to hear what he has to say.

"It's going to get worse, Corrie. I've been working in the Coding area, and the Rebels are more organized than the Alliance thought. They have been developing systems that mean they can counter what the Alliance is already doing to keep the insurrections at bay, and they are finding ways to disrupt Alliance communications."

Corrie is surprised. She hadn't realized that the Alliance wasn't fully in control again, as they are in her and Samuel's town due to the rationing system. That has been enough to keep her from thinking about challenging the status quo, and probably enough for everybody else in the town as well.

"I ... I didn't know," says Corrie. She works in the Communications Office. Surely, she would have noticed something if this was the case, or maybe she just wasn't paying attention ... too caught up in thoughts about Samuel and her wedding.

"Have you noticed anything happening in your area, anything different?" Samuel asks her.

"Silas Caine has been on holidays for the last month, and I am on holidays now. Another man came in to replace him, but he didn't dictate letters to me the way Silas Caine did. In fact, he has been sending me on lots of errands, to deliver messages to other Offices," says Corrie. She misses Silas Caine and is looking forward to seeing him when he gets back from his holiday.

"How does he send the messages, Corrie?"

Why was Samuel asking her this? Why was it important? She searches Samuel's eyes, trying to discover any kind of treachery that may be lurking there, but all she sees is genuine concern . . . for what or for whom exactly, Corrie doesn't know.

"He puts them into an envelope which he seals, and then has me carry them for him," Corrie says.

Samuel doesn't want to know any more right now, and she realizes he has been holding her tightly by her arms. He relaxes his grip and gently rubs her arm, apologizing, but Corrie has craved his touch since their last encounter at the Mill. She puts her hand on Samuel's chest and looks up at him, just before sliding her arms around his neck and kissing him. Samuel draws her closer, and into an embrace which makes her feel, for the second time, like she has come home. Samuel feels like home to her, and she lets his hands move over her body in a moment that ignites something deep inside. It isn't something she can explain, but she knows she wants more of this closeness, more of this comfort, more of everything Samuel seems to be able to give her that Nate can't.

Samuel slows his advances as they both realize that this is neither the time nor the place. There will never be a time or a place that the Alliance will allow for their affection, or for their love to flourish. The cold hard facts temper the flames of their desire, but not the flames of Corrie's anger.

"Corrie," Samuel says with sincerity, looking into eyes now filling with angry tears. "Do you think you can wait for me?"

"Wait for you? What do you mean?" Corrie asks swiping tears away from her face.

"I mean, can you wait . . . if somehow things change, if for some reason the marriages don't go ahead?"

"Oh, Samuel. Do you really think that things can ever change? That we will be able to marry people we want to marry, people that we love, and not just people who have been chosen for us?" There is quiet desperation in her voice.

"Yes, I do, Corrie" Samuel replies. "People were never forced into compulsory marriages before the Alliance increased its power and, if they are overthrown, there is the chance a lot of things will change, that people will be able to choose again who they want to marry."

"Do you love Selena?" Corrie asks him. She needs to know. She needs to hear it from him.

"No, I don't love Selena. I try to be a good fiancé and do what is required of me, but no. I don't love her."

"Do you love me?" Corrie asks quietly wanting to hear Samuel say the words again.

"Yes . . . I love you" he says, sealing his reply with a soft, lingering kiss that makes Corrie want more.

"Do you love Nate?" he asks in return. Corrie understands Samuel needs to know, too.

"Nate is a friend. He has been good to me and my family. So, I care about Nate and I am grateful for him. But . . . "

Corrie finally gets the chance to say to Samuel what she has wanted to say for a long time, words that Samuel once silenced with a kiss.

"I love you, Samuel." She wants to give herself to Samuel in a way she has never wanted to give herself to anyone before, and Corrie won't deny it to herself or Samuel any longer. He is hers and she is his. No matter what the Alliance has decided.

Samuel takes her in his arms again and holds her tightly. Corrie has tried in so many ways to ensure her last embrace with Samuel would be the final one. Yet somehow, whenever they meet, the invisible forces of the Universe seemed to draw them into another. It's a force that neither of them are able to resist . . . a force they don't want to resist any longer.

Samuel releases her and tells her to walk out of the alleyway ahead of him. Corrie doesn't see Seymour watching her from behind a market stall. She doesn't see him walk in the direction from which she has just come, and she doesn't see the Sargent push Samuel up against a wall as the two of them confront each other again. Corrie is buried deep in her own thoughts about Samuel, about what he has said, and about the thought that maybe she and Samuel could be together after all. The thought creates a lightness in her spirit, a spring in her step, and she imagines a future completely different to the one the Alliance has planned for them.

Twenty-Three

Corrie spends the rest of the week in a cheerful mood playing with Joseph and helping her mother around the cottage. Otherwise, she takes time to wander through the woods surrounding their home, watching insects dart in and out of the sunlight breaking through the canopy, as woodland creatures scamper at the sound of her footfall. She searches for, then picks, flowers to bring home to her mother. All the while, Corrie thinks of the beauty of nature and the beauty of love. She loves Samuel and he loves her. They have told each other that, and it's all that matters. How they orchestrate their coming together is an entirely different matter, and one that is beyond her comprehension, so she tries not to think about it, and just lets the feeling of being in love wash over her.

On Sunday, Nate is unable to visit with her. The demand for the Blacksmith is becoming overwhelming as more soldiers are called in to help fight the Rebels. Corrie is pleased that their meeting is cancelled. How can she face him? Knowing what she knows, feeling what she feels, having confirmed to Samuel that she loves him? Corrie will have to face Nate, and Samuel, on the first day back at school, but that is tomorrow. She begins working on her dress in the evening, not knowing what she will do with it, or if she will ever wear it. She has to keep up appearances, though, as she doesn't want her mother to worry.

Corrie marks out the material and cuts it carefully with the scissors before stopping for a moment to hold it up to her cheek, imagining Samuel's touch, a touch she wants to feel again. At the same time, she recalls the friendly hugs she and Nate shared, which were comforting in a way too, giving a sense of masculine strength. Corrie realizes again she doesn't want Nate's kind of physicality. She used to be attracted to it, his good looks and congenial nature.

When had it all changed Corrie wonders? When did she become more aware of her attraction to Samuel? She had done her best to avoid him, and not just after the Selections. During the Winter Ball they had avoided looking at each other when they had danced together and even before that, Corrie had tried at different times to lessen her contact with him. Maybe because she knew that being attracted to Samuel could lead her to a place it wasn't safe to go.

She had thought the same thing about Nate at one time, too. Even though she was attracted to him, she couldn't afford to make a Selection before the Selectors. And now look what had happened. She was connected to both of them . . . loving one, while being forced to marry the other. Corrie realizes she's been cutting the material with too much vigor and puts the scissors down. It won't do to ruin the dress while she is still unsure if she will ever be wearing it. She decides to go to bed where she can dream her dreams, and shed her tears, in private.

The next day, and the first day back at school after the summer break, Corrie enters the classroom to see Nate sitting in his usual spot. This is the spot he sat in last year, and the seat next to him is reserved for her. It doesn't have a sign on it, at least not a visible one, and Corrie can't help but look to the back where Samuel normally sits. He isn't here yet, but Selena Prescott has moved into the seat beside his, and Corrie notices that all the class has now paired off, each couple sitting beside one another, most of them looking fairly content. Corrie wishes she felt as content now as she had this time last year when she had been brave enough, or foolish enough, to take the seat next to Nate . . . an act of bravado that may have led to the conundrum she is in today. She realizes she has no choice and takes her seat beside him.

Just as the class is about to start, Samuel quietly enters the classroom with his head down. Corrie can see he has a swollen lip with a cut on the bottom and his fringe doesn't hide the bruise under his right eye. What has happened to Samuel this time, and who did this to him? Some of the class members let out an audible gasp as Samuel hurries in to take his seat at the back of the room. She turns around to see Selena asking him if he is all right and hears Samuel mutter something under his breath. The teacher looks at Samuel with concern but decides to draw the class's attention back to herself, and lessons begin for the day. Corrie can't focus, and notices Nate looking across at her at one point, raising his eyebrows in a gesture that asks Corrie what is going on. She will to have to answer him when the class takes their first break.

When the bell rings, Corrie wants to see Samuel, but of course, she can't. She has to walk out with Nate, and he brings her around to the back of the building, to the place where the two of them used to sit and wonder, looking down the road that leads to Louisville.

"Corrie, what's the matter with you? You've been distracted all morning."

"I don't know. I think I got a shock when I saw Samuel come in with his face all marked up."

"Samuel's father is always beating him up. He's a cruel man, and the sooner Samuel is married and out of that house the better!" says Nate.

Everyone knows about Samuel's father, but there isn't much anyone can do. Parents are in charge of their children and other people don't interfere, at least not when it comes to family business. Corrie isn't sure this is family business. Samuel's father hasn't hit him in a while, only once since the rationing began, and Corrie feels that something else has happened to Samuel.

"You're probably right," she says, not wanting to arouse any suspicion in Nate. "But, it's disturbing. How can a parent treat a child like that?"

"I'd say alcohol is Samuel's father's biggest problem. Not having a wife probably doesn't help either. There's no one to help rear the other children, and Samuel's caught in the middle trying to protect them. I feel sorry for him. Makes me wonder if Samuel's father used to beat his wife as well,".

Corrie had never thought about that. Maybe he did beat his wife, until she died, and now Samuel is the one left to fend off the blows. But Corrie is sure it wasn't Samuel's father who did this. She will go to the Mill after work today and try to find out. That's the only way she can have dealings with Samuel and not raise any suspicions. The day drags as Corrie waits for the final bell to ring.

When Corrie gets to the office, she sees that Silas Caine has returned. She's so happy to see him. The other Manager had been sour-faced and unfriendly, whereas Silas Caine always seemed to be approachable.

"Good afternoon, Mr. Caine" Corrie says cheerfully, and she is cheerful now that she has seen him.

"Good afternoon, Corrie." He has a look of concern on his face, which she thinks is probably due to workload that has built up in his absence. If what Samuel said is anything to go by, plus what she had seen with her own two eyes, Silas Caine is going to be carrying a much heavier burden in his role as Manager of Communications soon. "Sit down, my dear" he says as he offers her a seat.

Corrie waits for Silas to tell her what he needs. Does he need to dictate a letter? Then she will need to get her quill and ink.

"How was your holiday?" he asks her.

"I had a lovely time" answers Corrie. "I went to Louisville to pick up the material for my wedding dress and I've started to sew it. Otherwise, I just enjoyed long walks out in the woods, and spent time with my mother and brother".

"Corrie, you know the woods are still dangerous with the possibility of Rebel soldiers hiding out there. I think you need to be more careful these days," says Silas.

"Oh!" says Corrie, genuinely surprised. She hasn't really thought about Rebel soldiers being anywhere near her home since army reinforcements had arrived and continued to do patrols in the woods. "I hadn't really thought about it, Sir. I just assumed the Rebels would have left by now".

"Well, that may be, but you can never be too careful. I want you to remember that," says Silas.

"Yes, Sir."

"All right. Get your pen please, Corrie. I need to dictate a letter".

"Yes, Sir," says Corrie again. She hurries over to her table in the corner and gets what she needs.

"All right," Silas Caine says again. "This is important, so I will speak slowly."

Dear Ichabod,

I have received your enquiry about the Mill and intend to look into it. I have asked for the books from the Mill to be delivered to me by the end of the week, so a thorough investigation can be done. If, as you suggest, the books have been tampered with to allow extra grain to be given to those who are not entitled to it, then this will be a matter for the Law, and they will be duly notified.

Very respectfully,
Your Obedient Servant,
Silas Caine.

Corrie finishes writing in her beautiful hand and looks up at Silas Caine. He is staring directly at her, and she wonders if he has dictated this letter to her for a reason. He could have dictated it to one of the other women when she wasn't here during the day. Maybe she is just imagining things, but she needs to warn Samuel. He is already in bad shape, but things might get worse. She doesn't want anything to happen to him. He is Corrie's reason for getting up every morning now, just like the sun and, just like the sun, she can't imagine living without him.

Corrie wishes Silas Caine "Good Night," at 5.30 and hurriedly exits the office to make her way to the Mill. This time, she doesn't stop to enjoy the day. There is nothing Corrie can think of to enjoy right now, especially with the warning Silas Caine has just given her.

Twenty-Four

Corrie runs to the Mill. She knows Samuel usually works on a Monday and hopes to find him there. There's plenty of daylight left, and no sign of soldiers on the road, so Corrie runs with no regard for anyone else, except Samuel. She doesn't care who sees her or what they think. As she enters the Store, she sees Samuel standing behind the counter and all she wants to do is throw herself into his arms and tell him that he has to leave. Corrie can hardly catch her breath as she stops in front of Samuel. He moves to the other side of the counter to see if she is all right.

"Samuel . . . ," she says. "The Alliance . . . " Corrie is finding it hard to finish.

"What about the Alliance, Corrie?" he asks, helping her to stand up straight while she catches her breath.

"The Alliance . . . ," she begins again, "they're going to investigate the Mill. They suspect someone of giving extra rations and trying to hide the fact."

"How do you know?" asks Samuel.

"Silas Caine. He dictated a letter to me today. Someone reported the Mill and Silas had to reply to a communique from the Alliance saying the Mill would be investigated. They are going to ask for your books before the end of the week."

Samuel takes Corrie into the side room. He hopes no one has overheard what she has already said, but they are the only two people in the Store right now.

"Corrie . . . ," Samuel searches her face.

"You need to leave," Corrie says, the words catching in her throat, tears welling in her eyes.

"I'm not leaving, Corrie."

"Please, Samuel. The Alliance is going to investigate."

"Corrie. I'm not leaving you."

Corrie is getting frustrated with Samuel. He doesn't seem to understand that if he is the one who has been giving away extra grain, he will be punished. She doesn't know how severely. She decides to remind him that they still have no choice about their betrothals and that, even if Samuel stays, they won't be together.

"Even if you stay, Samuel, the two of us can't be together right now. That carries a punishment all of its own. Why risk your life for something that might never be . . . for me?" she asks.

"Because I want to be with you, and I'm going to find a way," he replies.

Corrie knows that Samuel doesn't have the means to keep that promise right now. Neither does she. If the Rebels continue their war against the Alliance maybe, in the future, things will change. But just being two young people in love is not going to change anything. She and Samuel will be squashed like bugs because that's what they are to the Alliance. They might as well be insects running on the ground, where the heavy boot of the Alliance will easily find them. In the shadow of the Alliance's power, their small, inconsequential lives will be brought to an end. It isn't possible to defeat the Alliance on just one front.

"Samuel, please don't make promises you can't keep. And besides, we can't get married if one of us is dead!" Corrie finishes, raising her voice, now on the point of hysteria. Neither one of them is touching the other as they stand as opponents in the back room of the Mill. A tear slides down Corrie's cheek as she looks at Samuel, the young man she loves, who is refusing to leave her side.

"Corrie, you need to buy some grain."

What is he talking about? She is here talking about life and death and Samuel is talking about grain.

"Look at me. You need to buy some grain. That is the reason you are here. I will meet you tonight, after I finish work and make sure my brother and sister are OK. You go home and do the same."

"Where will we meet?" Corrie asks him. It's dangerous to be out after dark and she doesn't want to take the chance of running into Rebels or soldiers.

"I will come to your cottage at midnight and tap on your window when I get there. There's a place in the woods I know, not too far from your home, where we can talk about what's happening."

"Do you promise?" Corrie asks him. This is a promise Samuel might be able to keep.

"Yes. I promise. Only death could keep me away," he says with an ironic smile. Corrie is not reassured. The promise of death is all around them, and Corrie doesn't want anything to happen to Samuel.

"Don't say that," Corrie whispers as she places a finger on his lips. She is also going to find out what happened to Samuel, how he got those marks. She still hasn't asked him.

They leave the back room to return to the counter after Samuel checks first to make sure the coast is clear. Corrie gets her pound of grain, taking Samuel's hand across the counter as he gives it to her.

"See you at midnight," Corrie says.

"See you at midnight," Samuel replies.

This is going to be the longest wait of Corrie's short life. Longer than the wait to hear about her job, longer than the one to hear about her Marriage Selection. This wait will be the wait that promises life or death, and Corrie wants Samuel to live.

Twenty-Five

Daylight is waning as Corrie makes her way home. She is no longer running. She needs to look calm and reassured, like nothing is wrong, as she heads back into the town and home to her family. As she steps onto the path just past the school building, Corrie bumps into Sargent Seymour.

"Well, well, well. Miss Tennant. How are we this fine evening?" he asks with a sneer in his voice.

"Fine. Thank you" Corrie answers nervously, as she feels her heart begin to pound in her chest. Most people are in their homes now preparing their dinners, and there isn't another soldier in sight.

"What have we here?" Seymour asks, indicating her bag of grain.

"Oh. I just had to pick some grain up for my family. We are running out," Corrie tells him.

"I see," says Seymour. "I guess these are the kind of supplies you don't have to go to the city to buy," he says.

"No. It would be too much to carry when you can get it right here," Corrie says, trying not to let her voice shake.

"That's true," says Seymour. "I wonder what a poor girl like you could afford to buy in the city anyway?"

Corrie looks at him. Up to now she has been looking away. She decides not to respond to what is clearly an insult.

"Well, tell me what you were buying on your trip to the city last week," he says gesturing with his hands, motioning her to hurry up and give him an explanation.

"How do you know I was in the city?" Corrie asks.

"Because I saw you there. Strangely enough, I saw the Mill hand there as well. Your friend, Samuel Jacobs. He didn't seem to like me asking him questions either."

Now Corrie knows where Samuel got his injuries. Seymour. He must have cornered Samuel somewhere in the city after she'd left, and she hadn't known anything about it. She couldn't. Today at school was the first time she had seen Samuel since then.

"Why were you asking him questions?" Corrie tries to sound innocent.

"Oh, because I thought maybe the two of you were meeting up, having a little Rebel rendezvous, and I couldn't allow that now, could I?" Seymour sneers again.

"I went to collect the material for my wedding dress. I don't know why Samuel was there. I didn't see him," Corrie lies.

"Apparently, he was there to pick up his outfit for the wedding. He showed me the receipt, but not before we ended up in a little altercation," Seymour says. Corrie isn't interested in hearing Seymour's version of events.

"It's a busy time of year and we don't have long to pre-pare now," says Corrie. "There were a lot of people in the town that day," she tells him, hoping that will satisfy his curiosity.

She can see a horse approaching, ridden by a more senior officer from the Garrison. Seymour sees it too.

"Run along now, Miss Tennant. You need to get your family's dinner ready. I'm sure we'll meet again," says Seymour.

Corrie walks as quickly as she can, back to her home, while darkness descends. She just hopes her legs will carry her, feeling weak at Seymour's revelation. He knows about her and Samuel. Not that they are Rebels, but that they are forming their own alliance, in opposition to the Alliance.

Corrie apologizes to her mother for being late, and her mother asks why she has bought another bag of grain when there is already enough to last them at least another week. Corrie says she thought she had forgotten to buy it last week. Her mother accepts her explanation without further comment. Thankfully, Corrie can use the excuse that she obviously has a lot on her mind with the start back to school, and her upcoming wedding.

After eating a dinner of biscuits and stew, Corrie stokes the fire and takes Joseph onto the armchair beside her. She tells him a story, another one of her father's old tales, while Joseph listens intently. So intently, that soon he can no longer keep his eyes open. She gets him to stir just long enough to bring him across to the bed where he snuggles in next to their mother. Corrie begins to sew. The rhythmic sound of the machine stitching the pieces of Corrie's dress together soon sends her mother off to sleep as well, and all is quiet in the cottage.

Corrie continues to sew for another couple of hours until she sees the skirt of her dress begin to take shape. It doesn't engender any emotion in her. It's just another task to complete right now. Her eyelids grow heavy, and she eventually she decides to lie down in her room and wait for Samuel. It shouldn't be long now until he arrives, so she stretches out on her bed and pulls the quilt over her legs to keep herself warm.

Corrie doesn't realize she's fallen asleep until a light tap on the window wakes her. Samuel! She jumps up and pulls the curtain aside to see him standing there with a lamp in his hand. She picks up her shoes, grabs the shawl from the chair, and quietly goes outside.

This time Corrie doesn't hesitate. She wraps her arms around his neck, and Samuel wraps his arms around her waist. They hold each other tightly before Samuel gives her a light kiss on the lips and takes her by the hand, leading her into woods. It's dark, but a dim lamp helps to light their way. As they walk, he removes his hand from Corrie's and places his arm protectively around her shoulders. Corrie's left arm circles Samuel's waist as she moves closer to him. After about twenty minutes, they reach a small cabin. It's in a very dense part of the woods where even horses would find it hard to travel. Corrie has never seen this cabin in the woods before and looks at Samuel with surprise.

"How did you know about this place?"

"A friend," is all he says. Corrie doesn't try to find out more. It's probably better if she doesn't know, and the main thing is they are together.

Samuel leads her inside, where a fire has been lit in a small stone fireplace to the right of the door. An old metal bed leans against the wall to the left, and opposite them is a table set with two candles. Between the candles is a vase filled with Daisies, reminding Corrie of her father. She begins to understand the significance of this moment and turns to Samuel.

"Did you do this?"

"No," says Samuel looking as surprised as Corrie. "Let's sit by the fire," he suggests and they each pull over a small stool. Samuel takes Corrie's hands in his, gently rubbing them, trying to warm them.

"I ran into Seymour in the town on the way home," Corrie tells Samuel.

Anger flares quickly in Samuel's eyes at the mention of Seymour's name, and he asks, "Did he touch you?!"

"No. He told me he saw you in the city. Is he the one who hit you?"

"Yes," says Samuel. "He told me he had seen you and asked if I had seen you, too. I told him I hadn't and that I was just in the city to pick up my outfit for the wedding. I said you were probably there to pick up yours. He didn't like the answers I was giving him, so he hit me."

"He hit you more than once, Samuel," says Corrie smoothing her hand over the bruised area around his eye.

"It doesn't matter."

"I'm so sorry, Samuel." She wishes she had brought some of Joseph's ointment as she smooths her hand over the area again, gently, and then puts her fingers to Samuel's swollen lip. Corrie leans forward and kisses him gently. It doesn't seem to hurt Samuel and he pulls Corrie closer to kiss her more deeply. The two of them are soon breathless, and Corrie pulls away momentarily. They still haven't talked about the Mill.

"Do you want to tell me about the Mill?" Corrie asks quietly.

"There are people starving, Corrie. They need to eat. It was the only way to make sure they could. Not everyone was fortunate enough to get a Ration Card."

She feels bad that she hadn't thought about this. Of course, there were people who got less, or nothing at all, being unable to prove their loyalty to the Alliance. Samuel had been doing what he could to help these people, trying to rescue them from starvation.

"What did you do?" she asks.

"I 'adjusted' the books to make it look like more grain had actually been sold, then gave the extra to the poor. It was such a small amount I didn't think anyone would notice. I wish it could have been more," Samuel says wistfully.

Samuel had put his life on the line and he still wished he could have done more. What more could any man do? Corrie doesn't know, but now she feels angry at the people starving, because Samuel will have to leave her, and she doesn't want him to go.

"Samuel, you are one of the kindest people I know. I never even thought about the people who might not have Ration Cards." Corrie knows she could have been one of those people, and Samuel had tried to help her once before by offering grain for less. Corrie loved him more than ever, and to think once she had wondered if he was an agent of the Alliance. She couldn't have been more wrong.

"I'm sorry, Corrie," he says. Now Samuel is apologizing to her, for being kind and generous and brave, but she would have none of it.

She gets up and lights a candle in the dying embers, bringing it back to the table where it spreads a soft glow over the small one-room cabin. Next, she takes Samuel by the hand, leading him across to the ramshackle bed. Samuel looks at her questioningly, but Corrie has only one thing she wants to say to him right now.

"I love you," she whispers.

"I love you, too," Samuel tells her.

Corrie draws Samuel down on the bed beside her.

"Corrie. I don't know what's going to happen after tonight."

"I know."

"You should save yourself for the man you are going to marry. Whether that's me, or Nate, you can't possibly know right now."

"I know."

Corrie knows she is being cryptic. She doesn't mean to be but, if she isn't going to see Samuel again, at least for a while, she wants to show him how much she loves him.

"I choose you" she says.

Corrie is making her choice tonight. In defiance of the Alliance, in defiance of her betrothal to Nate, and in concert with the Universe, which has drawn them together.

Corrie gives herself to Samuel as though it is their wedding night.

Twenty-Six

A gentle hand brushes the hair from her face. This coupled with a soft kiss, wakes Corrie. She is being held in Samuel's embrace, an embrace of love, an embrace of her choosing. Samuel draws Corrie closer as he looks into her eyes and tries to read her thoughts. She places her hand on his face, smoothing it over the yellowing bruise under his eye and the stubble on his cheek. Samuel leans in and kisses her again. Corrie responds. Finally, she knows what it is to be a woman, and what it is to love a man. She would not have wanted any other man to touch her the way Samuel had touched her last night. He was gentle and loving, kind and considerate. Corrie couldn't have hoped for more in the moment that she and Samuel had become one, but now it was time for her to leave.

Samuel moves his hands over her body one last time and Corrie tries to memorize his touch, as she senses Samuel trying to memorize her . . . the one he has chosen. They cling to each other in a final embrace and, as the sun comes up, Corrie rises from the bed to dress and return home. Samuel insists on walking her through the woods and as they get closer to Corrie's cottage the sound of approaching hooves forces them to move quickly, away from the oncoming patrol and deeper into the trees. The hooves thunder off in another direction and, when Corrie and Samuel feel safe to break cover, they continue toward the cottage.

When they reach Corrie's home, she pulls Samuel into the shadows, throwing her arms around his neck, and letting tears slide down her cheeks as she realizes this is their last opportunity to say goodbye. He holds her tightly. Neither wants to let the other go, but Samuel finally breaks their embrace as he wipes the tears from Corrie's eyes.

"It's going to be OK, Corrie" he tells her. "I am going to find a way to come back to you, so we can be together. I promise." Corrie has to believe him. It's impossible to imagine any other outcome, now that she . . . and the Universe . . . have chosen Samuel.

"Please come back . . . ," Corrie's tears are choking her now.

Samuel takes her hand and leads her to the door.

"I promise," he tells her again.

"I love you, Samuel . . . ," she tells him, and Corrie kisses him for the last time.

With that Samuel slips back into the woods, the way they had come, and away from the sound of the hooves they'd heard earlier. She is alone now. Samuel is gone, and Corrie is alone. She feels more alone than she has ever felt in her entire life.

Corrie opens the door as quietly as she can and sets the fire in the hearth. She might have time for a quick bath before she has to go to school this morning. As much as she wants Samuel's scent to linger on her body, Corrie knows, for his sake and for hers, she must scrub as much of Samuel from her body, and her life, as she can right now. It is the only way to keep him safe.

It doesn't seem that Corrie's absence during the night has been noticed, and she'd never intended to be gone this long. But, Corrie doesn't regret it. She hopes Samuel doesn't either.

Corrie tends to the fire and prepares breakfast after getting her bath. As she does this, she decides she wants to get a teacher for Joseph, someone who will come to the cottage and work with him. She knows he is bright, and Corrie does her best to help keep his mind active by talking to him, telling him stories and trying to enrich his understanding of the world, so much of which he has never seen. Corrie wants Joseph to have a life that doesn't just consist of the four walls of their cottage, to have a life that will give him what she knows he has to give to it in return. Corrie doesn't know how she can do this, but she is going to find a way.

Love is expanding Corrie's horizons and, walking to school, she realizes the world will never be the same for her again. She has been touched by something aligning her with all that is good in the world. . . love. And love is always a giver. That's how Corrie knows it's real.

Entering the classroom, Corrie looks to the back first, to Samuel's seat. He's not there and the sight of his empty seat opens a vast cavern in Corrie's heart. Samuel is gone, and she doesn't know when he will be back—if he will ever come back. Selena is sitting there, and she looks at Corrie. As their eyes meet, Corrie knows another heart will be broken today.

Corrie wonders how she would feel if Nate suddenly disappeared before their wedding day, leaving her alone and without a partner for the upcoming ceremonies. What will happen to Selena now? Corrie doesn't know. All the class has been paired up and there is no one left for Selena to marry. Corrie turns away quickly and notices Nate looking at her. Does she look any different now? Will Nate be able to tell that in her heart she is now betrothed to another, and that her body has betrayed him as surely as her heart? He doesn't smile at her but waits for her to take her seat beside him, and Corrie feels trapped again.

Classes begin, and Corrie does her best to focus, dreading the ring of the morning bell that will allow them out of the classroom, and Corrie into Nate's company again. It tolls too soon, and Corrie walks slowly out of the doors, alongside Nate, into the cool morning air.

"I'm sorry I couldn't make it on Sunday," Nate says looking serious.

"That's fine, Nate. I had so much to do. I've started working on my wedding dress," Corrie tells him.

"Oh. That's good" says Nate giving her a smile at last. He must have needed reassurance that Corrie wasn't mad at him, and now he knows she is enthusiastically preparing for their wedding. Corrie feels the burden of her lie, not about the wedding dress, but about her true state of mind. Nate deserves better.

"You were busy at the forge on Sunday," Corrie reminds him.

"Yes. More soldiers have joined the Garrison in town and more horses have been brought in, too. My father will probably need to apprentice me full-time sooner than he thought."

So, this is what is on Nate's mind. He may be forced to leave school before the end of the year to help his father. Now, Corrie is going to lose Nate, too. At least, during the week, when they were supposed to be at school. Things are happening too fast. They are being forced to grow up too quickly. Corrie isn't sure she is ready to lose the people closest to her in a war on the Alliance. She curses the Rebels and the Alliance as she fashions her response to Nate.

"I'm sorry, Nate. Maybe if you were going to be apprenticed anyway, it is better to start now rather than waste more time on the Alliance's indoctrination."

Corrie hopes she doesn't sound too strident and would never offer these thoughts up normally. But they are outdoors, and she is sure no one is listening.

"Well, if it wasn't for the Alliance, I might not have you Corrie" he says matter-of-factly. He is not defending the Alliance but seeing that something good has come out of it for him. Nate isn't aware that he doesn't really "have" her at all, and that Samuel had already taken her . . . far from Nate's grasp, and the intentions of the Alliance. Corrie can't help herself.

"Wouldn't you rather that you got to choose who you married?" Corrie asks him.

"I would still choose you," says Nate looking at her in the way that tells Corrie he is sincere in his desire for her.

Corrie regrets the turn of the conversation, and her deception. She decides to change the subject.

"I was thinking about trying to get a teacher for Joseph. Someone who could visit with him during the day and help develop his speech and learning. He's really bright you know."

"Yes. I know. Just because he is slow in his speech doesn't mean he isn't smart. I've noticed that when I've taken him out into the woods. He only needs to see or be told something once and he remembers all about it," says Nate.

"I know. And maybe the teacher can take him out. That way he won't be stuck at home the whole time lost in his own thoughts. I often wonder what he is thinking, and sometimes he tells me. They are happy thoughts, and in many ways, he is still a child, but he's growing quickly. He needs to have more than me and my mother to rely on. Thankfully, my mother is so much better now, too."

"I'm glad. A teacher would be expensive though, Corrie."

"I know. I can't do anything about it right now, but maybe in the future. If I do well in my job, there might be a chance I can help him." she says.

"I hope so," says Nate.

Their conversation ends just as the bell rings for them to return to class.

Twenty-Seven

After school, Corrie goes to the office as usual. Silas Caine is sitting behind his desk and looks up at her as she walks in. She reads a poignancy in his expression, one that matches her own, and Corrie wonders again about Silas Caine.

"Good afternoon, Sir," she says.

"Good afternoon, Corrie."

She walks over to her desk and finds a pile of filing waiting for her. She begins her tasks for the afternoon, and it isn't long before Tilly approaches her to ask for help in getting supplies from the storeroom. Corrie obliges and, when they get there, Tilly gives Corrie the good news.

"I went to see the doctor in the city again yesterday," says Tilly.

"Oh?" says Corrie. She had noticed Tilly wasn't at work but didn't really wonder why. Too much had happened to distract her yesterday.

"He told me I'm going to have a baby!" says Tilly excitedly.

"Congratulations, Tilly," says Corrie. "That's wonderful!" Corrie gives Tilly a big hug, and Tilly can't keep the smile from her face.

"I was so nervous walking into his office, but I knew already, I just needed the doctor to confirm it," she says.

"How did you know?" asks Corrie.

"Oh, there are signs. My mother had told me all about them and I just knew. My husband is so happy now that he knows we are going to have a baby. He said he doesn't care if it's a boy or a girl, but I'm sure he would like a boy," Tilly says.

Corrie looks at Tilly's belly but can't see a bump. Her dress is probably hiding what is not going to be a secret for much longer. Or is it a secret? Tilly is a married woman, and this is expected, even hoped for. Life is about to change for Tilly, and Corrie hopes for the better. This will improve her status enormously.

They walk back to the office with Tilly excitedly talking about her baby and how she is preparing for the future.

Corrie goes straight home after work and finds everything as it should be. Her mother is preparing the dinner and Joseph is sitting by the fire, humming to himself. Everything looks so normal, but Corrie knows things will never be the same again. She tries to take her mind off Samuel and feels like a traitor as she sits down to sew her wedding dress after dinner. How can she carry on this charade when she knows that's all it is? But Corrie knows she must, for Samuel's sake. Every push of the pedal on the sewing machine is like a knife striking deeper into her heart and, in the end, Corrie decides to go to bed early. Tragic tears soak the pillow as she remembers the previous night, when Samuel had held her in his arms, and told her that he loved her.

The next day when Corrie gets to school there is whispering among the classmates. Corrie isn't sure what it's about, but several girls are comforting Selena in the back row. She must have found out that Samuel has left, and she is no longer betrothed. Corrie can imagine the shock it must be for her and, in some ways, it's Corrie's fault . . . for telling Samuel what Silas Caine had dictated to her in a letter. But Corrie is glad Samuel has escaped and hopes no harm can come to him now.

Corrie sits down beside Nate and leans across to ask him what is going on. She has to pretend she doesn't know.

"Samuel Jacobs was arrested last night," says Nate.

Genuine shock registers on Corrie's face. Arrested?! But Samuel was supposed to leave. That had been Corrie's plan all along.

"Where?!" Corrie asks him.

"In the woods," Nate tells her.

"In the woods?"

"Yes. He was hiding out in an old cabin there when the soldiers found him," Nate tells her.

Was it the cabin they had slept in together?

"Why were they looking for him?" Corrie asks innocently.

"They suspect him of providing rations to the Rebels. They say someone had been giving portions of grain to people that weren't entitled to it, and the rations were finding their way into Rebel hands. I would never have guessed Samuel was the type to work against the Alliance," says Nate, genuinely surprised.

"Me either," says Corrie, which is the truth because she had never suspected Samuel either. "What will happen to him now?" she asks, her heart racing.

"I don't know. They are holding him in the Garrison until they make a decision. He will probably be charged with sedition and then, who knows? The Alliance has many different ways to punish people."

Corrie feels as though an icy hand has gripped her heart. Samuel has been captured and could soon be charged. Then he would be punished. Why had he gone back to the cabin? Why hadn't he just left like he was supposed to? What was he thinking? Instinctively, Corrie knows what he was thinking. The same thing she was thinking last night. That she wanted to be with him, and the cabin was the last place they had been together. He never had any intention of leaving.

Corrie doesn't know what she can do to help him. She can't visit him, only his father would be allowed to do that, so Corrie's only option is to rely on other sources to discover what is going to happen to Samuel now. Corrie also can't let anyone know that she cares about him more than she should because that would make things worse for Samuel. She is betrothed to Nate, and the Alliance doesn't tolerate dissent.

On Thursday, Corrie is pacing. She can't sit still and doesn't know what to do with herself. She has no idea what state Samuel is in, and she is afraid. Seymour is a Sargent at the Garrison, and Samuel has already had more than one altercation with him. Corrie tries to think of a way she can get more information, so at school she asks Nate if he knows any of the soldiers in the Garrison, since he and his father shoe the horses for them. He tells her he knows lots of them, but there are only a few he would call friendly. She asks Nate if it's possible to get any word on Samuel. Nate looks questioningly at her and asks Corrie why. She tells him that Samuel had helped her in the past and she wants to know that he is OK, if there is anything anyone can do to help him. Corrie hadn't told Nate the stories of how Samuel had helped her, and she doesn't want to go into it now. Those are private moments that belong only to Corrie and Samuel. Nate agrees to casually ask the soldiers, since Samuel is a classmate, and obviously his fiancée is distraught. Corrie thanks him and tries to stop her pacing. That's not going to help Samuel.

On Friday, Nate still hasn't had a chance to find out about Samuel, so now Corrie will have to wait until Sunday when she sees Nate with the Chaperone. Corrie tries to fill in her time with her sewing. The more the dress comes together, the more Corrie falls apart. Somehow, this wedding can't go ahead, but Corrie doesn't know how to stop it. Only the Universe can stop it now.

Sunday finally arrives, and Corrie is due to meet Nate in the afternoon. She decides to take a walk in the woods before they meet as she can't stand sitting inside any longer and wants to go back to the cabin where she and Samuel had spent their night together. Corrie takes the path leading into the woods, hoping she can find her way again, cautious as she wanders through the trees, mindful of Silas Caine's warning to her. Someone had set up the cabin for her and Samuel, but she doesn't know who. Perhaps it was Rebel personnel, who obviously know their way around these woods and could even now be close by.

As Corrie gets closer, she can smell embers, the dying of a fire. She walks faster, and then begins to run. Bursting through the undergrowth, she sees the smoldering remains of the cabin where she had become a woman in Samuel's arms. All that is left are some partially burned pieces of wood, and the stone fireplace. The bed on which they had lain is now a pile of ashes in the rubble, and Corrie can taste the ash as she stares at the remnants of her only moment of true love. There is nothing left, nothing worth salvaging, and Corrie wonders who could have done this. Then she remembers. The soldiers had found Samuel here, and must have set the cabin alight to prevent Rebels using it. Corrie feels like her first home has been destroyed—the only one she and Samuel might ever share—and she becomes angry. Thankfully, they didn't torch the cabin while he was still in it. How had they treated him when they found him here? She needs to see Nate.

Corrie runs back to the cottage and arrives just before Nate is due for his visit. She tidies herself up and tells her mother she had just been out for a walk and lost her way. Corrie's mother scolds her, telling her to be more careful in future. It's dangerous in the woods. Nate arrives with the Chaperone, but Corrie doesn't want to walk in the woods again today. She suggests a walk in the direction of the Mill. He agrees and, as they stroll along, Corrie asks him if he has heard any word of Samuel.

"He's being held in a cell in the Garrison with another prisoner. Apparently, he's pretty beaten up and they're going to transfer him, with the other man, to Louisville for trial."

Tears well in Corrie's eyes and her heart aches. Samuel is hurt, and she can't do anything about it. She can't even get a message to him, but she is sure he knows that she loves him, and that she would be there for him if she could.

"Do you know when they are moving them?" she asks trying not to let her voice catch as she tries to compose herself.

"No. Probably soon, although I'd say the city jails are pretty full now with the ongoing insurrections."

Corrie doesn't want them to move Samuel to Louisville, but she can't get to him either way. There's nothing else Nate can tell her right now, so Corrie doesn't ask any more questions. She just has to hope that the Universe will find a way to bring them together again.

She and Nate walk as far as the Mill, which tugs at Corrie's heart once more, and then turns around for the walk back to her home. Nate tells her that his father has applied for him to leave school and focus on the forge, but that won't have any impact on their upcoming marriage. The Alliance understands it's for the best.

Twenty-Eight

Now that Nate is no longer at school, Corrie will only see him on weekends. Both she and Selena have lost their partners, but Corrie only temporarily. Selena will never get hers back. Corrie carries out her duties at home, at school and in the office for another week and, on Sunday, Nate tells her that Samuel is being moved the next day. It is two weeks since their rendezvous in the woods, and now she doesn't even have the cabin to go back to as a way of remembering their stolen moments.

The following day, as always, Silas Caine allows the staff to leave at 5.30 pm on the dot, and Corrie walks to the edge of town because she knows they are taking Samuel tonight. When she reaches the Garrison, she sees him sitting in the back of a cart, with his hands and feet tied. A bloody bandage is wound around his head, and one of Samuel's eyes is swollen shut. Soldiers surround the cart, and she arrives just in time to see it pull away. As she mingles with the crowd of onlookers, Corrie wants to break away and run. Run after the carriage, call out to Samuel, tell him she loves him one more time. She can't, and his head is bowed so he doesn't see her.

A whole month goes by, and Corrie still has no way of getting any news on Samuel. It's mid-October, and only two and a half months to the wedding ceremonies. Corrie continues to work on her dress and sees Nate on the weekends, but she has shut herself off from the experience and wonders if anybody notices. Something else is happening to Corrie, too. She is experiencing changes to her body that don't make any sense, and sometimes she feels sick. She isn't eating as much because of the nausea overwhelming her, but her slender frame is padding out in odd places. Corrie wonders about these changes, and a disturbing, yet exhilarating, thought crosses her mind. What if this is what carrying a child feels like, and what if she is carrying Samuel's child? She has spent only one night with him. Was one night enough? Tilly spent lots of nights with her husband and it took them a long time to have a baby. Corrie decides to ask Tilly what it's like to carry a child.

On Friday evening, after the working day is ended, Corrie walks with Tilly as she heads out the door. She tells Tilly she has something she wants to ask her, something about babies.

"I'm nervous coming up to my wedding and I'm just wondering ... what happens to your body when you're going to have a baby?"

"Oh, you probably won't have to worry about that for a while," says Tilly.

"I know," says Corrie. "But I'm curious. Do people sometimes have a child right away?"

"Sometimes. I had a cousin like that. She went on her honeymoon and, a few weeks after they got back, she found out she was already carrying their first child. It happened so fast! She was lucky," Tilly reflects.

"So, how do you know when you are going to have a baby?" asks Corrie.

Tilly explains the signs to her, which correlate with what Corrie has been experiencing.

She looks pensive, and Tilly quickly tries to reassure her.

"Don't worry, Corrie. It'll probably be a while before you need to think about that, but it's something to look forward to, especially if the Selectors have chosen a good man for you to marry."

Their conversation ends as Tilly takes the turn for her home. Corrie's emotions seesaw between terror and joy. She's having Samuel's baby, but Samuel is in the prison in Louisville, and they aren't even married. Tears fill Corrie's eyes as her hand finds its way to her belly. Holding it there, she whispers to baby Jacobs that she loves him, or her, and she won't let anything bad happen to them, or their father.

Over the next couple of weeks, Corrie's mother notices her waning appetite and asks her about it. So far Corrie had been able to excuse herself by saying she is getting wood for the fire, or making up another reason to leave the cottage, when she feels sick. Corrie has to hide it from her mother, feeling sure she won't understand. In fact, no one will, especially Nate. Corrie tells her mother it's nerves coming up to the wedding and that it's to be expected. Apart from the sickness, Corrie isn't finding it difficult to hide her condition for now, but soon she won't be able to do that anymore.

She doesn't know who to turn to, and then one day, Silas Caine unexpectedly asks her to stay back after work.

"Corrie, I need you to stay back for a few minutes," he says.

"Yes, Sir."

"Have a seat," says Silas.

Corrie takes a seat opposite Silas who looks at her inquisitively.

"How are you feeling, dear?" he asks.

"Fine."

"Tilly tells me you are a little bit nervous about your upcoming wedding."

"Well, that's to be expected, I guess. I've lost my appetite lately, so I think that might be the reason why."

"Corrie, do you know that I have five daughters?"

"No, Sir."

"Well, I do, and there's only one that hasn't been with child so far. Two of them are expecting babies right now, just like Tilly."

Corrie's eyes fill with tears. She wants to tell someone about the baby, she wants someone to tell her it will be OK. But Silas Caine is her boss, and he might fire her if he knows.

"Now, now, Corrie. It's all right. I didn't mean to frighten you. I just wanted to tell you that you can always come to me if you have any concerns. I know your father died a few years back, and it's hard to be the one your family depends on."

"I'm going to have a baby," Corrie blurts out, not recognizing the sound of her own voice as she breaks the news to Silas. Tears stream down her face, and now she is sure she is going to be fired. He looks at her with sympathy and offers her his handkerchief. In this moment, Corrie realizes that somehow Silas Caine knew . . . because he has five daughters, and he is a loving father who notices everything.

"Whose baby is it, Corrie?" Silas asks her quietly.

"Samuel's. Samuel Jacobs. The boy who was taken to the prison in the city a few weeks ago. I love him, and he loves me, and we spent a night together just before he was arrested, when we knew we might never get the chance to be together again." Corrie finally confesses her sad, time worn story to Silas Caine.

"Corrie, this is a dilemma and it's not the first time I've heard a story like yours. First of all, I believe you are sincere in your affections for this boy. Secondly, I know about Samuel Jacobs, his difficult family life, and his efforts to help the less fortunate. He is a courageous young man, and I'm currently trying to find out more about his situation as a prisoner of the Alliance. I can't say anything else right now, Corrie. I hope you understand."

Corrie does understand. She understands that Silas Caine is not loyal to the Alliance, and that he might be her only hope of saving both Samuel and their unborn child. She doesn't know how, but Silas is about to tell her.

"Corrie, it's obvious that you can't stay here and have your baby. People will talk, and it's an offense to do what you have done. There is a possibility I could move you to the city, where you can be close to Samuel, and where there is someone who can look after you as well. With the help of some people I know, we should be able to get identity papers that don't hint at your real name or current circumstances. That will be important. You will no longer be Corrie Tennant, at least while the Alliance is still in power. Do you understand?"

Corrie is overwhelmed at Silas Caine's generous offer, as well as the thought of being someone else, not Corrie Tennant. It means she has to leave her family, Joseph and her mother. This is also overwhelming, but the thought of being able to be close to Samuel again, to tell him about the baby, is the one that captivates her. She wants to be where Samuel is, she wants him to know about their baby.

"Now, Corrie. I want you to go home but you are not to speak to anybody about this. It will have to be a secret between the two of us, that is the only way I can protect you, your baby and Samuel."

Corrie nods her head. She understands. She gets up and Silas comes around the side of his desk to put an arm around her.

"This is not going to be easy for you, Corrie. Making choices that go against the plans someone else has laid out for you is never easy. But, you need to remember this . . . love conquers all. I hope, one day soon, love will be the reason for marriage again, and not an Alliance edict."

Corrie remembers Silas Caine questioning her about love. She saw the fire in his eyes then, a conviction they both seemed to share.

Silas opens the door for Corrie to go. She thanks him, and begins to make her way home ... to her mother and brother who in the not too distant future she may never see again.

Twenty-Nine

Corrie is a mess of emotions by the time she arrives home. Walking through the door, she sees the family going about their nightly routine and feels the tug of familiarity, experiences the comfort of home. Corrie wonders exactly how many pieces her heart can be broken into before it can never be put back together again. She tries to think of the good things that have happened more recently. Since she had taken her mother to see the doctor in the city, her mother was feeling better, and was more capable of looking after Joseph and the house . . . Joseph finally had his mother back. Then there was her job with the Alliance. They had regular rations now which came with her job, and this has also improved the family's health.

Other, unwanted thoughts begin to crowd Corrie's mind. What is going to happen to them if she goes away? Without their entitlement to rations, her family might just starve. Corrie can't let that happen. And then there is Nate. What is going to happen to Nate? She can't marry him now, and he needs to be given an explanation. What is she going to say? And, how will Nate take the news? She can't tell Nate about the baby. That would be too much for him. It's bad enough that their wedding will have to be cancelled.

Corrie hopes Silas Caine has some of the answers to these questions because she doesn't. And she doesn't know what is going to happen to Samuel, what might have already happened to him. Corrie eats what she can of her dinner, gives both her mother and brother an extra hug, and goes to her room. She doesn't feel like working on her wedding dress tonight. She knows she won't be wearing it.

The week wears on, and then another, as Corrie waits for Silas Caine to give her more instructions. Samuel's empty seat in the classroom taunts her, and Selena has stopped coming to school as well. Corrie wonders if they are going to fashion her now as a Housekeeper, one of the women who looks after other people's families instead of her own. Corrie's condition right now, pregnant and unmarried, would place her even below the status of a field hand. If she were to be found out, it's almost certain that she and the baby would be left to starve. But Corrie has proved herself to be resourceful in the past and she hopes, with Silas Caine's help, she will prove her resourcefulness once more.

On the Friday of the second week, Silas asks Corrie to stay behind so he can speak to her again. She has still been seeing Nate on Sundays and is glad it is only for an hour at a time. It is so hard to fill the hour now, knowing what she knows, and Corrie wants to end the deception that surrounds their relationship. She sits when Silas Caine asks her to and waits for him to speak.

"Corrie, how are you feeling?"

"Sick. Not just physically sick, but heartsick . . . for my family, for Nate and for Samuel. I can't think of any way to do the right thing by them all, and then there's the baby. I have to put the baby first, but they all deserve so much better and I can't seem to give any of them what they need. I don't know what to do . . . ," says Corrie, as she starts to tear up again.

"I think we both agreed this wasn't going to be easy, Corrie, and we have to be realistic. If you really love this boy, and I believe that you do, then you are going to have to make sacrifices, just like Samuel did. He doesn't know about the baby, of course, but I have the feeling Samuel is the type of boy who would sacrifice everything for you. That is what happens when people love each other. They start thinking of the other, instead of themselves. But only you can decide if you love him enough to sacrifice this much for him. You can't go into this thinking you can blame Samuel later for the difficulties you are going to experience." Silas pauses for a moment to let her think about this. "You need to be prepared, Corrie, and it still isn't too late to back out."

Corrie knows Silas Caine is giving her the opportunity to choose a different path, maybe an easier one, a path that will ensure security, familiarity . . . and the status quo. It would be easy. Samuel isn't here, he is locked up in an Alliance prison, and Corrie could just pretend he never existed.

Except for one thing. Their baby. She could no more go back on the decision to leave than she could the night she and Samuel had spent together, and what it had created. Corrie prepares to move forward, into an unknown future, which means she must leave the comfort and familiarity of her past behind. She asks Silas Caine what she needs to do.

"Over the next two weeks I will be orchestrating a scenario that requires you to work in the city for an unspecified period of time due to the insurrections. This will be part of the war effort and will involve you being "incommunicado" for a while. Do you know what that means, Corrie?" Silas asks.

"Yes. I think it means I will be out of communication with people, and that they shouldn't expect to hear from me for a while."

"Exactly!" says Silas. "I will meet with your family and organize to meet with Nate to explain the situation."

"Can you do that?" asks Corrie.

"Of course. I will explain my role as your Manager, citing what an excellent job you have been doing, and stating that I need you to go to the city on important business for the Alliance. Of course, I will also have to give an explanation to the Selection Committee regarding your marriage. For that, I will fashion an official letter stating that you are required to fulfil duties in the city for the Alliance, and that your wedding must be indefinitely postponed. For now, we can only talk about postponing your wedding, but who knows what could happen in the meantime? So much can change in a short period of time, Corrie, and this doesn't mean you will never see your family again."

Corrie feels reassured that Silas Caine has a plan, and he is promising to put this plan into place over the next two weeks. She knows this is the only decision she can make ... she has had plenty of time to change her mind ... and thanks Silas again for his help. He tells her he will let her know about any arrangements he makes, and not to worry. The Universe has a way of working these things out.

When Corrie leaves there is a chill in the air, and she pulls her cloak more tightly around her. Rounding the turn that will bring her on the final leg of her journey home, she suddenly feels arms grab her from behind. It must be Nate trying to surprise her again, Corrie thinks, as she prepares to give him a piece of her mind. All too soon, she realizes the arms are not friendly as they pull her back roughly and spin her around. Corrie finds herself looking directly into the eyes of the man she despises, Sargent Seymour, and he is obviously drunk.

"What do you want?! Corrie demands.

"Is that any way to speak to an officer of the Alliance?" he says, grabbing her tightly by her arm and pushing his face into hers, the smell of alcohol on his breath invading Corrie's nostrils.

"I need to get home. My family are expecting me," she says. Maybe if he knows someone is expecting her, he will leave her alone, afraid that they might come looking for her.

"Well, they will have to wait!" says Seymour threateningly. "Because I am going to have my way with you first ... " Seymour leers at Corrie, and she is suddenly afraid.

With an aggressive movement, Seymour pulls the cloak from Corrie's shoulders. His intentions becoming clear, Corrie shivers as the cold night air wraps itself around her.

"Please . . . don't," Corrie whispers.

Without warning, Seymour uses both his hands to grab the top of Corrie's dress and rip it open. Just as he reaches for her, Corrie reacts.

"Get off me!" she screams, trying to push Seymour away while pulling the ripped fabric of her dress together.

A sudden, stinging slap across her face momentarily stuns Corrie before Seymour tries to push her to the ground. Not ready to give up the fight, Corrie drags her nails down his face as Seymour howls in pain, releasing his grip just long enough for her to start running toward home. He grabs the bottom of her skirt, preventing her from going any further, and brings her to the ground. Corrie screams, but she's not close enough to the house, or the town, for anyone to hear her. Seymour slams his hand over her mouth, which she promptly tries to bite. It isn't enough. Alcohol and adrenaline are driving him now. Seymour doesn't feel a thing as he drags Corrie further into the woods, where he can be certain no one will be able to hear her cries.

Thirty

arkness has fallen when Corrie comes to, lying on the
ground, shivering in the cold night air. There's terrible
pain all over her body, an aching and soreness, and
Corrie feels a sudden need to be sick. Rolling onto her side,
she throws up on the ground beside her before surfacing
more fully into consciousness. Realizing she is exposed
Corrie tries to pull her dress together to cover herself.
Seymour! Hot tears of shame fill Corrie's eyes as she realizes
what Seymour has done to her. He has taken her against her
will, and left her to wallow in the shame of his act, abandoning her deep in the woods . . . the place where Samuel had
loved her.

Corrie wonders how long she has been here and tries to
stand up. She tastes blood in her mouth and feels her
swollen lip. She remembers Seymour slapping her hard
across the face when she tried to resist him. It had all
happened so fast, and then Seymour used his superior

strength to pin her down, doing things to Corrie that make her want to weep. Tears come uninvited . . . tears of shame, sadness, and finally anger. She has been defiled by a monster and for that, Corrie decides, Seymour is going to pay.

She's not going to tell anyone . . . she can't. If a doctor examines her, they will realize she is carrying a child, and no one can know about that. Corrie would be punished, and probably get the blame for what Seymour had done to her. Assault of an unmarried woman who is pregnant would not garner any sympathy from those who would normally agree Sargent Seymour had acted in a despicable manner. No. Corrie can't tell anybody what Seymour has done to her, but she vows to hold it in her heart . . . he will not get away with the misery he has inflicted on her tonight, or the misery he has inflicted on Samuel . . . and what about the baby?

Corrie has been so consumed with what has happened to her that she hasn't considered the effect of Seymour's attack on the baby. Samuel's baby. She places a hand on her stomach and smooths it over the place where she imagines their baby lays. She holds her hand there for a long time, willing the baby to be all right, hoping that Seymour hasn't damaged either of them beyond repair tonight. Corrie can't go home, not like this. Too many questions will be asked, and there are just not enough answers to give, answers that will hide the truth and expose it at the same time.

Corrie slowly and gingerly tries to make her way to the remains of the cabin where she and Samuel had spent their first, and last, night together. When she eventually finds it again, she gathers wood from the burned-out shell, managing to light a small fire in the hearth that is still standing.

She uses this to warm herself as she sits, rocking back and forth, holding her knees up to her chest and thinking about Samuel.

As the fire begins to die down, Corrie lies down to sleep. Sleep is the only escape for her now, but in her sleep only dreadful nightmares exist.

Corrie hears herself shout as a hand touches her shoulder.

"Don't touch me!" she cries, startled out of her sleep, preparing to fight her would-be attacker.

"Corrie," a gentle voice says.

Corrie scampers back from the man that is standing over her.

"Leave me alone!" she shouts, trying to get to her feet so she can make a run for the trees.

"Corrie, it's OK. You don't know me, but I know who you are," he says.

Corrie is suddenly conscious of the state of her dress and tries to pull her clothes together as she struggles to stand. She watches the man closely, like wounded prey, trying to understand what is happening.

"I want you to come with me," he tells her.

"No!" she cries, fear rippling through every fiber of her body.

"Please, Corrie. I can help you. You need to trust me. I'm a friend of Silas Caine".

Silas Caine. He knows Silas Caine. There is only one reason for Corrie to trust this man and he has just given it to her.

"Who are you?" she asks, trembling, still hesitant to trust him.

"My name is John Brooks. I'm a friend of Silas Caine," he repeats.

"How did you find me?" Corrie asks, wondering how this man could possibly know she was in the woods. Then, she wonders if he knows what has happened to her.

"We saw the fire. There are places in the woods that you, and the soldiers, don't know anything about. Hidden places, where the Rebels are safe for now. Unfortunately, someone told the soldiers about this place, and that's how they found Samuel."

Samuel. Corrie's eyes fill with tears at the mention of his name, and then at the thought again of what has just happened to her. She doesn't want to go with the strange man who is now offering her his hand, but she doesn't know what else to do.

"Where are you taking me?" she asks.

"Somewhere safe. Somewhere that Seymour can't find you and Silas Caine can meet with you".

"How do you know about Seymour?" she asks, feeling sick at the thought that someone knows about her violation at the hands of the Sargent.

"One of our men saw him stumbling out of the woods with scratches on his face, and we knew you had just come from a meeting with Silas Caine. The fire alerted us to your presence here." Was this one of the men who had told Samuel about the cabin, and offered it to him for them to meet?

"Why did you come looking for me?" Corrie asks, still wondering why anyone else would care.

"Because Silas Caine asked us to watch out for you. He knew you could be in danger after Samuel was arrested."

"Well, you're too late!" says Corrie feeling the full impact of her assault at the hands of Seymour. "He_raped_me!" she cries as sobs wrack her body, and she doubles over in grief and pain.

The man approaches her quietly and puts his jacket over her shoulders.

"I'm sorry, Corrie," is all he says, as she allows him to lift her in his strong arms and bring her to the safe place he is offering where there is shelter, and respite from her ordeal.

Thirty-One

John Brooks carries Corrie a short distance to his horse. There are two other men on horseback waiting for him, and one of them leans down to take her in his arms. She shrinks back into John's arms and he tries to reassure her that everything will be all right, but Corrie won't budge. The other man leaves his horse and John Brooks asks her to stand while he mounts up, then she is carefully lifted into John's arms again. She doesn't know where they are going, but she needs to trust these men. They know Silas Caine. And Silas would never let her come to any harm. He is trying to help her.

Corrie realizes she is having her first contact with the Rebels, a contact she expected to be very different to this, and probably more like the altercation she has just had with Seymour in the woods. How strange that those who are officially meant to protect her did the opposite to what these people, called Rebels, are now doing.

After traveling for what seems like a long time, they reach the outskirts of the woods . . . Corrie doesn't even know if they are the same woods . . . and arrive at another small cabin, much like the one she has just left. A woman comes out to meet them as Corrie is helped from John Brooks horse. The woman is round and flushed, big-bosomed, with gray hair in a bun on top of her head. She wipes her hands on a dishcloth as she walks across to where John is supporting Corrie, now barely able to stand. After a quick look at Corrie, the woman places her arm around Corrie's back and helps John to get her inside.

They lay Corrie down on the bed in the cabin, and the woman walks John Brooks back outside to ask what has happened. Corrie can hear their hushed voices as intermittent words from their conversation reach her ears . . . soldier . . . in the woods . . . attack. She curls up into a ball and rocks, somehow trying to contain herself and all her feelings. Does everyone need to know about her shame? Is Samuel going to find out about what Seymour has done to her? How could he ever look at her the same way? Maybe Samuel will think of her as "dirty", too, and won't want anything more to do with her. Corrie's eyes fill with tears again. If Seymour has robbed her of Samuel's love, then she will surely find a way to hold him accountable.

The woman comes back into the room as Corrie hears the horses riding away. She realizes that no one else knows she is here. What will her mother be thinking? She must be worried sick, but Corrie knows she can't let her mother see her in this state. It would be too much for her, and her mother will have enough to deal with because of what Corrie has already done.

The woman sits on the bed beside her and tells Corrie her name is Martha. She brushes the hair back from Corrie's forehead and Corrie can see Martha taking in the marks on her face, her swollen lip, the tear tracks running down her face. Martha is shaking her head and tut-tutting, all the while looking sympathetically at Corrie. Then she tells Corrie it's not her fault. Corrie looks at Martha with wounded eyes and disbelief. Whose fault is it, Corrie wonders, if it isn't hers? Maybe if she hadn't answered Seymour back that first time, he would have just left her alone. Maybe he would have left Samuel alone, too. Thinking of Samuel makes Corrie think of the baby again. Her hand goes to her belly in an unconscious motion, which Martha notices.

"I hear you're going to have a baby," she says matter-of-factly to Corrie.

"Who told you that?" Corrie asks defensively.

"A little birdie," Martha replies, warding of Corrie's defenses.

The childish thought of a little birdie telling Martha something brings a wan smile to Corrie's lips. Birds don't talk to people, but people sometimes talk to birds. Corrie lets her mind drift for a moment, imagining the scenario, but she is soon brought back to reality by the sound of a kettle whistling over the fire.

"I'm going to make you a nice sweet cup of tea, and then we're going to get you cleaned up," Martha says.

Corrie doesn't argue as she watches Martha brew the tea and put some milk, plus two big spoons of sugar, into a cup. When the cup is in her hands, Corrie quickly brings it up to her lips before feeling the sting of Seymour's hand across her mouth again. She puts the cup down.

"I can't drink it."

"Let it cool down for a minute first," says Martha.

Martha fills a tub in the corner with water from a pot resting over the fire. Corrie sips her tea while she waits and, when the tea is finished, Martha invites Corrie to step into the tub. Corrie can't think of anything she would like more than to wash the stench of Seymour from her body, but she hasn't undressed in front of anyone for a long time . . . except Samuel. This is what she had done after she had lain with him. Corrie had been trying to protect Samuel. This is different. Corrie needs to wash away the fact that she can't even protect herself. How was she going to protect an unborn child?

Martha makes herself scarce, so Corrie can slip into the warm water unobserved. There are scratches all over her body and some of them sting as she slides in. She feels sick as she takes up the brush to begin scrubbing herself, noticing bruises forming on her arms where Seymour had grabbed her. Once she starts scrubbing, Corrie finds it hard to stop, moving the brush over her body punitively, even though the pain is excruciating. She is less vigorous as she reaches her stomach. It's not the baby's fault.

Martha returns to find Corrie red and raw and takes the brush from her hand. Corrie doesn't resist. She just brings her knees up to her chest as a way of hiding her body, and her shame. Martha gently smooths a soapy hand over Corrie's back and, after she tenses up at the initial sensation of Martha's touch, Corrie allows herself to relax a little. Her hand goes to her stomach again.

"Do you know how far along you are?" asks Martha.

"Ten weeks . . . ," Corrie tells her, dreamily, remembering back to that fateful day. She has been counting the weeks ever since.

"It might be a few more weeks before you start showing," says Martha. "I didn't show with my first baby until I was nearly four months along." But Martha is a big woman and Corrie has lost weight with the sickness. She is already beginning to show.

Corrie wants to get out of the bath and leave the stain of Seymour in the dirty water, so she asks Martha for another pot of water to pour over herself as she stands, just to make sure she is clean. Martha obliges, and Corrie steps carefully out of the bath when she is finished. Martha wraps a towel around her and helps her sit gently on the bed. After pulling on a nightdress Corrie lays down, turning her back to Martha who pulls a quilt up over her before she goes to stoke the fire again. Corrie listens to the crackling of the wood, smelling its sweet aroma, and closes her eyes, remembering another cabin in the woods where, not so long ago, she felt safe and warm and loved.

Thirty-Two

When Corrie wakes, night is falling. Pulling the unfamiliar covers more tightly around her, she is reminded again of the rupture from the life she once knew. That life is over now, as surely as the chose to bring it to an end, and Seymour, by his actions, has ensured she can never return. There is no going back. Samuel and the baby are Corrie's only way forward.

The sound of approaching hooves makes her sit up. Adrenaline rushes through her body, and the pain of Seymour's assault grips her again. Corrie signals to Martha that she is going to be sick, and Martha rushes over to hold a towel under her chin as she brings up what little is in her stomach. She hasn't eaten since yesterday and doesn't think she could keep anything down anyway. Martha disposes of the towel and gives Corrie a wet cloth to hold to her face. Appreciating its soothing coolness, she uses it to hide from Martha's sympathetic eyes. Corrie doesn't want sympathy. She doesn't feel she deserves it.

Martha goes to the door to see who is approaching, and Corrie can hear him before she sees him. Silas Caine. Corrie wants the bed to swallow her whole. She doesn't want Silas to see her like this. She doesn't want Silas to know what has happened to her. If her father were still alive, Corrie knows this is how she would feel with him, too.

Silas walks in the door and straight across to the bed, but Corrie keeps her back turned to him. Refusing to look at him, she buries her head deeper into the covers.

"Corrie," says Silas gently. He doesn't dare to touch her.

Corrie doesn't answer.

"Corrie," he says again.

She still doesn't respond. She can't. She doesn't know what to say to the man who has become just like a father to her.

"Seymour is going to pay for what he has done," Silas Caine offers. "A man like that is a disgrace to any army, and he won't be allowed to get away with it!" The anger is rising in Silas's voice now. Corrie remembers he has five daughters and knows this is how he would react if the same thing happened to any one of them.

"He has already gotten away with it," says Corrie quietly.

"He will be punished, Corrie. Take my word for it."

"No one can know what he has done to me" says Corrie. "Otherwise, they will find out about the baby, and then I will be punished. And Samuel, too".

"His punishment doesn't have to be official, Corrie. There are many ways to skin a cat."

Corrie thinks this is a horrible expression. She doesn't want to skin a cat but would gladly skin Sargent Seymour if she got the chance.

"I will deal with it myself," says Corrie, knowing that revenge is sweetest when meted out by the victim of the crime.

"All right, Corrie." Silas knows this is not the time to argue with her.

"I'm worried about my mother," Corrie tells him, finally turning over and letting Silas see the damage Seymour has inflicted on her face.

He gasps, taking a moment to gather himself.

"I spoke to your mother late last night Corrie. She was frantic with worry, but too afraid to leave Joseph alone to raise the alarm. I explained to her I had to send you away on urgent Alliance business and told her I was sorry you weren't able to see her before you left. That you might not be able to contact her for a while."

Corrie's mother had unknowingly acted wisely, but Corrie can't imagine not seeing her mother again. She can't imagine not seeing Joseph, either. They have been her whole world until recently, and she has been the main provider for her family. Now they won't have her or her rations. And Corrie won't have the comfort of their presence or the reassurance of their love. This is too much for Corrie. Silas Caine can see it is too much for her. He takes her in a fatherly embrace, smoothing her hair and telling her it will be all right, as Corrie sobs into his shoulder. She lets Silas hold her tight until her tears subside, and then lets him hold her a little bit longer. Corrie needs the reassurance of somebody's arms, somebody who cares about her, and she knows Silas Caine cares about her, she just doesn't know why. Eventually Corrie allows him to loosen his embrace as the kettle begins to sing over the fire. Martha makes tea for them all while Silas explains what he thinks they should do next.

"Corrie, your mother understands the importance of your job. It is the only reasonable explanation for your absence right now. I have assured her the family will retain your ration entitlement. I'm organizing that."

Corrie thanks Silas profusely after she hears this news. Her family are not going to become destitute without her, and her mother is much more capable now of doing what needs to be done for Joseph. Corrie no longer feels as if she is abandoning them to a worse fate, but she still can't imagine never seeing them again. Maybe they will find a way. Silas Caine obviously knows a lot of people, people that can help her and Samuel. Maybe they can help her family, too.

"I'm going to see Nate tomorrow. He is expecting to see you with the Chaperone, but he will be seeing me instead. I will tell him the same thing I told your mother, and explain that it is for an indefinite period, so your wedding will need to be postponed."

There's that word again . . . postponed. The truth is, their wedding will never happen. There will never be a Nate and Corrie Daniels, there will never be a wedding night where Corrie will experience the love of a man for the first time. She has already experienced that, and it wasn't with Nate Daniels. It was with Samuel Jacobs. She feels that aching emptiness in her heart again, the space that only Samuel can fill. She wishes he were here, but she wouldn't want him to see her like this. She wonders what Nate would do in the circumstances. Would he want to marry her still, knowing she had been defiled? Corrie isn't sure. But, no matter what, Corrie doesn't want Nate to suffer because of her.

"What will happen to Nate now?" she asks.

"He will be required to wait a certain length of time to satisfy the Alliance that there is reasonable cause for the postponement to be considered permanent, and then he should be free to marry somebody else ... of the Alliance's choosing, of course. They will have matched him up to several prospective partners at the Ball and have some idea of the type of girl he might be best suited to. These things happen from time to time ... like with Samuel and Selena ... where one partner becomes unavailable for any reason. The Alliance has a list of the people who become available again, and they use this to ensure their program of Selection continues".

Corrie hates the sound of this and wishes Nate could marry someone of his own choosing. Then she remembers that Nate said he would choose her. Would he still choose her now, after everything that has happened? Corrie doesn't want to be unfair to Nate. He is a good man. But if he knew what she had been thinking, feeling ... if he knew the truth ... he would never choose her. No man in his right mind would. And she couldn't let him either. Because her heart belonged to someone else. It belonged to Samuel, and now her body belonged to Samuel, too. She had given it to him, and they had created something precious that would forever keep Nate and Corrie apart—a child.

"Thank you, Silas," is all Corrie can manage to say.

"Do you want to know about Samuel?" he asks.

Corrie looks at him with surprise. Silas knows something about Samuel?!

"Oh, Silas," Corrie whispers as tears fill her eyes again. Of course, she wants to know about Samuel.

"I've finally got word back from the prison. Samuel's offense isn't seen as minor, but there are much worse offenses that have been committed, and these will all go to trial first. So, he is safe for now, as safe as he can be in an Alliance prison."

Corrie grabs his hand as tears flow down her cheeks again.

"When can I see him?" Corrie asks, trying to choke back the tears.

"We need to get you well again first, then move you into the city. We have to arrange your new identity papers before you go, but once all these things are in place you should be able to visit him."

Corrie forgets about what has just happened to her. Nothing else matters now. Just seeing Samuel again is all she wants. It's what she needs. He is her reason for going on now. Samuel, and the baby.

"Corrie, I want you to focus on recovering from Seymour's assault. The sooner you are well, the sooner we can get you into the city and away from here. That will be important for everyone's sake, especially yours."

Corrie thanks Silas again and gives him a big hug. He hugs her back tightly and kisses the top of her head before moving to the table to drink his tea. Martha brings a cup over to Corrie with cookies that she can dip into it and chew slowly. Corrie needs to eat. The baby, and Samuel are depending on her.

Thirty-Three

Corrie spends the next two weeks recovering from her injuries—the ones to her body, and the ones to her soul. Those to her soul are going to take a lot longer but being able to see Samuel again soon will help with that. Thankfully, Seymour's assault doesn't seem to have affected the baby. Corrie's appetite is slowly improving, and her belly is protruding a little more now. She spends a lot of time resting her hand there, telling the baby that everything will be all right, and that they will be seeing Samuel soon. Corrie can't wait to see the look on Samuel's face when she tells him.

Martha fusses over her and makes a fuss about the baby, too. She makes sure Corrie eats plenty, or as much as she can keep down, and takes her out for short walks in the woods to gather firewood. It's too cold to go very far, but the fresh air is invigorating, and Corrie feels her health returning. Every time she sees a bird in a tree, Corrie thinks of what Martha said, and imagines the birds whispering secrets to Martha. Secrets that people are afraid to share with anyone else. Corrie is glad her secret is out, the one about the baby, and asks Martha lots of questions—the kind she couldn't ask the girls at work. Corrie is excited, but she's also scared. The fabric of her life has been ripped away from her, and she doesn't know who is going to help her when the time comes for the baby to be born, where she will be, or if Samuel will be with her.

Late into the second week, Silas Caine comes to see her again. She is happy to see him, and this time she hugs him after he walks through the door. He can see she is beginning to blossom and tells her so.

"You're looking much better, Corrie," he says admiring the extra weight she is putting on.

"I'm feeling much better, Silas," she says. She has stopped calling him "Sir". They weren't at work anymore, and he had told her to call him Silas.

"Well, I have finally organized your trip to Louisville." His words are encouraging, now that Corrie is feeling better and has had time to prepare for what lies ahead, including the opportunity to see Samuel. "There are a few things we have to go over, and you need to listen carefully."

"All right."

"First of all, and most importantly, I have organized your identity papers. You will need to have the same surname as Samuel in order to visit him in the prison. We can't present you as his wife because they know Samuel isn't married."

The reality of their situation hits home again. Corrie and Samuel are not married, might never be able to get married . . .

as long as the Alliance is in power . . . and she has to pretend to be a long-lost relative, rather than Samuel's intended. Selena was Samuel's intended. That's what the Alliance had decided. Corrie listens intently to what Silas Caine has to say next.

"Your new name will be Ruth Jacobs," he tells her, as he hands her the papers with the name change. Corrie looks at them. Her age is the same, with a different date of birth, and her hometown is different, too. There are no more details apart from that. "You are Samuel's cousin by marriage and your husband's name is Joshua Jacobs."

"Why do I need to be married to somebody else?" asks Corrie.

"Because you are expecting a child, and it won't be long before people begin to notice. We need you to be respectable if you are going to have an opportunity to visit Samuel in prison," Silas says.

Corrie never thought about the issue of being respectable. Well, only once—when she realized she couldn't report Seymour for assault. But she had already decided that loving Samuel was the most respectable thing she could do, the thing that she would live or die for, and what was more respectable than that? Nothing, as far as Corrie is concerned, but she knows she needs to play by the rules the Alliance has set. She is to become Mrs. Joshua Jacobs, Ruth Jacobs, and she hopes Samuel understands how much she is willing to sacrifice for him.

Silas tells her he has organized accommodation close to the prison, and she will be staying with a woman named Gert. Gert has a couple of grown daughters of her own, so she will be able to take good care of Corrie while she is waiting for her baby to be born. Corrie looks at Martha. She wishes she didn't have to leave her too, but the only way for her to see Samuel is to leave her life here behind. There have been so many goodbyes for Corrie lately, she doesn't know how many more she can endure. Hopefully, seeing Samuel again will make up for them all. She is sure it will. Then she wonders about Nate.

"Did you see Nate?" she asks.

"Yes, yes," says Silas.

"And?"

"He was a bit surly at the news. He was obviously looking forward to seeing you and didn't take too kindly to the fact that I'd sent you away," Silas says raising his eyebrows.

She can imagine Nate, towering over Silas, maybe intimidating him a little with his size and his manner. She knew Nate wouldn't be happy. Who would be? First Selena, now Nate. The dominoes are falling all around her and Samuel, but Corrie must keep her focus on the future.

"You will be traveling on Saturday, Corrie. John Brooks is going to take you to the next County, and you will catch a train from there to go to Louisville. It means you will bypass your own town and shouldn't run into anyone you know. Here is the address for Gert's home. She is expecting you." He hands her the piece of paper with an address on it. "If anyone asks, say you are visiting your cousin in the city and Gert will go through the details with you regarding your visit to the prison. There are a lot of men being held there at the moment, and you are not the only one she is trying to help."

Corrie thanks Silas profusely for all his help. He promises to stay in contact and says that, if he can, he will make a visit to the city soon. He also tells her not to worry about any of the other details. Her family will be looked after, the Selectors have been informed, and Nate will have to deal with the circumstances as best he can. Just like Corrie. And just like Samuel.

Thirty-Four

Corrie boards the train the next day, taking leave of Martha at the cabin, and John Brooks at the station. There are tears at both partings. Martha has given her another dress, and pinned Corrie's hair up under her new hat, so she looks like a mature young married woman. The final touch is the official Alliance Wedding Ring which she must now wear. In a small bag, Martha has packed some clothes she's found to fit Corrie and given her a few cookies to nibble during the trip to Louisville. Silas has sent a message saying Gert will meet her at the station, and that he understands the whole ordeal could be quite overwhelming for her. After all, she is still only seventeen.

Corrie remembers back to the day she turned seventeen, the day Samuel had given her his mother's dress. She hadn't been expecting it and had almost refused his offer. Corrie also recalls his smile, the one she wanted to capture and keep, the one that sent butterflies fluttering in her stomach.

She had tried so hard to resist Samuel's friendly overtures and ignore her own see-sawing emotions at the time, deciding it was best not to entertain an interest in anyone in case the Alliance disagreed. And disagree they did, which is what led her to the predicament she was in today.

As the train passes small towns on the way into the city, Corrie sees more of the devastation and destruction she saw on her last train ride. It's everywhere. The Alliance could yet lose power, and Samuel could be freed but, fearful of getting her hopes up after everything she has endured, Corrie turns her face away from the terrible sights and closes her eyes. She draws up images of Samuel, not realizing she has dozed off until the train comes to a sudden, screeching halt.

Corrie looks out the window to see the imposing buildings of the Business Quarter, and prepares to step into her new life . . . her life as Ruth Jacobs, wife of Joshua Jacobs, Milliner. Silas added that to give her a background story, and even supplied her with the fancy hat so she would look the part.

Corrie doesn't know what Gert looks like so, after she steps off the train, she waits for Gert to find her. Standing alone, feeling small and insecure, she is surrounded by busy people who all seem to know where they are going. Once Corrie knew where she was going too, when she had come into the city to buy the material for her wedding dress. It seemed like a lifetime ago, and yet it was only a few months.

A tall woman with dark hair approaches her. The woman is wearing a fashionable dress, visible under a heavy winter coat, and Corrie suddenly feels cold. Her clothes are thin and made of much rougher material, the hat being the only fancy thing about her. Her boots are worn, and she notices the woman's clean, leather, button-up boots as she makes her way toward Corrie.

"Corrie?" she asks as they meet.

"Yes." Corrie's voice comes out in a kind of a squeak. She is nervous, and it shows.

"I'm Gert," says the woman smiling at her. It's such a radiant smile that Corrie can't help but think of Samuel. "Let me take your bag."

"Oh, that's OK. It's not heavy." Corrie clutches her bag as though she is clinging to life itself.

"All right. Then let me show you to your new home." Gert takes Corrie by the arm, as though they have been friends for years.

Corrie tries to walk in step with Gert but finds it difficult to keep up the pace as Gert is obviously a very energetic woman. She points out sights to Corrie along the way, and they head in a different direction from the places Corrie had visited in the city before. Coaches and carts pass them as they walk along the main streets, and then Corrie sees houses that remind her of the ones in the town center at home. They are three-story houses, with steps leading up to brightly colored front doors which create a welcome contrast to the cold gray buildings in the main part of the city. Gert's home has a green door with a gold knocker.

As Corrie is invited in, she observes a palatial home, decorated in the finery that only a city dweller could afford. Heavy drapes, crystal chandeliers, rich tapestried carpets, along with finely crafted tables and cabinets filled with delicate china pieces surround her. Paintings, beautiful paintings, hang on the wall. This is not what Corrie was expecting.

"It's beautiful," Corrie says with wonder.

"It was my parent's home. My husband and I came here with our children to care for them as they grew older. They passed away a few years ago now."

"I'm sorry," Corrie says.

She can't imagine losing another parent. Losing her father had been hard enough. Corrie was ten then, and old enough to remember it. Joseph was only four at the time. Her mother had been unwell since Joseph was born, so for those four years their father had featured large in their lives. Corrie wonders what their lives would have been like if he hadn't died. She wonders what her father would think of her now. He had been a Rebel of sorts. Was she following in his footsteps? Is that why she had fallen in love with Samuel? Corrie doesn't know what her father would think, but she does know he would love her no matter what. Just the way he had loved Joseph. And that was the way she loved Samuel.

"Let me show you to your room, Corrie," Gert says.

Gert leads her up a central staircase and they keep climbing until they get to the second landing, where Gert opens a door to the left of them. The room is large, with high ceilings and another, smaller, chandelier. An ornate canopied bed faces them, and beside it sits a heavy oak dresser topped with a mirror. To her right is a fireplace with delicate floral tiles embedded in its surrounds, and this faces a window which she assumes looks down onto the garden below. Dark green velvet drapes are pulled back to let in the light and Corrie thinks living here will be tantamount to living in a palace.

She turns to look at Gert, feeling as though she doesn't deserve this kind of luxury, and knowing she can never repay the kindness of these people who are allowing a young, unmarried, pregnant girl to stay in their home.

"Welcome to your new home," Gert says, and Corrie bursts into tears. She has left her mother and brother in a small two-room cottage with a Ration Card as their only means of survival, and Corrie feels ashamed. Gert puts an arm around her shoulders.

"Now, now, Corrie," she says. "It will be all right. Silas is looking after everything for you, and he wouldn't be doing that if he didn't think you deserved to be looked after."

"But, my family . . . ," says Corrie, thinking they deserve to be looked after, too.

"Silas is going to look after them for you," says Gert. "He always keeps his promises."

Corrie knows that Silas is the kind of man to keep his promises. She just wishes she could have brought her family with her. Feeling even further away from them now, she wonders if she was selfish in doing what she had done. She'd made an impulsive choice, which has put all their lives in jeopardy, and Corrie isn't the only one who will need to deal with the consequences. The circle of those affected is ever widening and yet, somehow, refusing to act as a puppet of the Alliance seems more important than ever. She wonders if her father would agree.

Gert offers her an opportunity to get settled and says they will be having dinner soon. Corrie is glad for a little time on her own again. No matter how painful it is, she needs to adjust her thoughts from what she has left behind to what now lies ahead.

When Gert comes to call her down to dinner, Corrie is lying on the bed, still in her traveling clothes, feeling tired and somewhat bereft. Gert walks across the room and throws open the doors to a wardrobe where all manner of fine dresses hang, in an assortment of colors and designs. Gert offers to help Corrie get changed, picking out a fashionable blue dress, then sits her at the dresser, taking a brush and gently pulling it through Corrie's long dark hair. As Gert pins it up again, Corrie looks at herself in the mirror and sees she's not the girl who was carried out of the woods two weeks ago . . . at least not on the outside.

"Silas said I'm to be known as Ruth Jacobs now." Corrie wonders how Gert knew her real name, and why she is using it still.

"I will call you Ruth in company, and for all other intents and purposes as necessary. Silas feels it's important, after everything you've been through, to continue to use your real name whenever possible. He doesn't want you to lose sight of your identity, and our names give strength to who we are as individuals, Corrie. Silas wants you to be strong."

She knows she needs to be strong and is glad that she doesn't have to forgo her old identity all together. She has so little to hold onto right now.

When Corrie is ready, they go downstairs. Seated at the large dining table are Gert's husband, their two daughters with their husbands, and two young children. The men stand up as Corrie enters the room and Gert's husband pulls a chair out for Corrie to sit down. After she is seated, a maid enters the room with the first course of their dinner—soup. She enjoys the vegetable broth which goes down easily. The main course is a large juicy turkey with sides of vegetables—potatoes, carrots and a variety of greens. Corrie takes plenty of these onto her plate because she knows they are good for her. Her father had told her so.

Dessert is a delicious pudding made with a caramel sauce and Corrie devours it. She is finally getting her appetite back. During the meal, there is light conversation around the table, mostly about family affairs, and no one presses Corrie to join in. She doesn't know what she would say anyway and is glad she doesn't have to explain her presence here. Gert has explained to the family that Corrie is visiting from a neighboring County, after her husband had left her pregnant and alone. Apparently, it isn't the first time Gert and her husband have brought a young woman in 'unfortunate circumstances' into their home, although it is always understood those circumstances align with current Alliance expectations. The fact that Corrie is unmarried can't be revealed, so the ring Silas has given her to wear confirms her expected status.

The children are curious and look over at Corrie often, but are told to mind their manners and eat their food. When dinner is over, the men retreat to the study and Corrie joins the ladies in the parlor as the maid clears the dishes from the table. Corrie feels she should be doing something to help but resists the temptation. This is how people in the city live and she must respect their way of life, even if it feels uncomfortable to her.

The children become more animated after the dinner table restrictions are lifted, and the little girl, who is about four years old, approaches Corrie to show her a doll. Corrie admires it and the child seems pleased. The boy, about eight, wants to know why he can't join the men in the den. His mother tells him he can join them when he is older, and he retreats to a corner where he begins to work on a puzzle. Gert's daughters, Annie and Belle, are tall and beautiful, like their mother. They ask Corrie how she likes her new home.

"It's beautiful. I've never seen anything like it. Well, I have seen less grand houses in my own town when I delivered the dresses I made," she says.

"Oh!" says Belle. "Are you a seamstress?"

"Of sorts," says Corrie. "My grandmother was a seamstress and her sewing machine came into our possession after she passed away. I learned some of my skills from her, and eventually became quite proficient. People from the town bring materials and patterns to me so I can make up their outfits. I deliver them after they are complete and help the ladies to try them on. None of them had a home as lovely as this though," Corrie says, looking around her again.

"Well," says Gert "maybe we could bring a sewing machine into your room and, if you are feeling up to it, we can have you make some dresses for us. All the women in the family, including yourself, will need new clothes for the winter."

Corrie is grateful that Gert is already finding work for her to do. She will feel better about staying here if she knows she can do something in return.

"That sounds wonderful," says Corrie, and means it.

The conversation then revolves around styles and materials, upcoming parties and visitors. Gert, and her daughter's lives are so different from Corrie's own, but she is enjoying their company and appreciates their kindness. She doesn't want to judge these people whose lives are obviously so privileged. Corrie wonders, though, how Silas Caine knows Gert, and why Gert would want to help her. So many things don't make sense right now. Eventually, the husbands come looking for their wives and it's time for the young families to leave. The little girl gives Corrie a hug, and a quick kiss on the cheek, before she goes. The boy is eager to follow his father and rushes out the door after him.

The sumptuous meal, the long day of traveling, and the baby, too, are all making Corrie feel tired, so Gert invites her to take her leave and go to bed early. In Gert's estimation, it was early. Corrie's family were normally in bed by this time, but then she often sat up until the small hours completing her sewing tasks, more out of necessity than desire. Now, Corrie doesn't need to do that, but she's glad she will have something to do to pass the time before she sees Samuel, and before the baby is born. Hopefully she can have a conversation with Gert about that tomorrow. Samuel is the reason she is here.

Thirty-Five

Corrie wakes up late the next morning. The heavy drapes still drawn across her window haven't allowed the morning sunlight into her room. A fire is set and crackling in the fireplace, and she assumes the maid must have come in while she was still asleep. There is a robe at the end of her bed and Corrie wraps it around her. Even with the fire, there's still a chill in the air. Her clothes from the previous evening have been put away, and there is a new set of clothes laid out for her. Corrie peeks outside of the bedroom and, not seeing anyone, wanders to the top of the stairs. She comes face to face with a maid carrying fresh linen. Corrie asks her if she knows where Gert is, and the maid tells her she is downstairs in the study. Corrie makes her way downstairs and finds Gert writing at a desk. She coughs slightly to make Gert aware of her presence.

"Good morning, Corrie," Gert says with delight in her voice.

"Good morning."

"How are you feeling, dear?"

"Very well. Though, I slept a lot longer than I thought I would."

"That's fine. You obviously needed the sleep. Babies do take a lot out of you, you know."

Corrie's hand immediately goes to her belly where she feels her precious bump getting bigger. She asks Gert what she has been wanting to know ever since she got here.

"Gert, do you mind me asking when I might be able to see Samuel?" Corrie asks, trying not to sound too demanding.

"I'm arranging for you to see him on Tuesday, if possible," says Gert. "The prison requires notice so that they can have the men ready for the visitor's arrival. It's part of their system to keep things running efficiently. There are allotted times for visits, and only so many visitors can be accommodated in a day. Someone else has offered to give you their place, so I am sending a letter requesting a change so that Samuel can be prepared."

Be prepared? What does Gert mean? How exactly do they prepare the prisoners? Is this an Alliance attempt to convince people that they treat their prisoners well? When Samuel was taken from the Garrison at Brookstown, Corrie saw that he had been brutally beaten and she feared for his life. What chance is there that a city prison will treat their prisoners any better? Corrie just wants to see Samuel, whatever state he is in.

Corrie also wonders who is giving their place up for her. All these anonymous people helping her, and Corrie doesn't know why. Maybe it is because of Samuel, because he is a 'rebel', too. But Corrie finds it hard to think of Samuel that way. His acts of rebellion were acts of kindness, generosity . . . acts of love.

He had loved Corrie in an act of rebellion, and she had loved him back. They were both "rebels", but Samuel was the one who had been caught, and Samuel was the one who was going to be punished because he wouldn't leave her. Now, Corrie has left her family because she wants to be with him. They were both suffering for the love they shared, and now someone else was offering to suffer for their love today, by giving up their place for her.

Love is a giver, Corrie remembers. It is always sacrificing for the sake of the other. She hopes she is up to the task that love requires of her again today.

"Thank you, Gert," says Corrie. "Is there anything I can do . . . I'm happy to help in any way I can."

"No, that's fine, Corrie. I'll ask the maid to prepare you something to eat and then perhaps she can draw you a bath. I'll let you know about Samuel as soon as I get word back."

"Thank you." She can't thank Gert enough. She is going to see Samuel on Tuesday for the first time in over two months. She hopes she can touch him.

Two days later, Corrie looks at the outfit the maid has laid out for her visit to the prison. There's a green velvet dress with black trimming, black boots and jacket to match, plus a muff—all designed to keep out the cold. Corrie hears a light tap on her door as Gert calls her name. "Corrie, your carriage will be here any time now, dear. Are you almost ready?"

"Almost. I won't be long," she calls back. In some ways, she's not ready to see Samuel, fearful now of the state he might be in, uncertain how he might be feeling after his ordeal. So much has happened during their time apart, but Corrie isn't going to tell him everything. She hopes she never has to tell him about Seymour.

A short while later the carriage arrives. Corrie's visit is at three o'clock, and she will be allowed twenty minutes with Samuel before the Guards take him back to his cell. Gert has warned Corrie that Samuel won't be expecting her, and that he will have no idea about her new identity. She will need to think on her feet to make sure the prison Guards don't become suspicious.

As the carriage approaches the prison, Corrie sees its outer walls are high and made of stone. The building behind the wall is several stories high, and narrow windows with bars look out onto the street below. A big iron gate fronts the prison, with a smaller one to the side, and she sees people walking in through the side gate after they have their papers checked by a prison Guard. She alights from the carriage outside the gate, thanks the driver, and walks up to the Guard with her papers.

"Name?" he demands in a gruff voice.

"Ruth Jacobs."

"Who are you here to see?"

"My husband's cousin, Samuel Jacobs."

"Go through," he tells her.

Corrie doesn't realize she's been holding her breath until she passes through the gate. Slowly exhaling, she continues along a path that leads into the main building where her papers are taken from her. They will be given back when she leaves. There are several people in the waiting area with few chairs available. Corrie sees a heavily pregnant woman sitting on one chair and thinks that could be her in a few months' time. She hopes Samuel won't still be here then, but she can't possibly know what the future holds.

As one visitor leaves, another is called in. Corrie waits as an elderly man, and then the pregnant woman, go in before her. Finally, as a tearful middle-aged woman walks back into the waiting area and past her, Corrie's name is called.

"Ruth Jacobs!"

Corrie's heart is pounding. She doesn't know what to expect, and knows Samuel isn't expecting her. It's the most daunting moment of her life so far . . . except, that is, for the moment Seymour had her in his clutches. She doesn't want to think about that now. She just wants to see Samuel.

A Guard leads her along a corridor where there are empty cells on the right, and small interview rooms on the left. The interview rooms are windowless and white, apart from what appears to be blood spatter in some places on the wall. Are these rooms also used for interrogation? Was Samuel interrogated in one of these rooms? Corrie passes by the first room where the old man sits across from a young man that could be his son. In the next room, the pregnant woman sits weeping as a man holds her hand across the table trying to comfort her.

Corrie is led to the room at the end where she sees another door opposite her for the prisoner to enter. In the center of the room is a small wooden table with chairs on either side. Corrie is invited to sit down while she waits for the Guards to bring Samuel to her, but says she will stand for now, stating she's not sure how long she is going to stay. This will give the Guard the impression that it is just a perfunctory visit and there's no need for him to pay too much attention to what is going on. As he leaves her, Corrie feels as though her heart is in her throat. She doesn't want to do anything that could hurt her chances of seeing Samuel again.

Suddenly, the door opposite her opens.

The moment Corrie's eyes alight on Samuel, she chooses him again. He is thinner, but not wretched in appearance, and there are no marks on him now—at least not marks that she can see. Samuel's trademark fringe still falls across his eyes, but it doesn't hide his surprise at seeing her. Before he can speak her name, Corrie says "I am Ruth, your cousin Joshua Jacobs wife. He asked me to come and visit with you as he is unable to leave his business to come to the city."

"Welcome to the family," Samuel says before the Guard leaves the room and, at last, they are alone.

Corrie takes the moment to throw her arms around Samuel's neck. She clings to him, and eventually his lips find hers, their longing intensified by the weeks they have spent apart. She has missed him so much. Before the Guard can pass by again, she takes Samuel's hand and places it on her belly, holding it there as she looks into his eyes. A startled expression crosses his face, before a question appears in his eyes. Corrie's answer is a simple nod of her head. Samuel takes her in his arms again before being forced to let her go as they hear the Guard approach. It will be safer if she takes a seat at the table opposite Samuel, which she does finally, and where they begin a perfunctory conversation about her imaginary husband, his business, and Samuel's family.

Their time together passes quickly, and so much needs to be left unsaid, but just seeing Samuel again strengthens Corrie's resolve. She can no more regret her choice to love him than she can the baby she is carrying. They have created a life together. A life that began when Corrie chose Samuel, and he chose her.

It takes all Corrie's strength not to cling to him when the time comes for them to say goodbye, and she promises to visit him again soon. Tears blind Corrie as she exits the prison searching for the carriage that will take her back to Gert's. When she finds it, she maintains her composure until she walks through the front door of Gert's home. Then, rushing past Gert and up the stairs, Corrie throws herself onto the bed and begins to weeps unashamedly. It will be two weeks before she can see Samuel again.

Corrie decides to take dinner in her room that night. She wants to be alone.

Thirty-Six

The next morning, the maid opens the curtains early to let in the weak fall sunshine. It's the end of November, and sunshine is a rare commodity as the days become short and dreary. Corrie is adjusting to the routine in Gert's house, rising at no given time in the morning for breakfast, perusing the papers, and completing any necessary correspondence. Around midday there is normally a light lunch, which Corrie shares with Gert, and then a brisk walk into the town for supplies.

Today, they are going to be looking for materials and designs for winter dresses, and Gert has already organized for a sewing machine to be delivered to the house. It should be arriving any day now. The evening, of course, means dinner with the family and that requires a change into evening clothes. That was two outfits a day ... no wonder the family needed more clothes for the winter.

When they arrive in the shopping district that afternoon, Gert takes Corrie to some of the stores she had visited when looking for the material for her wedding dress. This causes Corrie concern for two reasons. Firstly, she is probably not the only one who has shopped in the city for materials, or a dress, which means she might see someone she knows. Secondly, Corrie doesn't want any reminders of her "postponed" wedding to Nate. And it is only postponed for now. Corrie wants to be as far away from weddings and wedding dresses as possible, and from any classmates who are excitedly preparing for, and looking forward to, their weddings.

She knows only one other person who isn't. Selena. Corrie wonders if Selena has gone back to school yet, or if she is going back to school at all. Corrie knows she will never be going back. Nate has already left, so there was nothing and nobody to miss. Only Samuel, and she was much closer to him now. Corrie remembers how she felt, those first few weeks after he was arrested. His empty seat matched the emptiness in her heart. Corrie never wants to lose sight of Samuel again.

After their return home, Corrie asks Gert if she can speak to her. She explains the risk she thinks she is taking by going into the fabric stores and says she doesn't want to be seen by any of her classmates who are due to be married soon. Gert looks at her, and Corrie dreads what Gert is about to ask her.

"Do you ever wish you were still getting married?"

"Only to Samuel," Corrie says curtly.

Gert doesn't seem to notice Corrie's curt response.

"Didn't you like the partner the Selectors chose for you?"

"I liked him just fine. We were friends. But I didn't love him," Corrie answers more wistfully.

"My husband and I were free to choose each other," Gert says. "I don't know how you make a marriage last if you are not in love."

"When did your daughters get married?" Corrie asks, curious now.

"One of them got married before the Alliance edict was instituted. The other the year after," says Gert.

"Was Belle's a compulsory marriage then?" Corrie asks. She wants to know if privileged city children also had to follow the edicts of the Alliance.

"Yes. Her husband was chosen for her. Sadly, he's a cruel man, and that is one of the reasons I welcomed you into our home. We don't agree with the edicts of the Alliance, and we know firsthand how terrible the outcomes can be."

Corrie is shocked that Gert is willing to be so open with her about their family's secrets. It seems like Corrie isn't the only one with a secret.

"I'm sorry," says Corrie. She knows not all marriages the Alliance arranges will work out, but that isn't the reason she didn't want to marry Nate. If Samuel hadn't been her classmate, if he hadn't tried so hard to help her, if he'd never smiled at her or shown her how brave he could be, then maybe she would still be getting married to Nate and be none the wiser. Corrie is sure Nate will make a good husband for someone, just not her.

"We are, too," says Gert. "They have a daughter now and Belle has to make the best of it. We help her as much as we can, but as parents we feel powerless to change anything. If Belle left him, she would be punished. The child would be taken away from her, and she loves her daughter too much to leave."

This part of Gert's revelation makes Corrie angry. Not only can the Alliance force people into marriages they don't want to be in but, by means of blackmail, they can force them to stay together even if their marriage isn't working out. The Alliance can never be seen to be wrong. The Selectors are to be considered all-knowing. The partnerships formed are to bear the fruit of this knowledge. Smarter, stronger children. Future leaders to rule over the less fortunate, less talented, less able. Corrie, through sheer good fortune, or the design of the Universe, had been graced with certain abilities. Those abilities led to her being selected for further education. Unfortunately, that also led to her being selected for an Alliance imposed marriage. She had to marry whoever the Alliance chose for her, to suit the purposes of the regime. Nate had not been a bad choice, and maybe Corrie could have lived with that, but it still wasn't her choice, and nobody could tell her who to love.

After this conversation, Corrie is more observant whenever Gert's daughters come to visit. She notices little subtleties in the relationship between Belle and her husband. At first, she would never have guessed there was anything wrong. But, as the family relaxes more in her company, Corrie picks up on the furtive glances, the deliberate asides, and the lack of affection between them. He is unkind to his wife on so many levels, and Belle has no way to respond. She is a sitting duck, and duck-hunting season is probably going to last for the rest of Belle's life ... or at least as long as the Alliance is in control. It's sad to watch, frustrating, and Corrie wonders how Gert can tolerate this man in her house. Then she realizes. It's probably the only way Gert can see her daughter, and granddaughter, too.

Thirty-Seven

The sewing machine is delivered the day after Gert and Corrie's shopping trip for materials, and Corrie gets straight to work. She still takes time to read the papers in the morning and is waiting for Silas Caine to visit so she can ask him about writing a letter home. Gert insists that Corrie take a walk with her every day after lunch, but they avoid the shopping area and find quieter places to enjoy the brisk fall air. Corrie misses the natural beauty of the woods that were always on her doorstep, and when she thinks of the woods she thinks of home. This makes her think of her mother and Joseph. She wonders how they are getting on. It is almost too much to bear, thinking about them trying to carry on without her steady oversight. If her father had been alive, Corrie wouldn't have to worry. Her only option is to trust Silas Caine. He has done everything he can to help the family so far.

Gert remarks that Corrie is beginning to bloom with her pregnancy. It is nearly three and a half months since her fateful rendezvous with Samuel. Soon she won't be able to hide her burgeoning waistline, but Corrie doesn't want to hide it and she doesn't have to in the safety of Gert's home. She is happy to be carrying Samuel's child, even though others might say she should be ashamed. Nothing could make her ashamed of loving Samuel.

On the Friday before she is due to visit Samuel again, the family are preparing to sit down to dinner when there is a knock at the door. Tonight, it's just the four of them—Silas, Corrie, Gert and her husband. Gert's daughters are attending a soiree at a friend's home, so they might come for dinner tomorrow night instead.

Corrie isn't aware they are expecting any visitors, so when Silas Caine walks into the dining room she jumps up and runs to throw her arms around him. Silas opens his arms wide to accept Corrie's hug and returns it with vigor. Eventually he holds her out to look at her and smiles.

"Well, well, well. You look wonderful, my dear," he says, taking in her fuller figure and her rapturous smile.

"Thank you, Silas," Corrie says.

"I have something for you from your mother," he tells her. Silas pulls a package out from under his coat and hands it to Corrie. It is small and wrapped up tightly with a bow. "She told me it was your birthday recently, and she wanted to send you a small gift."

Corrie's eyes fill with tears. Her mother hadn't forgotten her birthday, but Corrie had been so preoccupied she had almost forgotten it herself. She turned seventeen not long before the Winter Ball, and now she was eighteen years old. She takes the gift from Silas.

"Would you like to open it now, Corrie?" Gert asks her.

"If you don't mind, I think I will open it in my room later," says Corrie, not wanting tears to spoil the happy occasion.

"All right," says Gert, and she asks the maid to take Silas's coat as her husband directs him to a seat at the table.

"How is my mother?" Corrie asks.

"She's doing very well, Corrie. I have told her you are fine, but that I can't tell her any more about the work you are doing for the Alliance. She seemed to be happy with that," Silas tells her. "She is happy as long as she knows you are all right. She misses you, of course."

Corrie feels bad about Silas having to lie to her mother. She wishes she could see her and explain everything to her, but that would be too dangerous for Corrie and for Samuel. She just needs to appreciate the fact that her mother is all right for now, and that Silas is taking care of things.

"What about Joseph?" Corrie asks, wanting to know that he is being cared for properly as well.

"He is fine, Corrie. In fact, your mother is managing quite well with him, and I've taken the initiative to organize a tutor to visit him twice a week, to give your mother a break so she can shop and do the things she needs to do. That way Joseph can begin to develop his faculties as well. He really is quite a bright and happy boy."

Corrie knows that. She has always known that and, while her father was alive, he never gave up on Joseph. He always tried to teach him things and increase his understanding of the world. Sadly, there wasn't much time to do that after her father died. There were so many things Corrie wished she could have done to help her family, and now she has virtually abandoned them. But it seems that, with Silas's help, they are managing just fine without her. Corrie doesn't know how to feel. They were unable to survive without her for so many years, and now they seem to be able to carry on with hardly a problem. In fact, things seem to be even better for them now she is gone. Maybe she should have left sooner, Corrie thinks in a moment of pure bitterness. She feels confused and bereft again at leaving her family behind. They needed her once, and now they don't seem to need her at all when she, in truth, needs them more than ever.

The maid carries in the food for the evening meal which brings Corrie out of her reverie. It smells delicious and will taste even better with Silas for company. He always makes everything better, and Corrie is grateful for his presence here again tonight. She will always be grateful to Silas Caine.

The four of them enjoy the meal as Silas gives them an update on what's been happening in Corrie's hometown. The Selectors have accepted Silas's explanation for Corrie's "unfortunate" departure before her wedding and agreed to postpone her marriage to Nate. She quietly breathes a sigh of relief. It's the best she can hope for right now. She wonders how Nate is feeling. She hopes he is being kept busy in his father's business, so he doesn't have too much time to think about it. At the same time, she wishes Nate could know the truth. That would give him an opportunity to get on with his own life. She knows the consequences of her choice aren't fair to Nate. He was her friend, and he deserved happiness, too.

Silas tells them that Rebels are continuing to fight Alliance forces across the Counties and, according to his estimation, the fight is fairly even. The Alliance have begun calling up young men who haven't been automatically enlisted, and Corrie remembers how she overheard the Captain's conversation with Nate's father. They had wanted to enlist Nate as well. Maybe, if they'd enlisted him, it would have been Nate who had to postpone their wedding. In a way, that makes Corrie feels better. It could have been Nate who brought this dilemma on them. But, in the circumstances, he would have had no choice, and his reason wouldn't have been deceptive like hers. Corrie knows she wouldn't have been as disappointed as Nate if that was the case, simply because she hadn't felt the same urge to marry in order to maintain the Alliance's status quo. She could wait. But the reality is she hadn't waited for Samuel—and he hadn't waited for her either. They had chosen to create their own marital bond, and it was sealed now with the child growing in her womb.

The next word Corrie hears snaps her out of her reverie. She freezes at the mention of his name. Seymour. Corrie loathes him, and what he has done to her. Her eyes drop down to her plate, and she feels her cheeks flush with the hot shame of his assault as anger rises in her chest.

"Just quietly, I heard that he boasted to other soldiers about what he did to you, saying that's probably why you moved away," says Silas.

Corrie feels her blood begin to boil, knowing Seymour has been able to get way with what he has done because she couldn't report it. And now he's adding more hurt to that despicable act by claiming he is the reason she moved away. Corrie feels she has no claim to justice, and worse still, there is nothing she can do about it. Seymour deserves to be punished, but for now he can't be touched. Silas Caine doesn't want to risk her welfare, or Samuel's welfare, but she knows he wants justice for her in the circumstances.

"He would like to think that!" says Corrie, spitting out the words.

"Yes, he would," says Silas. "Because that is the sort of man he is . . . believing that preying on the weak and vulnerable somehow makes him more of a man. But it is a weak man that uses his power to crush those less powerful. A coward, in fact."

Gert and her husband nod their heads. They are probably thinking of their daughter and her husband. Just because it is his wife he is abusing, doesn't make his actions any less offensive. In fact, it makes them more so.

"He's not just a coward," says Corrie. "He's a monster who enjoys seeing other people suffer." She knows. She had experienced her greatest moment of suffering at his hands.

"He won't get away with it, Corrie," says Silas.

"He already has," she replies, thinking about all the ways she would like to repay Sargent Seymour for the misery he had inflicted upon her.

Gert can see that the topic of conversation is upsetting Corrie and decides to change the subject. It won't do Corrie any good to dwell on these things when she what she really needs to do is focus on Samuel and the baby. She tells Silas that Corrie is going to see Samuel again on Tuesday and that their first visit had gone well. Corrie tells him that Samuel was thinner, but didn't appear to be injured, the way he had been at the Garrison before he left Brookstown. She can see Silas is glad to hear that. He has obviously been worried about Samuel, too. Corrie also lets Silas know that Samuel picked up on her ruse right away and, thankfully, hadn't given anything away during their visit. Finally, she tells Silas that Samuel knows about the baby now, too. As she says this, she puts her hand on her belly wishing Samuel was with them.

Silas nods his approval. He must think it is good for Samuel to know about the baby. Maybe it will give him hope. Corrie wonders how Samuel has kept himself going, not being able to communicate with anybody except his family and, even then, his father hadn't bothered to visit him. Silas tells them that Samuel's father thinks his son is a fool for putting their whole family in jeopardy, just to give a few starving people some grain, and a thought which had occurred to Corrie once before is now confirmed. Samuel is nothing like his father. She feels certain now that he is more like his mother, the woman who wore the beautiful green gown that Samuel gave her for the Winter Ball. A woman who, long ago, danced and smiled, and who Samuel felt sure would want Corrie to have her dress. Suddenly, Corrie feels grateful to Samuel's mother.

This reminds Corrie of her own mother's gift and, feeling tired now, Corrie excuses herself from the company telling Silas she will see him tomorrow. He is staying another couple of days, but it could be weeks before he is able to visit again. He told Corrie they were very busy at work now without her, and of course Tilly will be leaving soon to have her first baby. There would be fewer people to do more work, and Corrie hopes Silas Caine is looking after himself as well. She doesn't know where she would be without him and is sorry now that her departure has put more pressure on him.

The number of casualties around the choice she and Samuel made are starting to mount. Corrie needs to be alone. She doesn't want to confront the magnitude of that choice in the company of others whose kindness she feels she doesn't deserve. Corrie wonders why the Universe has chosen her for this role, and why it couldn't have chosen another. As soon as Corrie thinks this, in her heart she knows the answer. She wouldn't want to love another, and she hopes Samuel wouldn't either. There had to be a reason, a purpose, for their love. Maybe it's the child she is carrying.

Thirty-Eight

The next day passes quickly with the immediate family gathering to see Silas. It isn't until Gert's oldest daughter Annie arrives that Corrie finally understands the connection between Silas and Gert.

"Uncle Silas!" Annie cries when she sees him. Gert is Silas's sister. Annie and Belle are his nieces. Corrie is beginning to understand the passion she'd seen in Silas Caine's eyes when he'd talked to her about love. He knows the consequences of being forced to marry someone you don't love. Silas Caine hadn't wanted Corrie to experience a loveless marriage like his niece. Corrie had not wanted that either. She and Silas Caine understood each other, and now she knows why.

To say there is tension between Silas and Belle's husband during the evening meal would be an understatement. Corrie can see Silas attempting to hide his distaste for the man for Gert's sake, but to Corrie it is palpable. Silas is normally jovial, but not tonight, and she's relieved when the

231

meal is finally over, and she can retire to bed. She hopes Silas will be in a better frame of mind tomorrow before they say goodbye.

Corrie hasn't been able to bring herself to open her mother's gift yet, and it is still sitting on her dresser when she goes to bed. Just seeing it there is making her homesick. Opening it might make things worse. Corrie wants to let her mother know she has received it, and tonight is the last chance she will have to write a letter home, in the hope that Silas can take it back with him.

As she tugs on the bow, it is as though she is tugging on her own heartstrings. With tears in her eyes, she opens the small box to see what's inside. After unwrapping a pretty floral handkerchief, staring up at her are the pair of faux pearl earrings she wore on the night of the Winter Ball. As she lifts the earrings out of the box, memories of that night come flooding back. It was all she could afford to buy for the occasion, and she bought the earrings to go with Samuel's mother's dress. Was her mother trying to tell Corrie something by sending her the earrings? Perhaps they were meant to be a reminder of her betrothal to Nate, and the outcome of the Selectors' decision. That was the whole point of the Winter Ball after all. Maybe they were a reminder about what hard work could achieve, and that Corrie could do whatever she put her mind to. For Corrie, they would always be a reminder of Samuel's generosity, when all she needed to do was supply a pair of earrings to match the dress he had given her.

She wishes again that she had been more generous to him on the night. Maybe, if the Selectors had chosen

Samuel as her Marriage Partner, they wouldn't be in this predicament. She would be betrothed to Samuel, not Nate. But it would still be the Selectors' choice, and Corrie wanted to choose for herself. She had no idea at the time that her desire to choose would lead her to Samuel. At least this way, without the Selectors' interference, Corrie could be sure. Maybe that was her problem with Nate. She had chosen him as a friend, but they had chosen him to be her husband. Could Corrie have made that choice on her own, given enough time and opportunity? Anything was possible. Still, what was possible then had become impossible now ... and what was impossible before has now become possible. All because Corrie made a choice. She thinks again of the ripples on the water when she, Nate and Joseph had been tossing stones into the river. Corrie's realizes her choice is having a ripple effect with far reaching consequences, not just for herself. She walks to the window and looks out at the stars. Corrie asks the Universe to help her tonight. She asks the Universe to help them all.

The following day, in the lead up to Silas Caine's departure, he takes Corrie aside for a chat.

"So, you are going to see Samuel again on Tuesday?"

"Yes, in the afternoon," says Corrie as her eyes light up at the thought of their visit. Silas notices.

"I know you will be happy to see him again, Corrie, but you need to be careful. Don't give anything away. The Alliance have spies everywhere."

"I know," says Corrie. "Samuel knows, too. He was very careful on our last visit".

"Well, this time it will be different. I need you to carry a message to Samuel for me."

"What kind of message?" she asks, sounding a little alarmed. She doesn't know how she will get a message to Samuel with the Guards watching them, and bodily checking Samuel after their visit.

"I have written it on a piece of paper. It's very small and will be hidden inside a sweet concealed in a bag of sweets I want you to give to Samuel."

"I don't think they will let me give him sweets," she says, sure that the Guards will probably take the sweets for themselves. Corrie is certain she will have to hand them over when she arrives.

"I will mark the sweet, so you know which one it is. It will be your job to get this sweet to Samuel somehow. He will know what to do after that."

Corrie feels uncomfortable with the idea of taking such a risk. What if she is caught? What if Samuel is caught with the message? And what exactly does the message say?

"Silas, I don't want Samuel to come to any more harm. What does the note say?" asks Corrie.

"The less you know, the better, Corrie. Just trust me. It's for the good of both of you, and it's the only way," Silas tells her.

Everything Silas had done so far was to help her and Samuel. Corrie is going to have to trust him again. She hopes Samuel trusts him, too. He is their only hope right now, so she agrees to bring the note to Samuel. Before Silas leaves, she gives him the letter for her mother. They are exchanging items to be given to others, neither knowing what is contained within. Silas will have to trust Corrie, too.

Thirty-Nine

When the day finally arrives for Corrie to visit Samuel again, she chooses the green velvet dress once more. Its color is the closest thing she has to match the dress Samuel had given her for the Winter Ball and, after putting it on, she places the pearl earrings her mother sent into her ears. She wonders if Samuel will notice, wanting him to remember what his generosity meant to her at the time. She also wants Samuel to know that her regret has now become her desire . . . her regret at not acknowledging him has become her desire to acknowledge him always.

The carriage arrives, and Corrie is nervous, as well as excited, but at least she knows what to expect this time. That will help, especially as she has to deliver Silas's message to Samuel today. Her anxiety heightens as she makes her way through the prison gate and holds the sweets Silas has given her tightly in her bag. She will need to present it to the Guards when she enters the building and isn't sure what their reaction will be. Corrie can only hope she has the quick thinking to do what is needed when the time comes.

She presents herself at the desk once inside, and the Guard attempts to take the small velvet bag containing the sweets from her. Corrie tells him she has brought some sweets for Samuel she would like to give him. She opens her bag to show him the sweets, but the Guard orders Corrie to hand it over. She was hoping this wouldn't happen but has a sudden thought which may be a way of obtaining the one sweet that Samuel needs.

"May I please take one sweet before I go in. I'm feeling a little faint. I haven't eaten this morning because the baby is making me feel unwell."

Corrie opens her coat to show the Guard her slightly protruding belly, smoothing her hand over her dress to make it stand out even more. The Guard doesn't look happy at Corrie's request and hesitates, but another Guard standing beside him tells him to hand over the bag so Corrie can take a sweet.

"My wife was the same with our first baby. She was sick all day long, and sweets were often the only thing she could keep down."

Corrie gives him an understanding smile as the original Guard passes the bag back to Corrie. Thankfully, the sweet she needs is marked, so Corrie quickly searches for it, takes it out of its wrapping, and pops it in her mouth. She nods to the Guard who has agreed she should be allowed to take the sweet, then takes a seat in the waiting area. There are different people waiting to visit prisoners this time, but Corrie's name is called right away. Maybe the sympathetic

Guard had decided that a pregnant woman with morning sickness should have the privilege of making her visit first. Corrie looks around to see if the other visitors are annoyed, but they are deep in thought and don't seem to notice.

Corrie is brought to the same room where she saw Samuel on the previous visit, and the Guard leaves her to suck on her sweet as she waits.

When he is brought in, Corrie wants to immediately throw her arms around him, but remembers to act with decorum until the Guard closes the door behind him. As soon as he does, Corrie jumps up and clasps Samuel around the neck, holding him tight. He wraps his arms around her waist, pulling her close, before bringing his lips to hers. Corrie takes the opportunity to transfer the sweet from her mouth to his, and Samuel accepts it seamlessly.

"It's from Silas" she whispers quietly in his ear.

After slipping the sweet to the inside of his cheek, he gently lifts one of the pearl earrings and gazes into Corrie's eyes.

"They're from the Winter Ball," he says.

"You remember?"

"You looked so beautiful that night."

"I know."

He kisses her again, moving his hand to rest gently on her belly, and Corrie knows the memories of that night, memories that have haunted her, are not going to come between them. Only one thing is coming between them right now, and that is the Alliance. They hear the Guard moving in their direction, so Corrie takes her seat again opposite Samuel.

All too soon, their time together is over, and the eternity Corrie feels she has waited to see him begins again. Corrie leaves Samuel holding the sweet with the message she has delivered in his mouth as she departs for another two weeks.

She wishes she knew what was in the message. What did Silas Caine want to tell Samuel? What would that mean for her? For them? Corrie just wants Samuel to be safe. But how safe is he in an Alliance prison waiting to stand trial? There has been no further word on the date of his trial, so Corrie doesn't know how long Samuel will be here. Their baby is due in a few months and she wants Samuel to be with her when the baby is born. Their time apart already seems like a lifetime. Corrie hopes Samuel will be coming home soon—she just doesn't know how.

Forty

The next two weeks are the final ones for those preparing to get married and, toward the end of them, Corrie thinks of Nate and wonders how he feels, knowing their marriage has been postponed indefinitely. She wonders how Selena feels, too. Have they found her another partner? They thought she was suitable for marriage, so the Alliance probably won't downgrade her status to that of a Housekeeper yet—unless they can't match her to another suitable partner.

Corrie tries not to think too much about either of them, but somehow thoughts of what could have been keep intruding. How much simpler would it have been for Corrie and Samuel to accept their fate, the fate determined for them by the Alliance? How much simpler would their lives be now if they had lived them according to the plans of the Alliance, not taking risks, not confronting the possibility of making the "wrong choice", not opening themselves up to the potential of Alliance retribution?

In the end, choice is all people have, Corrie thinks. There is nothing else to separate them as individuals, except the choices they make. Those choices say something about them: who they are, what they desire, the things they value in life. Without choice, people became puppets, allowing others to direct their lives, taking away their meaning and purpose. Under the Alliance, they were all puppets. If you dared to cut the strings, what was there to hold you up, to keep you from collapsing once the tensile strength of Alliance edicts and propaganda were removed? Corrie is no longer a puppet in the play of the Alliance, thanks to Silas Caine and the Rebels. Samuel isn't a puppet either, but his strings are still being held by the Alliance in their city prison, and they can still control what happens to him.

As Corrie wrestles with these thoughts, Gert knocks at her door and asks Corrie if she can come in.

"Corrie, I need to go into the town, dear, and I was wondering if you want to come with me."

"The weddings are only a few days away, Gert, so I'm not sure that's a good idea. What if I run into somebody I know?"

"Oh, they should have all had their final fittings by now and picked up their dresses. That's normally organized well in advance to save any last-minute hitches. I think you'll be fine."

Corrie isn't as confident as Gert, in fact she's not confident at all, but she doesn't want to disappoint Gert after everything she has done to help her. She has taken Corrie in and looked after her when she had nowhere else to go. She has given her a place to stay where she could be close to Samuel. Corrie reluctantly agrees to accompany Gert on her venture into town.

Their walk is brisk as the wind is bitter, and Corrie is glad to finally reach the shelter of the first store when they arrive. She's cautious as she enters, looking around for people she might know, but thankfully there are none. Corrie and Gert inspect the materials on display. Those designed for weddings seem to continually attract her eye. She wonders what has happened to the partially sewn wedding dress she has left behind at her mother's cottage. Corrie had put it in a box under the bed and she guesses that's where it will probably stay. At least until her mother realizes that she isn't coming back to get married, and then her mother will have to decide what to do with it. Hopefully she can get something for it—the material at least. It's worthless to Corrie now.

Gert orders materials for delivery and then offers to take Corrie to a café for some pastries and tea. Corrie's appetite has been increasing now that she has stopped feeling sick, and her mouth begins to water at the suggestion. The cafés are a couple of streets away, and after hastily making their way through the crowds, they step into the nearest one just as a light snow begins to fall. A bell rings as they walk in the door and a girl offers to take their coats as they search for a place to sit down. The smell of freshly baked goods tantalizes Corrie's nostrils and, after giving the girl her coat, she rubs her hand over her stomach just as she comes face to face with Selena Prescott.

They both look startled, but it's too late. Corrie can see Selena has taken in her protruding belly and her worst nightmare suddenly becomes a reality. Selena Prescott knows that Corrie is going to have a baby. Selena doesn't know whose baby, but the look on her face tells Corrie that her secret is out, and the first thing Selena will do is tell everyone in Brookstown.

She feels the color drain from her face as a look of triumph crosses Selena's. But Selena doesn't know that the baby is Samuel's, and that in truth it is Corrie who has triumphed. Her sense of victory feels hollow as Selena passes her by without a word and exits the café.

Corrie needs to find a seat. She feels faint. Silas Caine is the only one in their small town who knows about the baby. Now everyone will know—including Nate.

Gert asks Corrie if she is all right when she sits down, noticing how pale she looks and that her hands are shaking.

"I've just seen the girl Samuel was betrothed to," says Corrie in a whisper.

"It's all right, Corrie. She doesn't know anything about you and Samuel, or why you are here."

"She knows about the baby," Corrie tells Gert numbly.

"How could she know about the baby?" Gert asks her.

"Because I had my hand on my belly when she saw me. She knows that I'm carrying a child. The boy I am betrothed to . . . she will tell him. She will tell everyone. What will happen to my mother and my brother if the Alliance find out I am here under false pretenses? What will happen to Silas?" Corrie can't control the hysteria gripping her, so Gert waves the waitress away and takes Corrie's arm to lead her out of the restaurant. Corrie can't breathe and feels like she wants to run. She wants to get away from here, away from the Alliance, to get away from the consequences of her actions which are now going to reverberate around her small town, her family and Nate.

Gert makes her walk to try and help quell her anxiety, telling her to take deep breaths as they make their return to Gert's home. Corrie can't seem to get enough air into her lungs and stops several times, gripping a lamppost while she attempts to slow her breathing down. Gert puts a protective hand on her back and when she sees a free carriage hails it to take them the rest of the way. Corrie is in no state to keep walking.

When they arrive at the house, Gert asks the maid to draw a bath, to help Corrie relax, and brings in lavender to add to the water which might soothe her as well. For all Corrie knows, Selena Prescott could be on her way back to their town already, and by tomorrow Corrie's secret will have spread far and wide. It doesn't bear thinking about. But they have to think about it, and they need to get word to Silas somehow before that happens.

By the time Corrie gets out of the bath, she still has no idea what to do. She can't go back to her hometown and reveal herself. If she did what would she tell people . . . her mother, Nate? They would be shocked, angry and she would have no explanation to give them—at least not one that was acceptable. Corrie realizes her whole situation is unacceptable, except maybe to herself and Samuel, and the people who are trying to help them. And there were so many people trying to help them.

Why? Corrie knows she's not the only one feeling the way she does about the Alliance and their dictates, that other people also find their edicts oppressive. That doesn't mean they need to help her or put their own lives at risk. It also doesn't solve her problem, which is about to become even more momentous now that Selena Prescott has seen her and become privy to Corrie's secret.

After finishing her bath, Corrie heads downstairs. Gert is nowhere in sight. She approaches the maid and asks where she can find her, and the maid tells her that Gert has ordered a carriage to take her to the station. Corrie runs outside to find Gert waiting and takes her by the arm, asking Gert where she is going.

"I'm going to see Silas, Corrie. To warn him. It's my fault that Samuel's betrothed saw you, and I realize the danger I have put you all in, including Silas."

"Oh, Gert. I'm sorry. This is my fault. I should be the one going back."

"No, Corrie. It's not your fault, and I want you to stop thinking like that. Silas will know what to do. He will come up with a plan and the best thing you can do is stay here, rest, and let Silas and I worry about it for now. You can't go back. It's too dangerous—for you and for Samuel. Please, go back inside and I will try to get home tonight so that you'll know what's happening."

Corrie looks at Gert with appreciation and gives her a big hug. She hopes Gert is right, that Silas will come up with a plan, and she hopes her mother will understand whatever Silas is going to tell her. It had taken her mother so long to get well, and Corrie knows Joseph needs her now more than ever. Whatever explanation Silas gives her will need to make her mother stronger.

Corrie goes back into the house, knowing there is nothing else she can do to help untangle the web she has unintentionally woven, with more people caught in its intricate grasp than she ever imagined.

Forty-One

It's late at night when Gert finally returns. Corrie hears the carriage pull up outside—she hasn't been able to sleep yet—and jumps out of bed to go downstairs and meet her. The maid opens the door and Gert sweeps in, light flakes of snow dotting her heavy winter coat falling to the floor. As she releases the pins holding her hat in place, Gert sees Corrie standing at the bottom of the stairs and, stopping mid-task, she takes Corrie in her arms. They hold each other for a moment, and then Gert tells Corrie she will see her in the study as soon as the maid helps her out of her traveling outfit.

Winter is descending on the County, and there is a chill in the air as Corrie enters the study. The fire is dying down, but it isn't long before the maid appears to stoke it again, bringing light and heat into what feels like a sacred place. The study is a place for contemplation, where decisions are made, and fates are sealed as letters are written, signed and sent. Books designed to hold the wisdom of the ages line the walls in large bookshelves, and Corrie feels their weight pressing down on her as she contemplates her current situation. With only an impulsive notion of choice, and what that might mean, she doesn't feel she has the ability to see her choice through to the end. Corrie feels overwhelmed.

Gert steps into the study with a robe wrapped tightly around her. She takes a seat in front of the fire beside Corrie.

"I managed to see Silas just before he was finishing work. He took me aside while I explained to him what happened today." Gert pauses.

"Is he all right?" Corrie asks anxiously.

"Yes, yes. He's fine. He's upset, of course, that you've been exposed, but has come up with an idea that he hopes will keep you, and your family, safe a little longer."

Corrie is relieved that Silas Caine is all right for now, and wonders what his plan could be.

"Did he tell you what he intends to do?" asks Corrie.

"He is going to tell the Alliance about Seymour."

The moment seems frozen in time as Corrie's heart skips a beat and she can't keep the fear out of her voice.

"What is he going to tell them?"

"That Seymour raped you, and that you are carrying his child."

Corrie gasps. Feeling violated again, she tries to comprehend what Gert has just told her. Silas using Seymour's vile act as an explanation defiles the moment she and Samuel shared to create the child she is now carrying. It both shocks and infuriates her.

"He can't do that! I am carrying Samuel's child, not Seymour's!" Corrie can't keep the anger, and shame, out of her voice. The thought of what could have happened, if she and Samuel had not encountered each other sooner in an act of love, doesn't bear thinking about.

"Corrie, I know you're upset. Silas is upset, too. He couldn't think of any other way to keep you or your family safe. If you have been taken against your will, which you were, then the judgement of your pregnancy prior to marriage will be much less harsh . . . "

"But, it's Samuel's baby . . . " states Corrie tearfully, knowing that she wants others to understand that her child was conceived in love, not an act of lust.

"I know. I know, Corrie. The most important people know that it is Samuel's baby, but the ruse will buy us time. It will also create an opportunity for Seymour to answer for his crime. Silas told you he had been boasting about it to other soldiers, so he has confessed by his own words what he has done."

"I don't care about Seymour. I want to forget about his filthy hands touching me. Samuel doesn't know about what Seymour did to me. I don't want him to ever know. If he finds out he will think I am vile, too." Corrie can't stand the thought of Samuel knowing that another man has put his hands on her, doing things to her that Samuel did with gentleness and love.

"We can't worry about what Samuel will think right now. If he loves you, and I believe he does, then he won't hold Seymour's evil act against you. And there are witnesses who can attest to the fact that you were already carrying Samuel's child when that happened. Samuel will know this is his baby. But accusing Seymour is our only hope of protecting you both for now."

Corrie knows Gert is right. They have to offer an explanation for her pregnancy, and there is no other explanation that can possibly be offered except that she was taken against her will. Then she remembers Nate.

"What about Nate?" she wonders thinking aloud.

"Silas was going to see your family to talk to them, and then he was intending to call on Nate. He knows that Nate deserves an explanation as well."

Corrie wonders how Nate will react to such a damning revelation. Will he search for Seymour, attack him? Will he despise her for her deception? Corrie doesn't know. What she does know is that the world they all knew is crumbling under their feet, and she is the reason. Corrie lets Gert hold her as she sobs for all that is lost. A huge wave is now breaking on the shores of so many people's lives in the aftermath of the choice she has made to love Samuel.

Forty-Two

Corrie falls into bed exhausted. Gert's revelation of Silas's plan invokes nightmares where she finds herself once again fighting Seymour, trying to remove his weight, struggling to breathe, feeling his hands gripping her, holding her down, refusing to release her. Waking up in a cold sweat, Corrie finds the drapes open, and a fire burning in the grate. She rises weakly from her bed, wondering how she will get through the next few days, and how she will face Samuel on her next visit which is only three days away. Corrie seeks out the maid and asks if she will bring breakfast to her room. She doesn't want to see anybody right now.

After struggling to get down a few bites of egg and toast with a sip of tea, Corrie sits at the sewing machine. There is plenty of work to do, and she is grateful for something to take her mind off the anguished thoughts swirling in her head. It's lunchtime when Gert finally comes knocking at her door.

"Corrie?"

"Come in," says Corrie, sounding defeated.

"How are you dear?" Gert asks her as she steps into the room.

It takes Corrie a moment to answer. She feels over-whelmed but knows that Gert is trying to help.

"Exhausted. I didn't sleep very well last night."

"I'm not surprised. Neither did I. I can't help wondering how everyone is taking the news, and what the Alliance will do . . . "

Corrie can't help wondering either. Whatever the out-come, it isn't going to be good, and there is nothing Corrie can do about it.

"When do you think we'll hear from Silas?" asks Corrie, hoping it will be soon.

"He has promised to get in touch as soon as possible," Gert tells her.

It can't be soon enough for Corrie, who doesn't know how long any of them can hold out with all the questions now being raised about her current situation, and therefore her future.

"The sooner, the better," says Corrie, feeling the burden of both these things, and dismissing Gert with her words.

Anger rises again in Corrie as she thinks of Silas's plan and what it could mean. Exposure, revelation of the fact she has been raped, rumors about her pregnancy and who the father of her child might be. It is all too much, and Corrie spends the weekend in her room, with the excuse she is feeling unwell. Gert doesn't disturb her, except to occasion-ally look in on her, and the maid tends to all her needs without question.

By Monday, the sense of isolation is becoming too much for Corrie. The memory of her ordeal is invading her thoughts and dreams, promising to enslave her if stays alone in her room any longer. Choosing to leave her self-imposed exile, Corrie decides to join Gert for lunch. Gert doesn't comment when Corrie walks in but makes sure she has something to eat and hands her a paper to read. As Corrie flips through the pages, not really taking in any of the articles, Gert finally speaks.

"You know that's all Alliance propaganda," Gert says.

"What?" answers Corrie, her thoughts far away.

"The papers. It's propaganda. They never tell the people in Louisville what is really happening in the townships."

This seems obvious, but somehow Corrie hadn't really thought about it before.

"What do you mean?" asks Corrie, sensing there is something more Gert wants to say.

"The newspapers only report in a manner that would have us believe that the Alliance is overcoming the Rebels. Silas tells me that isn't true. I saw it with my own eyes again yesterday."

Corrie remembers how she had once seen a different landscape on her visit to the city. Destruction had been all around and yet, somehow, their little town seemed to be sheltered from what was happening. Corrie thinks there are probably a lot of little towns like hers . . . separated from the trouble in more populated areas, silent. People simply trying to survive on Alliance Ration Cards. They were in the iron grip of those in power, and starvation was their only alternative. Corrie had felt the full force of that grip when she had agreed to work with the Alliance. At the time, it meant survival.

Samuel had tried to loosen the Alliance's grip by offering extra grain to those who needed it. Corrie ponders Samuel's selflessness, and how he had helped those in need. He probably hadn't thought about those extra rations going to the Rebels, but it was obvious they had appreciated his non-compliance, which is why they were helping her now. Samuel was an unintentional "rebel". The truth is all it took to be a Rebel these days was to offer starving people some grain. In this moment, Corrie loves Samuel as much as she hates the Alliance . . . it is the Alliance that should be paying for their misdeeds, not Samuel.

"I saw it once, too," Corrie says softly.

"The Alliance can't keep people in the dark forever," says Gert. "The Rebels are on the march, and things are going to change. I feel certain of it."

"I hope so," says Corrie not feeling as certain as Gert.

Her father had been party to the last Insurrection. It had failed, and he had lost his life, but Corrie needs things to change . . . for her sake, for Samuel's, and the baby's.

Corrie wonders what her father would think of Samuel. She is sure he would like him and respect him for his efforts to help the poor. But, would her father be warning her, warning them both, of the possible consequences. Samuel is already suffering in an Alliance prison, just as her father had, and her father had never returned. That's all Corrie knew.

Word had come to them one day that her father was dead, but they were never told how he died. They would probably never know. Corrie doesn't want that to happen to Samuel. She doesn't want to have a child without a father. She wants their child to know Samuel, to know how brave he is, how much he loves them. She also wants their child to know that Samuel let his love be known, in spite of the fact the Alliance forbade it, and in spite of Corrie turning him away time and again. Corrie wants Samuel to know his child as well. He will be a good father. She can't wait to see him tomorrow.

Forty-Three

The next day it's raining as Corrie steps out the door.
The carriage that will take her to see Samuel is waiting,
and Corrie lifts her dress carefully to avoid the puddles
at the side of the road. There are no messages to bring to
Samuel this time, and Corrie wonders again what was in the
message she had offered to Samuel with a kiss the last time.
That kiss left an indelible taste of conspiracy in her mouth
which was both frightening and exhilarating. She had been
more frightened at the time but, if the Rebels are on the
march, then that is exhilarating. She doesn't want to get her
hopes up though, and for now she just wants to see Samuel
again. Seeing him allays so many of her fears.

The same Guards are not at the desk as she walks into
the prison, and Corrie is required to take a seat as usual
while she waits to be called. She hasn't seen the pregnant
woman again . . . maybe she's had her baby by now . . . nor
the old man. Each time she comes the visitors are different.

Maybe it all depends on when people are able to travel, as most of the Rebels are from outlying areas.

She hears her name called, and her heart begins to beat more rapidly in anticipation of her visit. The Guard brings her to the room at the end of the row to await Samuel's arrival.

When the door opposite her opens, a Guard shoves Samuel into the room. He is bloody and bruised. Corrie is shocked and moves to go to him just as the Guard speaks.

"You might want to tell your husband to come next time, so he can tell Jacobs to treat his captors with a little more respect!"

Pushing Samuel into the chair, the Guard spits in his direction before slamming the door behind him. Samuel's hands and feet are shackled, and Corrie goes straight over to him to look at his wounds.

"Samuel . . . what happened?!" Corrie cries, her voice catching as she speaks.

It takes Samuel a moment to answer, his eyes downcast as he refuses to look at her.

"He raped you . . . ," Samuel says.

Tears begin to form in Corrie's eyes. She was hoping Samuel would never need to find out.

"I couldn't stop him," she says. "I tried . . . " A small sob catches in her throat.

Samuel finally looks up at Corrie with a wounded expression in his eyes.

"Why didn't you tell me?" he asks in a whisper.

"I didn't know how to tell you . . . I was afraid." Corrie still doesn't know how she could have told Samuel about what Seymour had done to her.

Samuel looks at her questioningly.

"I was afraid you wouldn't love me . . . ," Corrie tells him, tears now streaming down her cheeks as she wonders what Samuel will say next.

He reaches across for her hand, and Corrie looks up to see tears in Samuel's eyes now, too.

"I will always love you, Corrie," Samuel says gently.

It's what Corrie needs to hear, laying her fears to rest. She is unprepared for his next question.

"Is it mine?" Samuel asks so quietly that Corrie can hardly hear him, but the words are like a knife to her heart. Corrie had thought the wounds from Seymour's assault couldn't go any deeper. She was wrong. In spite the pain she feels, Corrie understands that Samuel needs to know.

"Yes," she answers quietly. "I was carrying our child when he raped me."

Tears spill onto both their cheeks as the horror of Corrie's ordeal takes its full effect. Corrie feels Samuel's grip on her hand tighten as something else flashes in his eyes. Corrie has seen that look before, the first time Seymour confronted her on the road to the Mill when she sought Samuel's help and he comforted her.

"I'm going to kill him," Samuel says, his manner cold, hard, determined.

"Samuel, you have to be careful. Look at what they've done to you already . . . ," says Corrie, now concerned that Samuel will overlook the most important thing at the moment—their baby.

"I don't care what they do to me. I care about what Seymour has done to you!" he says, his voice rising just as the Guard approaches the door.

"Everything all right?" questions the Guard, looking in on them and raising his eyebrows at Corrie.

"No. Everything is not all right. Look at the state of my cousin! He is hurt. Has he had any medical attention?" she asks.

"He'll get medical attention when he learns to show a bit of respect to his captors!" counters the Guard.

Corrie decides it is best not to anger the Guard further.

"Well, I hope that will be soon. He's only here because he fed starving people some grain."

"That may be so. But, if he's not careful we'll bring other charges against him, and he could be here a lot longer."

Corrie can't stand the thought and turns away from the Guard who leaves them again for a few moments while he checks on the other prisoners.

"Samuel, please. I am fine, the baby is fine. We need you to be fine, too. Seymour will get what he deserves. In fact, he may be getting it already. You would never have known, except for the fact that Selena Prescott saw me in the town and saw that I was carrying a child."

Surprise registers in Samuel's eyes. Then he frowns. He knows the weddings have taken place over the weekend, and she wonders if he feels any concern for Selena Prescott. He was betrothed to her after all.

"She never liked you," he says.

"I never liked her either," says Corrie, and they smile briefly at each other. Samuel knows why Corrie doesn't like Selena. Now he has a reason not to like her as well but, knowing Samuel, he isn't going to hold it against her. He is much too forgiving. Seymour will be a different story.

The Guard walks by, and Corrie lets him pass before she speaks again to Samuel.

"Please, Samuel. You need to look after yourself. Forget about Seymour. It's more important that we get you home, safe and sound . . . " Corrie still doesn't know when that will be, but she hopes it will be soon. She doesn't want Seymour to ruin that for her, too.

Corrie gets up and moves to Samuel's side.

"We need you . . . ," she tells him, taking his shackled hands and placing them on her pregnant belly.

"I need you, too . . . ," he tells Corrie, holding her gaze as he rests them there. She knows he means it.

They need each other. But, for now they must separate again as the Guard comes back to lead Corrie out of the room. She doesn't look at the Guard, but keeps her tear stained eyes downcast for fear he might read more in them than Corrie is willing to share. She doesn't want to share her pain or sorrow with anyone, except Samuel.

Forty-Four

Corrie finds it hard to focus on anything else after the visit apart from Samuel and his safety. She isn't sure of her own, but they haven't had any more news from Silas, so Corrie assumes she is safe for now. Selena had seen her in the city, but Silas Caine is the only one who knows the full details of her whereabouts. She wonders what the Alliance will decide to do after learning of her assault, and the fact she is now carrying a child. She hopes they will be more concerned about dealing with Seymour first, and that there won't be too much pressure on Silas Caine to produce her for questioning. There is nothing she can do but wait.

On the Saturday night, after finishing dinner with Gert and the rest of the family, Corrie retires early. She is emotionally drained, and tired, due to the ordeals of the past week, and not in the mood for conversation, especially superficial chit chat, while Samuel's life is hanging in the balance.

Corrie settles into her bed and is just drifting off to sleep when she feels a strange sensation. It's not something she's ever felt before and then, it happens again. Corrie puts her hand on her belly. A fluttering sensation emanates from somewhere deep inside. It takes Corrie a moment to realize . . . the life inside her is reaching out and making its presence known. Corrie is feeling the first movements of their baby.

She keeps her hand over her belly and thinks of Samuel. Corrie wishes he was here, so she could share the news with him, but another week isn't too long to wait. Then she wonders how long it will be before Samuel will be able to feel the baby move. She hopes he will get the chance.

Several nights later, Corrie is woken by the sense of a presence on her bed. Startled from her sleep, she moves fearfully from the figure turned toward her, pulling the covers close to her body. A hand reaches out to her.

"Don't touch me!" she cries.

"It's me, Corrie."

The voice is unfamiliar in Gert's home, but not to her heart.

"Samuel . . . ? Oh! Samuel!"

She throws her arms around him, then kisses him. . .his lips, his eyes, his forehead, his cheeks.

"Samuel, how did you get here?!" Corrie asks.

"By hook or by crook." Samuel answers cryptically.

Corrie frowns, then smiles. Samuel is teasing her.

"I love you, Corrie."

"I love you, too," she whispers.

As they cling to each other Corrie decides to allow her unanswered questions to rest until morning.

Light filters into the room the following morning as Corrie wakens to feel Samuel's arms wrapped around her. A hand rests lightly on her belly and she places her own hand over it. She doesn't want to disturb him and remains in Samuel's sleepy embrace while her silent tears of gratitude dampen the pillow.

When he finally begins to stir, Corrie turns over to face him. She rests her hand on his unshaven face and feels the roughness of his skin. Samuel, only recently turned eighteen, is a man already . . . life had made it so. At eighteen, Corrie is a woman, and soon to be a mother. She moves closer to Samuel and kisses him gently on the lips. She still can't believe Samuel is here with her and wonders again how it happened.

Samuel puts his hand over Corrie's, then turns his head to kiss her palm.

"Good morning."

"Good morning." Corrie offers him a smile, and he smiles back.

"How are you feeling?" Samuel asks her, more serious now.

"Like all the stars in the Universe are aligned."

Samuel gives her another fleeting smile and then frowns. "I've been worried about you, Corrie, with everything that's happened . . . the baby . . . "

"I felt the baby move a few nights ago, for the first time," she says. Corrie doesn't want to talk about Seymour.

Samuel looks at her with surprise, then with a sense of wonder. He puts his hand back on her growing belly.

Corrie laughs.

"You won't be able to feel it yet, Samuel. I can hardly feel it. It's like a soft fluttering in my tummy. But the baby is telling me it's here and it wants to say hello," she says, holding his hand in place. Samuel bends his head down to Corrie's belly and whispers.

"Hello, baby Jacobs".

"Samuel . . . " Corrie laughs again. "It can't hear you, you know".

"Maybe it can," says Samuel seriously.

"Maybe it can," Corrie agrees before Samuel kisses her again.

There's a knock at the door.

"Breakfast, Ma'am," says the maid.

"Thank you. Can you leave it at the door, and I will collect it in a moment," Corrie replies.

"Yes, Ma'am," says the maid.

Samuel raises his eyebrows and looks at Corrie questioningly.

"This is the way they live in the city," says Corrie, feeling as though she has to explain how Gert runs her household.

"I know. My mother came from the city. She used to tell us how city people lived," Samuel tells Corrie wistfully.

"Do you miss her?" Corrie asks.

"Sometimes. But she died seven years ago now, just before we started school together. I missed her a lot at the time . . . "

"I miss my father. But since he died, I've been so busy just trying to look after my family, I haven't had a lot of time to think about him. I wonder what our lives would be like now, if our parents were still here?" Corrie says.

Samuel doesn't answer right away.

"I wouldn't want mine to be any different, now that I have you," he says.

"Me, either," she agrees gazing deeply into his eyes. "We're going to be parents ourselves soon . . . ," she reminds him.

"I know," Samuel says, gently stroking her belly as they both think about the life they have created together.

"I'd better get the breakfast, Samuel. You need to eat".

"You do, too, Corrie. You're eating for two now," he reminds her.

Corrie slips on her robe and collects the breakfast from outside the bedroom door. There is food for two, and Corrie realizes that the household knows Samuel is here.

Forty-Five

After breakfast, Corrie tells Samuel she is going downstairs to see if she can find Gert. She wants to talk to her. If Gert knows Samuel is here, then she also knows how he got here, and Corrie wonders why she didn't tell her anything about what was happening.

Corrie makes her way down the stairs and eventually finds Gert in the study. She must have eaten her breakfast already and is now preparing her correspondence.

"Gert," Corrie says, beckoning Gert out of her reverie.

"Corrie!"

Gert gets up from the desk and moves across to her, taking Corrie in her arms. Corrie hugs her tightly for a moment, grateful for whatever intervention Gert has been able to engineer which has brought Samuel here, to her.

"Samuel . . . ," she begins, but Gert doesn't give her the chance to finish.

"I know. He arrived in the middle of the night, and I was

hoping he would get here safely," she says.

"How did he get here?" asks Corrie.

"There was a breakout at the prison last night, and Samuel escaped with a number of the other prisoners. It's been planned for a while, but only certain people knew when it would take place." Corrie thinks of the sweet she had transferred in a kiss to Samuel, the one with a message from Silas Caine.

"I got word last night to prepare to take some men in, and I am so glad Samuel knew where to find you. He wouldn't take anything to eat or drink when he got here, he just wanted to see you."

Corrie feels that breathless feeling again, the one that tells her that she and Samuel are meant to be together. No one else takes her breath away like Samuel.

"What will happen now, Gert? There will be people looking for Samuel and these other men ... what are they going to do?" asks Corrie, realizing that Samuel's escape is not going to make things any easier for them. In fact, their being together always seemed to be riddled with complications.

"For now, Samuel is safe here. The soldiers will be looking for the men in outlying areas ... no one will suspect they have traveled deeper into Alliance territory to hide. We will need to wait a few days, until all the furor over their escape dies down, and then we will move them, one by one, to safe houses".

"I'm not leaving Samuel again," says Corrie stubbornly. She's waited so long to be with him. She isn't going to let him out of her sight again after what had happened the last time. Corrie doesn't care about her own safety. She has already left everything else behind to be with Samuel.

"Corrie, we can talk about this later. For now, the two of you are together, and both of you need to rest. Spend time together and enjoy each other's company. I will make sure you aren't disturbed."

Corrie decides that she can no more look ahead than she can behind and decides to take Gert's advice. She is going to spend as much time with Samuel as possible now that she has him back and will do whatever she can to make sure she never has to leave him again.

Corrie and Samuel spend the day exchanging stories. Some of it is spent crying in each other's arms. They have both been through so much while they've been apart, and it isn't going to get any easier. Corrie and Samuel realize they made choices which will result in sacrifice and suffering, intertwined with their sense of joy and fulfillment. They also understand they will need courage to see their love through to the end. The opportunity to hold each other eases the pain of their past separation, and their future fears. As long as they are together, as long as the Universe holds them in place, nothing will ever be able to come between them again. Not even the Alliance.

As daylight wanes, Gert comes to the door to invite them down to dinner. Corrie is hesitant, but Gert assures her it is just going to be the four of them: Gert, her husband, Corrie and Samuel. Samuel thanks Gert for her offer and tells her they will be down in a few minutes.

"Samuel, I'm afraid. What if someone comes to the door and they find you here?"

"It's OK, Corrie. Gert knows what she's doing, and I trust her. Her husband is a friend of the Rebels, too, and they are the people who will make sure we get away from here safely."

Samuel had said "we". He had no intention of leaving Corrie behind. This reassures her. Samuel is not going to leave her, and she is not going to leave him. Gert and her husband will make sure that they can make their escape together.

Escape. It isn't a word Corrie had really thought about before. They had to escape. They weren't going to walk out of Gert's door hand in hand like a normal couple going about their day-to-day business. Samuel is a fugitive. Corrie is a fugitive now, too. The Alliance will be asking all sorts of questions about Samuel's cousin's wife, the one who came to visit him in prison, and wonder whether she had aided and abetted the "rebel", Samuel Jacobs. These thoughts over-whelm Corrie, and she knows Samuel can see the trepidation in her eyes.

"Corrie, it's OK. We're going to be OK. These people will help us, and we are not the only ones. I promise. We need to be strong while we wait for the Rebels to overcome the forces of the Alliance. It's the only way."

Corrie knows there is no other way. The Alliance must be defeated so that people can live in peace, and have the ability to make choices about their own lives. It isn't just marriage that the Alliance controls, but it is one of their most powerful weapons, used to manipulate the population and further their own agenda—an agenda that Corrie and Samuel now stand firmly against.

Samuel gives Corrie a reassuring hug, then takes her by the hand and leads her downstairs to dinner. As they enter the dining room, Samuel walks across to shake Gert's husband's hand before hugging Gert and thanking them both for all they are doing to help. Corrie thinks she sees tears in Gert's eyes, and wonders if she is thinking about her daughter, the one who was forced to marry against her will and is now destined for a life of misery unless the change Samuel is promising comes about.

The couples sit across from each other at the table and the maid begins to bring out the food, serving delectable courses of soup, roast lamb with vegetables, and finally chocolate pudding for dessert.

Corrie always thinks of her family when she sits down to eat, and wonders what they are eating tonight. She knows it won't be anything nearly as nourishing and delicious as what is being served at Gert's table. At the same time, Corrie is unable to curb her appetite as the baby demands what it needs. Samuel encourages her to eat, and Corrie realizes it's probably a long time since he has eaten this well, too. She notices that he takes a second helping of the main course, and then the chocolate pudding. She's happy to see his appetite is healthy and hopes Gert and her husband's hospitality will help them both gain strength for what lies ahead.

Suddenly there is an unexpected knock at the door, causing the group to stop in the middle of their conversation. Corrie looks at Samuel. They aren't expecting any of the family after Gert had told them she and her husband were going to be away over the weekend. The servants were told Corrie's husband had returned seeking her forgiveness. That explanation should keep any suspicions about Samuel at bay.

Gert's husband excuses himself and waves the maid away while he prepares to answer the door. The maid scurries back to the kitchen and all is quiet as they listen for voices that Corrie feels are sure to come, with demands to gain entry to search the premises.

What they hear is the hearty greeting of Silas Caine as he makes his way directly to the dining room. Corrie realizes she has been holding tightly to Samuel's hand, and they stand up together as Silas enters the room. He comes straight over to them and rather than shaking the hand that Samuel offers Silas takes him in a big, fatherly hug, patting him on the back several times just for good measure. When he lets go, he sees the receding bruises on Samuel's face, causing him to frown, but only for a moment before he turns to Corrie.

She immediately throws her arms around Silas Caine as tears of relief spill down her cheeks, and thanks him for all he has done. He holds her tightly and tells her it has been his pleasure and he would do it all again for this outcome. She knows he means it. Finally, Silas moves to a seat at the table and the maid sets a place for him, so he can have some of the dinner the family have already enjoyed. Silas tucks in with gusto and Corrie watches him, grateful for the day she met him, and accepting that there are some good things that have come out of her affiliation with the Alliance after all.

It doesn't take long for Silas to finish his meal, and Samuel is invited to join the men for brandy and cigars in the study. He looks at Corrie, and she nods her assent. He is a man now and needs to be in the company of men, at least for a little while, as they determine what Samuel needs to do next. Corrie and Gert go into the parlor where they silently warm themselves before the fire. There is little to be said right now as they wait to hear how Silas intends to help the couple.

After what seems like an eternity, the men appear in the doorway of the parlor and Gert invites them to have a seat to discuss their deliberations with her and Corrie.

"Now, Corrie, Samuel," Silas says nodding in their direction. Samuel is standing beside Corrie and offers her his hand as Silas begins. "You have a long way to go in this journey that the two of you have undertaken. The Alliance is looking for you, Samuel, and they will be asking questions about Corrie as well. But, of course, they only know you as Ruth Jacobs, Corrie, and it will be a long time, if ever, before they discover that you are one and the same." Corrie breathes a sigh of relief. That gives them a little more opportunity to avoid detection for now. "We need to get both of you to a safe place, and I know you want to be together, but it would be better if we moved you separately," Silas finishes. He is giving Corrie an opportunity to think about what he has just said.

"I want to be with Samuel," says Corrie, not even considering Silas's wisdom.

"We need to think about the baby too, Corrie," Samuel says. "And about what is best for the baby."

"I am thinking about the baby. What is best for the baby is that the two of us are together," retorts Corrie, dogged now in her determination not to separate from Samuel again.

Silas intervenes.

"I know you don't want to leave Samuel again, Corrie. Samuel doesn't want to leave you, either. But it's safer if you separate for now and then meet up at a rendezvous point when we are sure there is no danger to either of you."

"No! I won't leave Samuel," says Corrie stubbornly. "The last time I left him he ended up in prison. It was months before I could see him again, and then only for a little while." Tears well in Corrie's eyes as she remembers how it felt to be without Samuel, how she feared for his life, and how desperate her longing was to see him again.

Samuel decides to try and reason with Corrie. He kneels beside her.

"Corrie, I felt the same way. You went through a terrible ordeal while I was gone, and I am sorry for that." Corrie can see the sadness in Samuel's eyes. He blames himself for what Seymour did to her. "I don't want anything like that to ever happen to you again, but we have to trust these people. They are the only ones who can help us right now."

Corrie holds Samuel's hand tightly and looks directly into his eyes.

"I want to be with you," she says as she looks imploringly at him.

"I know. And you will be. We will be together, I promise."

Samuel wipes the tears from Corrie's eyes. She needs to trust Samuel, too.

"I plan to meet you at your destination," says Silas Caine. "In the meantime, we think it would be better to move Samuel first, Corrie, and then bring you a couple of days later."

272

"Where are you taking us?" Corrie asks tentatively.

"You will know when you get there," says Silas cryptically. "Don't worry. I have it arranged."

Corrie wishes she didn't have to keep relying on other people to arrange things for her. She wants to be able to make some decisions for herself and Samuel, and the baby. But this is too important, and Silas is the only one who knows how to keep them all safe for now.

"When?" asks Corrie, wanting to know how long she still has to spend with Samuel before he must leave her again.

"Two days from now, under cover of darkness," Silas tells her.

If Samuel gets caught again, things will be a lot worse the next time. Corrie doesn't want to think about that, though. She just wants to spend as much time with Samuel as possible.

Gert decides it is time for everyone to retire and offers to show Silas to his room. Corrie knows she will have more questions for him tomorrow, but they will have to wait.

Forty-Six

C orrie wakes early in the morning. The maid hasn't opened the curtains yet, and Samuel is still fast asleep, but Corrie wants to see Silas before he leaves. She grabs her robe from the chair by the fireplace and goes downstairs. Finding no one in the dining area or the study, Corrie follows the sounds she hears to the kitchen where the maid is preparing the breakfast. It smells delicious, and Corrie's stomach rumbles, but she has other things on her mind right now.

"Good morning Ma'am," says the maid.

"Good morning."

"Would you like your breakfast now?" the maid asks her.

"No. I was just wondering where everyone is."

"Madam and her husband are still in bed," says the maid.

"What about Mr. Caine?"

"Mr. Caine left some time ago. He said he had to catch an early train and asked me to pass on his goodbyes to the family."

It takes Corrie a moment to digest what the maid has just told her. Silas has left. He has gone, and Corrie isn't going to get a chance to ask him all the questions still hovering on her lips and requiring an answer. For only the second time she can remember, Corrie is annoyed with Silas Caine. The first time, not long ago, was when he urgently engineered an explanation for her pregnancy. That rocked Corrie to the core and resulted in Samuel's finding out about Seymour's assault. Now, Silas was leaving her in the dark about his plans—plans that will have a dramatic effect on her and Samuel's future. Plans that could, in fact, mean life or death for them, and for their unborn child.

There is so much more at stake now. Corrie wonders if Silas is avoiding her, and her questions. Is it because he doesn't have the answers? What could that mean for her, Samuel and the baby? She grapples with the uncertainty surrounding these thoughts as she moves her hand to her belly. There is a life depending on her and she is depending on Silas Caine. She hopes he will be able to keep them safe, and she hopes Silas will be safe as well. He has taken enormous risks for her, and there is nothing she can do to repay him. In fact, she is doubting him, and Corrie feels bad that her sense of trust is lacking. She must accept that she is not yet the author of her own future and will need to depend on others for a little while longer until she reaches the place her heart desires, the place where she gets to determine her future. The choices she has made so far, to act against the Alliance, have only brought her deeper into their clutches. If they are not defeated, there will be a very high price to pay.

She sits at the kitchen table. No one else is up yet, and

Corrie wants to take her mind off all the thoughts disturbing her, so she offers to help the maid prepare some of the food. The maid politely refuses, saying she appreciates the offer, but she would get into trouble if the Housekeeper found a guest helping her in the kitchen. Corrie doesn't want to get the maid into trouble and asks her name.

"Atlanta."

"What an unusual name," says Corrie.

"Yes," says the young woman. "It comes from a story. It was a lost city. . . the lost city of Atlantis. My mother named me after that."

"Atlantis . . . ," murmurs Corrie. "Where is the lost city supposed to be?" she asks with curiosity.

"Under the sea, Ma'am," the maid tells her. "It's called Atlantis, but my mother thought that sounded too much like a boy's name, so she changed it to sound more like a girl's."

Corrie thinks of the stories her father told her. She hadn't heard the story of the lost city of Atlantis and wonders if her father had. Once, long ago, he told Corrie her name meant "love" or "heart". It came from another language, Latin, and her father had chosen it especially for her. He said when she was born it was as though all the love he and her mother shared had been poured into Corrie, and she became the heart of their relationship. She knows that she and Samuel will feel the same about their child.

When she returns to her room, she finds Samuel awake, sitting up in the bed with a paper resting beside him. Samuel was always so studious, and it seems some things about him are never going to change. She remembers, with a smile, how Samuel sat at the back of the classroom with his head over his books, and that trademark fringe falling into his eyes. It seems like an eternity ago . . . and an eternity since Corrie dropped the eggs on the floor at the Mill . . . an eternity since she and Samuel had been unable to acknowledge each other as they danced together at the Winter Ball, since Corrie had been betrothed to Nate, and Samuel to Selena Prescott. It also seems like an eternity ago that Corrie and Samuel had forged the intimate bond which had brought them to this very moment, in this very place. Samuel pats the space beside him, holding out a hand for Corrie to take as she climbs back onto the bed.

He wraps his arms around her, and Corrie relaxes into Samuel's warmth and his presence. It's a presence she hopes will stay with her forever. She has given everything up for it, and she knows Samuel will steady her in the days ahead, reassuring her that she is not alone. His is the presence that will help Corrie meet the challenges she will have to face, and the next challenge is only two days away . . . when Samuel will have to leave her again.

Corrie decides she wants to focus on the time she and Samuel have left together, so they spend the next two days immersed in each other's company, and in each other's arms. Making up for lost time, the two of them forget about the world outside of Gert's home, the world outside of Corrie's room, and delight in their opportunity to be alone together in a place that is safe from the Alliance's prying eyes, and its oppressive edicts.

Far too soon, that time is ripped away from them as the night arrives for Samuel to leave and travel to their next destination.

Corrie is distraught. For a long time, she refuses to let Samuel go. In the end, she knows she doesn't have a choice. This is only the first leg in a long line of journeys Corrie and Samuel will need to make in order to be safe.

Clinging to him at the end, her arms wrapped around his neck, Corrie kisses Samuel deeply, wanting to remember the taste of his lips. She places her hands on either side of his face, wanting to remember the feel of his unshaven skin at midnight. For a long time, she gazes into his eyes, wanting to remember the love she sees residing there. In their final moment together, Corrie allows Samuel to wipe away her tears. He moves his hand to her belly, bending down to say goodbye to baby Jacobs, before kissing Corrie swiftly on the lips once more, and then he is gone.

Samuel leaves under cover of darkness, and on foot, disappearing into a heavy mist to travel alone through the dark, dank alleyways of the city in order to meet a companion who will take him to their next destination. As the mist envelops Samuel, the hushed silence of the winter's night muffles his footsteps. Corrie hopes it also keeps him safe from prying eyes. She won't know if he has arrived safely until she arrives at their destination herself.

It's the second time Samuel has left her, in fear of the Alliance, and in an attempt to evade capture. Corrie vows to herself it will be the last time. When they meet up after this, she is never going to let him leave without her again. By hook or by crook, as Samuel would say, she will remain by his side. There is a gentle flutter in her tummy. The Universe has a plan for them . . . and their unborn child.

Forty-Seven

Two days later, Corrie is preparing to travel in the full glare of the midday winter sun. Gert has dressed her in a black mourning outfit and accompanying the outfit is a wide-brimmed black hat with a veil that covers her face. No one, not even a soldier, will disturb a woman in mourning.

The carriage waits for Corrie in the street below as she takes one last look around the room that has become her home, and her haven, in the last few months. She will miss the temporary security it provided, and the solace of knowing Samuel wasn't far away, even if she couldn't see him every day. Gert and her family have provided Corrie with comfort, and an opportunity to regain her strength, as well as her sense of purpose, after Seymour's assault. They have given Corrie what she needed to embrace her impending motherhood—food and shelter, companionship and concern. It will be hard to leave.

Carrying her bag, packed with just a few essentials, including the gift her mother sent, Corrie turns to Gert and her husband at the front door. Hugging Gert tightly, she tells her that she doesn't know what she would have done without the hospitality Gert's family had shown to both her and Samuel. They had given them the opportunity to be together, moments that were only snatched before, and moments that now will become more meaningful in the fight against the Alliance.

Corrie wonders silently . . . if she hadn't conceived a child with Samuel, would her fight be over already? Would she be married to Nate, maybe even carrying Nate's child? She still doesn't know what's happened to him and determines to find out from Silas Caine the next time she sees him. She knows she must have hurt Nate deeply, but also knows there was no way she could have avoided hurting him in the circumstances. Not if she was going to be true to herself. She had to choose. She wanted to choose. And she had chosen Samuel.

Taking her leave from Gert, Corrie tearfully, but resolutely, steps into the carriage that will bring her to her next destination. It is another step into the future, one that she and Samuel have chosen, and there is no turning back now.

The carriage pulls away slowly, making its way outbound from the city. It passes the imposing buildings and busy marketplace. As it does, Corrie sights the back alley where she and Samuel had embraced, the place where she'd shed angry tears, and Samuel had asked her to wait for him. It was also the place where Seymour had seen them, and confronted Samuel.

She wonders if Seymour was the one who insisted there should be an inspection of the Mill's books. It wouldn't surprise her. Seymour despised them both. And then he had tried to ruin her in the worst possible way. Seymour didn't know at the time it was impossible to ruin her because she had already experienced the true expression of love in Samuel's arms. Not even Seymour could take that away from her.

Corrie rests her head against the back of the seat. She still doesn't know where she is going, but she knows Samuel will be there to meet her at the end. It reminds her of the first time they kissed, how she experienced that frightening, yet exhilarating sensation of falling into a chasm, a deep and seemingly endless place where no boundaries existed. In that moment, Corrie was able to believe that anything was possible. She also knew the person she wanted to carry her safely out of that experience was the one who dared to bring her there in the first place . . . Samuel. She places her hand on her belly. She had dared, too. Neither of them yet knew the price they might have to pay.

Corrie wakes suddenly as the carriage comes to a halt. Dusk is falling and with it, snow. She isn't sure where she is, but the driver opens the door to the carriage and offers to help her out. The sound of an approaching train, and the sight of people making their way toward a platform, causes Corrie to realize she is at a train station and, as the driver hands her a ticket, she understands she is meant to get on the train. The ticket says Brookstown, but that can't be. It's Corrie's hometown. She looks at the driver questioningly, not sure now whether he is friend or foe, but he just nods his head in answer to her unspoken question. She is to catch the train to Brookstown, and somehow, someway, this is meant to keep her and her baby safe and lead her back to Samuel.

Corrie takes the bag she has packed and steps gingerly across the slippery path marked by other traveler's footsteps. People look at her sympathetically as she enters the platform. It takes her a moment to remember that she is dressed for mourning, and those around her are acknowledging her misfortune. She hopes she is not tempting fate, allowing others to believe that she has lost someone she loves, and a tiny knot of dread settles itself in the pit of her stomach. She and Samuel have tempted fate so many times in their love for one another, and in their desire to be together. Corrie doesn't know if fate will yet smile on them, but it had brought them together and sealed their relationship with the child Corrie is carrying. She feels fate must be on their side. To imagine anything else is unbearable.

The acrid smell of smoke from the locomotive's chimney fills the air as Corrie takes her seat in the carriage. Hidden under her warm winter coat is her and Samuel's secret, and she just hopes she doesn't see anyone she knows on the way back to Brookstown. The station sign says Hooperstown which is close to the northeastern edge of the County.

The train slowly makes its way out of the station and, as Corrie looks out the window at the passing scenery, someone takes the seat beside her. She doesn't turn around immediately but feels the sensation of something being pushed into her hand. Startled, Corrie reacts, and tries to pull her hand away, but it is held in place and she turns to see John Brooks sitting beside her. A sense of relief floods through her. John Brooks is a friend, one who helped to rescue her after her ordeal with Seymour. She knows she can trust him. John doesn't look at her, but slowly removes his hand from hers, giving her an opportunity to see what he has placed there. She discreetly unfolds the small note he has given her and reads what it says.

Disembark at the third stop – Woodridge. I'll meet you there.

Woodridge is about halfway to their hometown, Brookstown. So, she isn't going all the way home. A sigh of relief escapes Corrie's lips. She couldn't imagine alighting from the train at Brookstown. Now she doesn't have to.

At the next stop, John Brooks gets up and moves from the seat beside her. She sees him use the connecting door to step into another carriage before the train moves off again. More people enter the carriage, and she looks at them closely from behind her veil, to see if there is anyone she might know getting onto the train. Thankfully, there isn't, and Corrie relaxes a little as the train recommences its journey.

The train rolls on to their next stop, the last one before Corrie is required to alight. Here, there are soldiers waiting to board the train and Corrie's heart begins to pound. The soldiers are carrying rifles and have pistols at their waists. Young and old alike climb aboard, bearing worn expressions, some of them demanding seats from the passengers. Corrie's hands begin to shake, and she clasps them tightly to keep herself from being noticed. John Brooks has left a free seat beside her, and she is terrified one of the soldiers will sit there, maybe paying her unwanted attention.

An older soldier eventually takes the seat after the younger ones have forced passengers to stand and taken seats by the carriage door.

"I'm sorry for your loss Ma'am," the old soldier says congenially.

"Not as sorry as I am." Corrie sparks, remembering her assault at the hands of Seymour, and seeing how the other passengers are being treated by the soldiers.

As she turns toward the soldier, she remembers that these men are also victims of the Alliance and their dictates. She knows the younger ones have been enlisted into the Army, and that things are so bad they had tried to enlist Nate as well. Corrie wonders how older men, men who had not been forced to join the ranks of the Alliance Army, still end up fighting for them.

"Do you mind if I ask, how long have you been a soldier?" she asks him.

"All my life. I joined up as a young man, and I have been fighting in one war, or another, ever since."

"Did you have to pledge allegiance to the Alliance?" Corrie asks him.

Corrie is moving into dangerous territory. This man has always been a soldier, but not always a soldier of the Alliance. He seems to want to talk and is not disturbed at Corrie's line of questioning.

"Of course. That's how it works when you're a soldier. You fight for whatever government is in power. You don't question anything. You just follow orders."

Following orders mindlessly doesn't make sense to Corrie. What if the government is wrong? A soldier's job should be to protect and defend the people, not just follow the government's orders. What if the government was more interested in its own power than in the people? And, as a means to maintain that power, it had to control the people, just like the Alliance was controlling them?

"What if the government's orders are wrong?" Corrie asks him boldly.

He looks at her, without being able to see her face.

"It's not our place to decide if the orders are wrong or right. It is our place to follow them. That is what you are taught as a soldier and that's what you are trained to do. You have to confront the enemy boldly, without any hint of wavering, otherwise you are lost."

The train slowly pulls into Corrie's stop. She excuses herself as she gets up, and the old soldier stands for her. He sees her reach for the bag above her head and lifts it down for her. Corrie and the soldier nod to one another, each having given the other food for thought on the journey today. She wonders what will happen to him, but she will probably never know. The battlefield is becoming too vast, and Corrie and Samuel are trying to remain hidden for now.

None of the other soldiers interfere with her as Corrie alights from the train. Some look at her sympathetically, probably imagining their own families in a potential moment of grief, depending on the outcome of battle. Corrie's initial fear of the soldiers, having turned to anger, now leads to a fleeting moment of sorrow—for these men, for their lives, and for their lack of choice.

As she exits the station, the Station Master advises her that she has alighted before her intended stop. Corrie tells him she will be visiting a relative here for a short while and so will catch another train to take her all the way to her destination. She says she hopes the ticket will still be able to be used for the next leg of her journey. He tells her it can be, if it is used within the week. She thanks him and moves out into the muddy street. She looks to her left and then her right but sees no sign of John Brooks. Where could he be? A carriage approaches, comes to a stop, and the driver asks if she is Ruth Jacobs. She says she is, and he gets down to help her in. There is still no sign of John Brooks.

The carriage takes her to a small Inn at the edge of town. John Brooks is standing outside when they arrive and hands the driver a few coins for his trouble before bringing Corrie inside to seat her at a table. He orders food and drink for her, and a glass of ale for himself. The Inn is crowded. Winter is keeping the County in its pristine grip, and a fire blazes at one end of the room to keep the customers warm. The serving area is in the center of the Inn, and Corrie and John are tucked away closer to the entry, which also serves as an exit. She keeps her coat on. She doesn't want to reveal her condition to these people, and she is impatient to continue her journey to meet Samuel. After John returns with the refreshments, she decides she can't wait any longer.

"Is Samuel all right?" she asks without hesitation.

"Yes. He arrived two days ago. He's waiting for you now," John Brooks tells her.

Tears spring into Corrie's eyes. She is so grateful that Samuel has made it safely. She's so glad she will be seeing him soon.

"How much further do we have to travel?" she asks, now willing to taste the food she has been offered.

"You will need to ride with me. It will probably take about two hours."

She has ridden with John Brooks once before. That time she had been riding away from her attacker, Seymour. This time she would be riding toward her lover, Samuel.

She eats as much as she can to give herself strength for the rest of the journey. John Brooks has also given her a strong, dark, slightly bitter ale to drink, which he tells her is good for the baby. The baby needs its strength too, Corrie decides, and drinks the ale before they rise to prepare for the final leg of her journey.

Forty-Eight

John Brooks helps Corrie onto his horse. She sits sideways in front of him and grips the saddle, while John takes up the reins. He is an experienced rider and helps her manage her discomfort.

As they draw near to their destination, Corrie senses familiar sights, sights she had forgotten, or imagined she would never see again. There it is. The cabin at the edge of the woods. And there is Samuel, waiting for her with a lamp at his feet.

Corrie sees him get up from the stool at the entry as John slows his horse to a stop in front of Martha's cabin. Reaching up for her, Samuel gently brings Corrie into his arms.

"Oh, Samuel!" Corrie cries as she wraps her arms tightly around him. The feeling is new every time they embrace.

Samuel slowly lifts the veil from Corrie's face and looks at her in a way that makes her knees go weak. When Samuel kisses her, he takes Corrie's breath away. Samuel looks up at John and asks him if he would like to come inside for some refreshments, but John kindly declines telling Samuel he needs to get back to the village. The two men shake hands, and Corrie thanks John again for all his help. They both tell him to stay safe.

After John rides away, Samuel turns back to Corrie and takes her by the hand. She lets him lead her to the cabin and, when they reach the door, he lifts Corrie to carry her across the threshold. She buries her head in Samuel's neck, feeling his strength, and their purpose in coming together again.

When they are inside, Samuel gently lowers Corrie to the floor and stands facing her. He loosens the pins holding her hat in place, and gently releases it, causing her hair to fall full and loose around her shoulders. Samuel gently runs his hands through it, before lifting her left hand and slowly removing the ring Silas has given her. She won't be needing it anymore. Corrie doesn't ask about Martha. Not yet. In this moment, all she wants is to be close to Samuel, and she knows he wants to be close to her.

Their reunion is blissful. Corrie, nearly halfway through her pregnancy, has been feeling the first movements of their baby for several days now. Samuel can't feel them yet, but that doesn't stop him from wrapping his arms around her to feel what the two of them have created. They are bringing a new life into the world. It's a dangerous, damaged world but, hidden at the edge of the woods, they are safe for now.

Corrie wakens the next day feeling refreshed and invigorated. She wonders where Martha is and, when Samuel finally opens his eyes, she asks him.

"She's visiting her mother who isn't well right now. She might be away for a while and offered her cabin as a safe house to the Rebels. Silas thought it would be a good opportunity to provide us with the hiding place we need—at least until she returns."

"What if the soldiers find us here? They were always searching the woods at Brookstown and managed to find the cabin where you were hiding even though it was deep into the woods where even horses couldn't pass."

Corrie is worried. If they found Samuel there, the soldiers could find them here.

"Unfortunately, not everyone in the ranks of the Rebels can be trusted, Corrie, and that's how they found me. Someone told the soldiers about the cabin. But it was my choice to stay. After that night, I knew I couldn't leave."

Corrie looks at Samuel. He couldn't leave because of her. She had to leave because of the baby. The choices they made on that night had changed everything.

"Besides, Corrie, the fighting is around the major towns right now. Soldiers are only passing through the smaller towns to head to those areas. We're a two-hour ride from the nearest town, not close to any other dwellings. I think we will be safe here."

"I hope so," she says wanting to be convinced of all Samuel is telling her. There is nothing else they can do, so she accepts that they must make the best of it.

Corrie and Samuel enjoy the next couple of days undisturbed, and in each other's company. They take walks in the woods, and gather firewood, which he chops so they have a constant supply. Corrie notices he's looking healthier since his escape, with more color in his cheeks and extra weight added to his slim frame. His appetite is healthy, and Samuel is attempting to hone his survival skills for their benefit.

Corrie finds it amusing at times and tries not to laugh. She probably knows more about the woods than he does, having lived at the edge of them for years, but had relied on her ability as a seamstress to ensure her family's survival. Corrie never felt she could go far from home, or for too long, with her mother and brother being so needy.

Both she and Samuel have a lot to learn, but she enjoys watching Samuel learn at his own pace. He must catch and kill whatever they are going to eat and is using every ounce of his common sense to try and do that now. Fortunately, the cupboards are stocked with basic items while Samuel attempts to develop his hunting and foraging skills.

On the Sunday, Samuel chases a ground bird for a fair distance until he finally corners it and snatches it up by its feet. It's a good size, and Samuel tucks it up under his arm to prevent it escaping until they arrive back at the cabin. He takes the hatchet he uses to cut wood and asks Corrie to help hold the bird while he does the honors. She has never been involved in killing an animal this way, but they have to eat, so she turns her head. After what seems to be a long time, she turns back, trying to determine the reason for the delay. Samuel has lowered the ax and tells her he can't kill it. He feeds it some grain instead. His gentle nature wins out again and, if it is left up to him Corrie thinks, they are not going to survive for very long. A hearty soup will have to do for dinner tonight.

Just as they sit down to eat, they hear hooves approaching.

Samuel tells her to wait inside while he goes out to see about their unexpected visitor. They are isolated here, so both hope it is friend, and not foe. Corrie pulls back the curtain at the window and immediately recognizes the large figure dismounting from a sturdy steed. Silas Caine.

She watches as the two men hug before Samuel leads the horse to a rail by the side of the house. Corrie has already opened the front door for Silas and runs to throw her arms around him.

"Well, well, well. I see everyone has arrived safely," says Silas.

"Thanks to you," says Corrie smiling at him as Samuel comes in.

"Welcome to our new home," says Samuel inviting Silas to take a seat by the fire.

"Something smells good," says Silas, noticing the dinner laid out on the small table.

"There's plenty, Silas. I will get you a bowl, and then you can give us an update on all the news," says Corrie, part of her wanting to hear what Silas has to tell them, and part of her dreading any bad news he might bring.

Silas first asks the young couple how they are settling in, and Corrie tells him about their "hunting" expedition today.

His loud laughter at Samuel's attempts to provide food has Corrie and Samuel smiling, too, and Silas ends by telling Samuel he will send someone out who can show him the finer skills of catching and killing prey. He will need a gun, Silas tells him.

Corrie doesn't like the idea of Samuel needing a gun, even if it is just for hunting. He will need to learn how to use it, and she doesn't want him to have to use a gun, ever. She wants him to remain the gentle and thoughtful young man he is now. He has matured, but not hardened, in prison, and she is glad of his escape.

Corrie is lost in thought as Silas and Samuel carry on their conversation.

"They haven't been able to find Seymour," Silas says.

Corrie's attention snaps back at the mention of Seymour's name.

"What do you mean they haven't been able to find him?" says Corrie with an edge of fear to her voice. Samuel has a dark look on his face as he waits for Silas to answer.

"As word spread about what he had done to you, along with the fact you were carrying a child, Seymour absconded from the town. They haven't been able to find him. He can't return to the Army, so he's a fugitive now, too," says Silas.

Corrie is glad that Seymour is on the run. He didn't deserve the status that being in the Army afforded him, and now he would know just how she and Samuel feel, running from the Alliance, afraid for their lives.

"I'm going to find him," says Samuel, the dark look becoming more menacing as he is forced to confront what happened to Corrie again.

Before she can say anything, Silas cautions Samuel.

"He will be found, Samuel, and he will answer for what he did to Corrie. The Alliance are not the only people looking for him . . . "

"I want to look him in the eye," interrupts Samuel "and then I am going to kill him."

"You need to be more concerned about Corrie and the baby right now, Samuel. Their welfare is your main priority. They need you, and you are responsible for them. Don't let Seymour drag you down with him. He's not worth it," says Silas.

Some of the darkness leaves Samuel's face as he looks at Corrie. He takes her hand under the table and she brings it up to rest on her belly. She holds it there to remind him of all that is good in the world . . . and to remind herself as well.

"Have the Alliance asked any more questions about me?" asks Corrie, knowing that she is implicated in Seymour's crime.

"For now, they have accepted my explanation around your pregnancy, the fact that you were too afraid to report the assault, and the need for you to remain in Louisville for your own safety. I told them that if Seymour can't be found, it's impossible to know if he is looking for you, so I explained you were currently being cared for in a safe house under my watchful eye. They've got bigger problems to worry about with the mounting insurrections around the country, so they haven't tried to take the matter any further for now. As compensation for Seymour's actions they've also agreed to continue the ration agreement they already had with you, so your mother and brother are not in any danger at the moment either."

Corrie eyes fill with tears. Her mother and brother are safe. That's all she wants to hear. Telling the authorities that she was carrying Seymour's child was a master stroke by Silas. Samuel squeezes her hand to tell her that he understands.

"What did my mother say?" asks Corrie, uncertain how her mother would take the news of her pregnancy.

"Your mother was devastated to learn of Seymour's assault. She couldn't understand why you hadn't come to her after it happened, but I was able to explain the rest of your and Samuel's story to her. Despite her sense of shock, she understood the difficulties confronting you. I explained I have everything in hand, telling her that you're in a safe place being well looked after and, though she wants to see you, she understands your safety is paramount."

"Was she angry at my deception?"

"No, Corrie. She was more incensed at the Alliance for forcing you into this position. She understands what the Alliance had planned for you was not what your father would have wanted. Now she sees there is another way and is sworn to the secrecy that we all share".

Corrie remembers Nate—the only other person she is concerned about in the situation. She's reluctant to ask in front of Samuel, and she doesn't have to as Silas answers her unasked question without prompting.

"I tried to see Nate after Gert came to see me, but he was already gone," says Silas.

"What do you mean . . . already gone?" asks Corrie with alarm in her voice.

"I'm sorry, Corrie. His father couldn't stop him. He left to join the Army."

"Why?" Corrie whispers.

Silas takes his time to answer her question.

"He knew you wouldn't be getting married. He said he didn't want to marry anybody else. That's what his father told me."

Corrie gets up. She can't stay here in this room with Samuel and Silas. She has sent Nate to his certain death, fighting against the Rebels, because she wanted to choose. Because she wanted to decide who she would marry. Her decision has broken Nate. If he knew the truth about her love for Samuel and that she was carrying Samuel's child, what would the consequences be? Could they be any worse? She doesn't think so, as she walks out the door, then runs blindly into the woods not wanting anyone to find her. She is guilty . . . as guilty as Seymour . . . and Nate should have his revenge, too.

A short time later, Samuel finds her sobbing under a tree and takes her in his arms. Corrie is bearing the burden of a thousand different wounds, to herself and others, and there is no consoling her right now. The Rebellion against the Alliance is escalating, and Nate has joined the forces aligned against them. Future confrontations, even violent ones, are imminent.

The choice Corrie and Samuel have made to love one another at best secures them an uncertain future. At worst, it lays them open to unimaginable retribution.

About the Author

Debra Calhoun discovered her passion for writing in the world of fan fiction. This combined with her nearly 'empty nest' inspired her to hone her skills at the Sydney Writer's Centre, and Corrie's story was born. Currently based in regional Victoria with her family, she continues to journey with Corrie and is preparing the second part of her trilogy for publication.